THREE M

BOOKS BY SANDRA BOND

The Psychopath Club
The Devil's Finger
Poetry Slum
Three Men in Orbit

Three Men in Orbit
SANDRA BOND

To Peter

Glasgow 2024

[signature]

THE CANAL PRESS

THREE MEN IN ORBIT
Sandra Bond

Copyright © 2024 Sandra Bond. All Rights Reserved.
Published by The Canal Press, Lititz, Pennsylvania (*www.thecanalpress.com*).
For information, email *editor@timespinnerpress.com*.
Author's website: *www.sandra-bond.com*.

BOOK DESIGN | John D. Berry
COVER ILLUSTRATION & FRONTISPIECE | Dan Steffan
AUTHOR PHOTO | Oliver Facey

*Dedicated to the memory of Jerome K. Jerome,
who would probably have been taken quite aback*

THREE MEN IN ORBIT

1

It is a most singular thing to relate, but everything that you are about to read – the story of our trip to the Moon in a bathysphere, the story of how the bank was robbed at Oakapple Orbital, the story of how Selene City came within an ace of utter destruction – occurred solely because Harris craved hot coffee.

Those devotees of literature who have already met Harris, upon the Thames or in the Schwartzwald, will already be raising their eyebrows and muttering to one another in sinister tones. "Harris!" I seem to hear them say. "Coffee! Surely those two words should never be permitted to appear in one and the same sentence." And at the same time I imagine Harris's voice, counterpointing them in a dry and what one might call a forthcoming bass-baritone, chiding me for what I have just written. "Good lord, J.! Do you want all of London to think I subsist on coffee and weak lemonade, like a Sunday-school treat? If the word gets about, I don't know what will become of my reputation."

Well, Harris himself has done more ill to his own reputation than any words that my tongue or pen could conjure up; but the man, despite everything, has been a bosom pal of mine for nigh twenty years, and so I feel obliged to point out that Harris is often seen holding a beer in a casual kind of a way, and not infrequently a whisky. Even on a raw winter day, such as that on which this narrative begins, Harris is far more likely to keep his temperature and his spirits up with a hot toddy than with a mere humble cup of coffee.

But there we are; I must set down facts as they occurred, and the fact is that upon that particular morn, Harris decided he wanted a coffee.

What had happened was this. The weather, as I have already mentioned, was perfectly frightful; it was a Saturday morning in November, with fog swirling up off the River Thames as though it aspired to feature in one of Mr. Dickens' novels, and a cold grey drizzle of precipitation. It was hardly distinct enough to call it 'rain'; instead of separate drops, between which a man with a narrower waistline than Harris might have hoped to dodge, this came down like the curtain at a music-hall, except instead of being plush velvet and pleasing to the eye, it was chilly and lent an air of colourlessness to the whole of London.

Harris had gone to bed the previous Friday night, looking forward to a comfortable night's repose after a week at the proverbial grindstone, only to find that the bathroom tap had started to drip. The sound it made by dripping was barely above the liminal threshold of human hearing; but it is a peculiar trait of our auditory systems that they work at their peak of efficiency only when we do not desire them to.

When an old friend hails us from across the street and invites us out to dinner at Belbrough's, we fail to hear his call, and trudge onward and homeward, to discover that the landlady has prepared for us a repast of undercooked mutton hash. When the driver of a hansom cab, having broken a rein and lost control of his horse, hollers to us to "get out of the way, quick!" as we cross the road in front of him, we are oblivious to his warning, and have to spring aside at the last second, whereupon we slip and fall in the mud, ruin a good pair of trousers, and lose our umbrella.

But when we are snug in bed of a night, and seem to feel the very brush of the arms of Morpheus about us, and a tap starts to drip, that tap will make a noise louder than an artillery shell.

Harris said that the worst part about it was the lack of rhythm.

If you are but lately escaped from education, you may cherish fond memories of having to work out how long a tap takes to fill a bath if it provides x gallons per minute, whilst the bath's owner has negligently omitted to insert the plug so that y gallons per minute run out again. I remember suggesting that surely it would be a more fruitful use of time to just put the plug in the hole, rather than fool around with arithmetic and algebra and all those things. My mathematics master adopted a contrary point of view on the issue, and sad to relate, I did not carry off the maths prize that year, or any other.

But if a tap must drip (as Harris said), why can't it at least drip steadily, like a tap in a mathematical problem? This tap was simply cussed about the whole thing. To begin with it sent a few drops out with a second or two between each. Then it would stop, and Harris would half go back to sleep telling himself that he had imagined the entire affair. Then the tap would wake up again, and allow a pitter-patter of liquid out, and Harris would also wake up again, and stumble into the bathroom, swearing, and screw the tap so tightly closed that Samson would have been hard pressed to draw water from it.

Then the tap would wait until Harris was back in bed and his toes had gone from icy to cosy once again, before delivering a volley of droplets so loudly that one might have thought they were landing on a tin tea-tray, rather than a porcelain wash-hand-basin. And Harris would pull the pillow over his head, and swear some more, and say he was not getting up, not he! – not if the whole bathroom, or the entire city of London, were to flood.

And so that Saturday morning, while more fortunate fellows than Harris were still clad in their dressing-gowns and enjoying their breakfasts while perusing their newspapers, Harris set to fixing that tap.

When Harris related the story to George and myself that night, I confess that, at this point, I leapt to a certain conclusion.

"Good Lord, Harris, old man," I interjected, "don't tell me that you started to dismantle the tap without turning the water off first, and got water all over your house?"

Harris looked at me over his beer. (The reader will note that his earlier aberration of coffee had quite passed off by this point.)

"What kind of a fool do you take me for, J.?" he grumbled.

This is not a question to which a ready answer suggests itself, and so I avoided a direct response. "I'm sorry; do please go on."

And Harris went on, to explain how he had taken good care to turn the water off at the stop-cock, having first filled several containers lest any of his household should require to drink or wash whilst he should be at his labours; and how he had taken that tap apart into its constituent parts; and how he had unerringly located the problem as being the simplest of things – a worn washer in the internal workings of the faucet.

Congratulating himself on having achieved the domestic saving of not calling out a plumber, Harris carefully placed all the components of that tap save for the washer upon a sheet of clean newspaper, and not forgetting to take with him that washer safely tucked inside a used envelope, ventured forth to seek a replacement.

He remembered that there was a plumber's supply shop only a few streets away, and presented himself at the counter thereof, with his washer.

"I need a new washer to replace this one," he said, shooting it out of the envelope in front of the storesman, who looked at it with suspicion, picked it up, bit it as though it had been a bad half-crown, held it up to the light and looked through the hole in the middle, and finally shook his head at Harris.

"Not in this size," said he. "There's no demand for them in this size."

Harris pointed out, with considerable tact (at least by Harris's standard), that he was here, now, and demanding such a washer.

But all the storesman could do was to suggest Ponsonby's in Rook House Street.

Harris and the washer went on to Rook House Street and sought the advice of Mr Ponsonby, who eyed the washer with disdain and asked whether Harris's plumbing had been fitted by a Frenchman. Upon Harris confessing his ignorance of this point, Mr Ponsonby explained that the washer was in a French size – a metric size, in fact – and that no true Briton would fit such a washer to any tap in the land.

Resignedly, Harris asked Mr Ponsonby whether he knew of any French plumbers. Mr Ponsonby did not.

Visits to three further plumber's storesmen met with similar failures, and Harris was wondering whether he was to be faced with the choice of ripping out every water pipe in the house and replacing them with new pipes that were certified as British made throughout, or of never washing or having a shave again. By now he had walked almost as far as the City, and the sound of Bow

Bells chiming was growing fainter and fainter behind him every quarter-hour, when he finally found a plumber's sundries shop somewhere just off Houndsditch where the proprietor allowed that he might just have one or two of those washers somewhere "out the back".

Harris waited with breathless impatience until the storesman returned with the news that he had three washers – no more, and no fewer – in that singular size.

"I shall take them," said Harris.

"All three of 'em, sir?"

"All three." Harris had concluded, with a speed of thought really remarkable for him, that to procure two spare washers in case of future problems was the act of a sensible and prudent man.

The storesman scratched his head and looked at Harris. "But what if some other gentleman comes here requiring this size washer?"

"Then," said Harris, "he must go to France, or to Germany, or to Timbuktu. I do not care what any other gentleman may do to obtain a washer. I want all three of those washers, and I am ready to pay cash – cash on the nail – for them."

He took a ten-bob note out of his pocket, which seemed to have a positive effect on the storesman, and left that shop with three washers in that envelope where previously there had been but one.

"And I suppose," said George, "that you got the worn-out washer mixed in with the new ones, and went home and fitted it back into the tap, and had to do your work all over again."

"Now it's you who are taking me for a fool," Harris sighed. "Upon my word, I don't see why you and J. have such a low opinion of my wits. Of course I left the worn-out washer in the shop, to avoid just such a mix-up. Upon emerging, rather than go straight home, I realised that I was feeling cold and lethargic – you'll remember I had scarcely slept – and I determined to get myself some hot coffee to take the chill out of my bones, and wake my thoughts up a jiffy."

"Are the coffee-shops open on Saturday mornings in the City now?" I enquired.

Harris smiled in response, which I found worrying, and I began to wonder if I had better not have asked that question; for I know that smile of Harris's, and he only trots it out when he thinks someone has played into his hands.

"That's the curious thing," he said. "It's a few years since I was in that district, and I realised as I stood there thinking of coffee, that there was much more hustle and bustle going on there than ever I saw it before on a Saturday. I found a coffee-house, and got my coffee, and mighty welcome it was too; and just to pass the time, I asked the coffee-man how the street came to be so busy on a Saturday when the City clerks were all at home."

"'Why, sir,' said he, 'they'll all be going to Fenchurch Street to take the train to Maplin.'"

"Why Maplin?" asked George. I never knew such a fellow as George for not knowing things. If the Prussians were to invade England, I fancy that George would wander along two months afterwards and ask an officer in full uniform whether he was going to a fancy dress ball, and compliment him on how well and idiomatically he could swear in German.

"That's what I asked him," Harris said. "Of course, it's from Fenchurch Street that you take the train down to the Essex coast, to London Spaceport. At the weekends, when the offices are closed, it's almost all that the station is used for. I expressed a polite interest, and the fellow went on to tell me about how he and his Amelia and their youngster had visited there only that summer, and how they'd gone up in one of the pleasure-ships, and what a jolly spectacle it had been to see all the people dwindling out of sight below, and to rise up until you could see the curvature of the Earth itself, and all the stars twinkling away like a politician's smile (these were the coffee-chap's words, you understand), and how when you came back down to land, there was scarcely so much as a bump."

George gave a little exclamation, and told us of how he had gone up from Maplin for an hour's trip himself on one occasion, and what a splendid view you got from the portholes, and how easy it was to steer the ship by adjusting the Cavorite shields which block off gravity from attracting it to Earth.

Then George and Harris both looked at me with what I thought a worryingly optimistic expression upon both their faces.

"Please don't tell me," I said, "that you want to take me up in one of those infernal contraptions. I have walked the earth all my life, or at least, such of it as was not spent in my cradle. I prefer to reserve soaring through the air with no means of support to the birds, the bats, and the daring young man on the flying trapeze."

"Oh, if you're going to be a stick-in-the-mud about it," said George.

"Mud? Don't mention mud," said Harris. "Why, I remember times only a few years ago when we were up the river and we had to positively wade through acres of mud. Don't you recall, J., when we got grounded off Wallingford?"

I did remember, but rather wished I didn't.

"Well," Harris continued, "there's no mud in a space-ship, nor yet any way of grounding. You just float merrily along and let Science do her stuff. You don't even have to scull, and if that doesn't mean anything to you, J., it means something to me. I'm not as young as I used to be, and oarsmanship doesn't come as easily to me as it did once upon a time."

In my secret heart I found myself agreeing that Harris had a point there. Sculling is all very well when you are young, fit and twenty, and can row cheerfully along all day while still retaining enough energy of mind and body to appreciate the scenery, or a passing boat with pretty young people in it. But Father Time has a way of placing his bony hand on your shoulder, once you get to about thirty-five years old, which reminds you that you are mortal and that breezing from Kingston to Oxford in a mere week or so looks a somewhat steeper proposition to you, now.

But it doesn't do to let Harris know you agree with him, of course. It only encourages him. So I said "Oh, stuff. There are accidents in space. You can die of suffocation if the air gets out. What if a meteorite hits you?"

"Meteor," said Harris. "They're only meteorites when they land here on Earth, you juggins."

I did not feel sufficiently learned to contest the point, so I leapt spryly over it. "And what about that space-ship that fell out of the sky on top of Hamburg and knocked half the city to matchwood?"

"You can have accidents on the river, too," George interjected. "Why, even now I sometimes think of that time we were almost drowned in the lock because of that tom-fool photographer."

I felt equally disinclined to agree with George as with Harris, and shook my head.

"That could have happened to anyone; and we were all right in the end, you know, apart from having to argue with the photographer about us getting our feet in the way of his focus. And even if we had gone into the drink, there were plenty of people around to heave us back out. If that had happened in space, we should have been done for."

George merely pointed out that so far as he knew, there were no itinerant photographers hanging around in the aether to try and make you pay two-and-six for a plate that cut off your right ear and gave you a squint.

While George and I were debating this, Harris had fallen quiet. It may be a mistake to let Harris believe he is correct on any point, but it is a greater mistake still to let him think. He does come up with such confoundedly wild ideas – ideas that would make a cat laugh.

"You know," he said, as soon as ever George and I fell silent for the briefest second, "you don't have to restrict yourself to a footling little two-hour pleasure trip. You could hire a space-sphere for a week or even more – easily enough time to do the tour of the orbital stations. Why, a fellow could go as far as the Moon and see all the sights up there. I know a man who had a week on the Moon and came back saying it was better than a month in Margate."

"I've heard similar tales," I said. "The gravity up there gives you a spring in your step. Everyone knows that. Why, they even use it as an advertising slogan for patent medicines. 'Better than a Trip to the Moon'. What they don't tell you is that when you come back down again, you feel as though you have the weight of the world on your shoulders for days afterwards."

I could see that George was about to continue this unwelcome topic, so I hurriedly went back to Harris's original story. "Anyway," I said, "what happened to the tap?"

"I got home with the washers," Harris said, "and my confounded cat had decided that the bits of tap laid out in the bathroom on newspaper were toys, and he had scattered them all over the shop, and it took me half an hour to find them all. I don't even want to think about it."

Which George, of course, saw as his cue to chime back in.

"Even if we didn't go as far as the Moon," he said, "the orbital stations are very fine, they say. They have restaurants, and shows, and casinos, and all manner of entertainment."

"They have restaurants, and shows, and casinos, and all manner of entertainment in London," I pointed out; but I couldn't help but feel that I was fighting a losing battle.

"I was only thinking the other day," mused Harris, "that it had been far too long a time since we three had taken a holiday together. Why, it's years since we rode around Germany on those bicycles."

"I grant you, with reservations," said I, "that it has been too long since this – this triumvirate – was united in its leisure time. I grant you that we have enjoyed a good many trips up the Thames in one another's company; I grant you that our excursion upon the bummel in Teutonic parts was not without its high points and its happy memories. I do not rule out a pleasant holiday with you twain playing golf, or rambling the Scots highlands, or sketching and painting in the Wolds. But I regret to inform you, with polite firmness, that I decline to go soaring off into orbit in a bathysphere with you. You may break each other's tom-fool necks if you so desire; but you are not about to break mine."

2

On my way home that night, I wondered how I was going to tell Ethelbertha that I was planning to take a pleasure-trip to the Moon with Harris and George.

Before I reached my front door, I had progressed to thinking out how best to mention the situation to Ethelbertha in such a manner that she would put her foot down and forbid it. Ethelbertha is not one of those modern, beefy women who wears knickerbockers in lieu of a skirt, and can hit a hockey ball further than some men – well, I say 'some men', but of course I mean myself – can make a golf ball travel. But when she puts her foot down, she can do so with a firmness out of all proportion to its dainty size.

I considered various angles. The danger; the expense; the thought of two full weeks of my being away from home and leaving her to deal with the family, the tradesmen, the thousand everyday cares and worries of domestic life. By the time I turned in at the gate, I was confident that I had a whole array of different concerns, any one of which might cause her to jib.

Ethelbertha was in the drawing-room. Some might call it the parlour, or the sitting-room, but we refer to it always as the drawing-room, for it is there that Ethelbertha likes to work on her sketches; she says the light is better in there. The sun having long set, she was working by gaslight. I personally do not think that any one gas-jet in our abode produces more light than another, but I suppose that force of habit compels her.

"Good-evening, J., dear," she said, setting aside her brush. "Did you have a pleasant time with your friends? How are George and Harris?"

"They are much as ever," I replied, "though possibly there is a little more of Harris today than there was a month ago. We enjoyed a most convivial reunion. How is your current sketch?" I looked at her paper. It seemed hardly changed from when I had looked at it the night before; but then, how often have I sat down at my writing-desk and scribbled a thousand words or more, only to sigh and shoot them into the waste paper basket?

"It is not yet," she said, "at the stage where I loathe it and am shamed by its faults. But that will come, I am sure. It always does."

"George had a rather peculiar notion," I ventured. The concept of the pleasure-trip skyward was as much Harris's as it was George's, of course, but George is a bachelor, and consequently Ethelbertha is rather more prone to disagree with an idea of George's, than she is one which originates from a married man like Harris. I can't think why; she knows both George and Harris well enough for reflection to show that any idea springing from either of them has a better than even chance of being perfectly preposterous.

"Oh? Don't tell me he threatens to set up in mushroom-farming in disused railway tunnels once again."

"He seems to think that the three of us would enjoy a jaunt up to the Moon in a Cavorite bathysphere," I said, and paused, hoping for a reply which would make further debate unnecessary.

But she arched one eyebrow, and merely said, "What an interesting notion! They say the lower gravity on the Moon is frightfully good for the health, and you know you've been prone to liverishness lately."

"We were thinking," I said, passing on to my first baited trap, "that it would be best to do it properly – to take two weeks about it, or even three. That way we could see all the Lunar sights, and still have time to take in some of the delights of the orbital stations, too."

"The orbital stations? Pray, my dear, does one not hear that some of the – the entertainment to be found in orbit is altogether lacking in taste and decency?"

This sounded promising, and I hastened to agree with her. A thoughtful air came over her for a second.

"Ah, well, my dear, I know that I can rely upon your discretion, and upon Harris's, to refrain from patronising any such establishment, not to mention discouraging George from doing likewise."

In other circumstances I would have been touched by Ethelbertha's staunch faith in my moral fibre; but at this particular juncture,

I could have wished that the spectacles through which she viewed me were of a less vivid rose in hue.

I dared not suggest that our plans were to visit the lowest and vilest continental burlesques we could find the moment that we arrived in orbit. Apart from anything else, it would have been untrue, and that marriage is upon the rocks in which a husband tells a lie direct to his wife.

"Naturally, my dear," I said instead, and pressed on to another stratagem. "I only wish that I could take you, and the children, also; but I scarcely think that the stratosphere is a fit place for young people, and of course, we should need to hire a larger craft at a prohibitive cost."

"Why, J.," she exclaimed, "how very like you it is to place your family before your own pleasures! But I sha'n't hear of it. It has been years, now, since the last time you and your gentlemen friends took a holiday without us womenfolk to encumber you. When you three went to Germany upon your bicycles, Clara Harris and Kate Pole and I took a house in Kent, if you recall; and we had such a jolly time there, the children and we, without you men always under our feet. Now don't start to think that I do not care for you," she added; "but a wife sometimes finds that a little spell away from even the dearest husband serves to make a marriage stronger, not weaker. I am sure our budget will run to one-third of a nice house somewhere, especially at this season, as well as to one-third of a space-sphere for a couple of weeks."

I began to object feebly. Somehow the words all got jumbled up in my throat, and I could say nothing coherent; but Ethelbertha evidently gathered a tone of protest in my stammers.

"You are the most thoughtful of men, J., my dear," she said, "but I insist upon it. I have sometimes thought myself of a trip to space, but I always assumed that you had no interest in such a venture."

I felt that I could hardly point out, now, that her assumption was correct, and could only smile weakly at her.

"I tell you what, J.," she said, grasping me by the hand. "You shall go to space this year while I and my lady-friends stay on solid ground, and if you come back and tell me what a wonderful time you've had – why, then next year, perhaps we shall go up into the sky together!"

I hope I may be forgiven for saying "Perhaps!" without adding "And perhaps not" at this point.

It seemed plain, now, that I was spaceward bound, whether or not I desired to be; and I retired to my study with my pipe and a sense of forboding.

Seizing upon a sheet of foolscap, upon one side of which I had lately jotted down notes for an article which I now perceived to be the most childish twaddle, I turned it upon its other side and began to make a list of provisions and other essentials for a trip to the Moon. I began thus:

"6 bt. whisky"

After a second of reflection, I deleted the '6'.

"12 bt. whisky
1 crate bitter beer
1 crate India Pale Ale
1 crate brown ale
½ crate porter
½ crate stout
1 crate Pilsner"

Both Harris and George have a weakness for German beer – it is so readily found in London now. It is little wonder that both my friends are more inclined to embonpoint, as a consequence of the improvements made by Cavorite to shipping and importing of perishables.

I thought it very noble of me, at a moment such as this, to consider the needs of my fellow-passengers as well as my own.

Inspiration failing me at this point, I laid my pen down, and determined to trouble myself about more solid provisions upon the morrow.

I awoke the next morning to a pleasing aroma of bacon drifting up the stairs.

There is no other scent so calculated to make a man throw off all vestiges of sleep, and hop out of bed feeling as though the world is turning at exactly the correct speed.

By the time I reached the top of the stairs, I had recalled to mind recent events, and the upshot of them; and instead of heading straight down to the dining-room, I turned right instead, into my study, and took up my pen, and the list I had begun the night before.

I added to the list bacon, sausages, eggs, mushrooms, and toast. Then, cursing myself as an ignoramus, I deleted 'toast' and substituted 'bread'.

Finally, my mental facilities having recovered a little, I wrote next to 'bread' the words 'and toasting fork'. After which I permitted myself to go down for breakfast at last.

All through the week I added entries to the list as they occurred to me, and I took to carrying it around in my jacket-pocket, a practice recommended by my late Uncle Podger when planning a long journey.

"Prepare your list a week in advance; and that done, always carry that list round with you," he would say. "Then, whenever you think of something to add to it, you can pull it out and jot it down as soon as the thought occurs. If you don't, you are sure to forget it again before you can find the list and add it."

This advice in itself was excellent; and I venture to say that my uncle's journeys should have been the best equipped and provisioned ever.

But when Uncle Podger wanted to add something to his list, he would take it out, and reach for his pen, only to discover it was not in its accustomed top pocket.

"Confound it!" he would cry. "Where the dickens is my pen? I had it only an hour ago."

And we would all scatter, to look for his pen, and bump into each other, and knock things over, and look in places where others had already looked, and mock each other for doing so, and my Uncle would finally find his pen himself in his inside pocket, and try to write with it, and discover it was out of ink.

"Wherever can the ink be?" he sighed in despair. "You all know perfectly well that the inkpot ought always to be on my desk."

It ought, but of course it never was. We would scour the house for the inkpot, without success, and my Uncle would find a stub of pencil, and snap its point off. Then he would attempt to sharpen it with a pen-knife, and break the blade, and cut himself.

And by now he had forgotten what he wanted to add to the list anyway.

I made sure, that week, that my own pen accompanied me always, and that its little india-rubber reservoir never thirsted for ink.

Somehow, though, I found it difficult to plan for a trip away from the surface of my planet. I could not help but keep thinking that there must be articles one could not do without in space, of which a neophyte was utterly ignorant. I envisioned my arriving at Maplin without these items, and George and Harris mocking me.

"Why, J., you utter ass!" George would laugh. "You mean you haven't brought a set of bing-cubblers? What sort of damn fool goes on a space voyage without a single bing-cubbler!"

And Harris would snort with laughter in that way he has, and people around us would look away in embarrassment for the poor soul who thought he could go into space without his bing-cubblers.

So I determined to go to my favourite bookshop, and to seek advice there on a good, inexpensive manual for the chap about to embark upon space travel.

When I explained what I wanted, the bookshop's proprietor looked me up and down, as if to say 'This man, at his time of life, wants to go jaunting off to the Moon?'; and I felt less inclined than ever to accede to George and Harris's plans. But I left the bookshop with Baedeker's "Luna", and a modest booklet entitled "A Pocket Guide To The Moon And Orbital Stations". I asked about the availability of a book about how to fly a Cavorite craft, but the bookman's face took on so horrified an expression at the suggestion that

I might wish to pilot one myself, that I did not pursue the question.

Arriving home and taking a comfortable seat, I first opened Baedeker, and found a wealth of information in the most impeccably translated English about the delights round and about the space-port at Zwickau. No doubt that information was accurate to a nicety, but to a man about to depart from Maplin space-port in England, I thought it less than helpful. Turning to the end of this section, I found one ill-written page "specially prepared for the English edition" dealing with Maplin. I closed the book sharply in annoyance, and turned to "A Pocket Guide".

This, I soon learned, was evidently aimed at a target reader somewhat younger than I. A bright child of ten, off to visit Luna with its parents, would probably have found it of immense benefit. I did not; I do not care for pages of gush about the amounts of steel, and tin, and aluminium, and india-rubber, that go to make up an orbital station. The matter is of perfect indifference to me, provided only that there is enough india-rubber at the joints to stop the air from leaking out, and suffocating everyone on the station. I had voiced this concern when the suggestion of a trip to the cosmos was first mooted, and George and Harris had both told me not to be such an old woman, – that there had never been a life lost aboard Oakapple Station in all the years it had been operating.

"How many years is that?" I had asked, distrustingly; and George said he thought it was about three.

"In which case, it can only be a matter of time," said I. But Harris pointed out that you could take out life-insurance before you left. There was an advertisement for space-travel policies printed – nay, embossed – on the rear cover of Baedeker, to which I now turned once more, deciding to forgive it its lapse in covering England's major space-port, and see what it had to say about the trip from there to the orbital stations.

There was nothing; not a word, not a syllable. Herr Baedeker evidently held the belief that the way to conduct a pleasure tour in space, was to purchase a ticket on a full-size passenger ship, proceed directly to the orbital stations without so much as troubling to peep through a porthole, and once there, to enjoy one's vacation as though one were in any tourist resort or seaside town on the surface of the planet – with, presumably, the trifling additional factor of the lack of gravity.

And so the days passed, until the time should come for me to take my farewells of Ethelbertha and my young ones, and travel to Maplin.

3

I would never have known it from Baedeker, but since the port of Maplin was first created for space-craft to arrive and depart, several hotels of greater or lesser stature have arisen there, just as they did fifty years ago around London's great railway stations. It seems peculiar for them to spring up there, like mushrooms, set apart from normal dwelling houses, shops and markets.

One can take a steamer down the Thames to Maplin, if one is not in a hurry; but the Thames east of London is not the pleasant river one can enjoy further upstream. It is a depressing sight, painted in greys and browns, and the country either side of the river is flat and reedy, like Harris's voice when he tries to sing.

So I travelled instead by train from Fenchurch Street; from which the view is scarcely any more desirable, once one leaves London's suburbs and enters Essex proper, but at least it is over more quickly.

The only town of any size on the way to Maplin is Southend. Before the coming of Maplin, Southend was a seaside resort. Nay; it was the seaside resort, to which flocked countless East Enders in the summer; in its way greater even than Brighton or than Blackpool. Now that space-vessels take off and land nearby, the town has swollen, with new houses appearing to the west of the old town, like soldiers growing from Cadmus's teeth. But there are none to the east of the town; only such few buildings as existed before Maplin are permitted there. As much emptiness as possible is maintained around Maplin; nobody wants to see a second Hamburg disaster. The railway line has been built onward from Shoeburyness, and ends at a spacious if rather gaudy terminus right at the space-port gates.

Into one of the hotels I have already mentioned we had booked for the night, taking the sensible view that it would get us off to a bright, early start in the morning. Harris had engaged us rooms at the Kepler Hotel, while George had been entrusted – despite qualms from both myself and Harris – with dealing with the actual hire of the Cavorite sphere, on the basis that he "knew a man who knew a man".

It is a failing of mine that when looking for any one thing, I cannot see another, though it be under my nose. So it was that while peering around for the Kepler Hotel, I felt a sudden pain in the region of my bottom waistcoat button; and, giving a start, ascertained that the cause thereof was that Harris had come up alongside me, and prodded me with the end of his walking-stick.

"You don't need to look for the moon yet, J.," he said; "that only comes after we leave Earth."

"I was looking for the hotel."

"Oh! the hotel. George is there already, and I also; I only came out to see where you could have got yourself to. Come along, do."

So Harris walked me there, and as promised, George was in the hotel; in its saloon bar, to be quite precise.

"Hullo, J.!" he called out as we approached. "Bless my soul, I had quite made up my mind that you'd decided against joining us."

This I found hurtful. I reminded him that I had vowed to accompany him, and that my word once given must not be broken, though the heavens fall – or the bathyspheres fall out of them. "Besides," I said, "if I must die in space, far from my loved ones and my planet of birth, the only comfort I shall be able to gain in my final seconds is the knowledge that you, who got me into such a pickle, are there and about to expire also."

"Come, come," Harris cried, "let's not start to quibble before we are even in orbit. J., do take some refreshment, and you'll feel less worrisome in a jiffy."

I suppose that mathematics and the law of averages dictate that even Harris must be correct upon occasion; and having taken the suggested refreshment, I was able to conclude that this was one of those scarce occasions.

We annexed a table to ourselves in a quiet but well-lit corner of the room, and I ventured to take out my list and offer it around.

Harris took it, and gave an exclamation of surprise.

"Why, J., we sha'n't be able to take a quarter of these."

George snatched the list from his hand, and laughed.

"Well, the list begins well, but –"

"But what?" I said, removing my glass from my lips and looking at George over the top of it.

"You can't cook bacon and eggs in space, you ass."

"Whyever not?"

"To begin with," Harris said, "once you got out of gravity, they wouldn't stay in the pan."

"Not to mention," said George, "that cooking involves flames, and flames use up air."

"And if something went wrong," said Harris, "which knowing you and George is more likely than not – if one of you chuckle-heads contrived to overturn the stove, or set light to your sleeve, or something – the consequences wouldn't bear thinking of. Space isn't the Thames, J., and you can't just douse a fire with river water if you manage to set your own craft blazing."

"I heard a story once," George said, a melancholy look forming in his eye, "about a man who was almost marooned in space by his own beard."

This seemed to me to have little or no relevance to the list I had made, but I was sufficiently taken aback by the discovery that I would not be permitted bacon to break my fast while aboard the ship that I made no protest.

Harris's hand went to his moustache, in a kind of protective way. "However did that occur, George?"

"This chap," George said, "went up to space with a full beard, but for some reason while he was on one of the stations, he bought himself a safety-razor as a souvenir."

"A safety-razor?"

"You can buy almost anything as a souvenir on an orbital station," George explained. "It's like Paris. But this man decided on a safety-razor rather than a pair of nutcrackers, or a money-box in the shape of the satellite, – I don't know why. But buy it he did. And after leaving the station, finding time hanging slowly on the trip, he thought he'd try the razor out, and shaved his beard right off, there in his sphere."

George paused at this moment, and shook his head, as though to wonder at the folly of this formerly bearded traveller.

I still failed to see George's point. "But how could that maroon him?"

"He had enough of a beard," George said, "that the trimmings from it floated everywhere, because of there being no gravity, don't you see? And some of them got into the controls and jammed the gears that operated the Cavorite panels, so he couldn't steer the thing properly, and he was stranded for days until they found him, and then they had to come and tow him back into the station, before he drifted off into the ecliptic never to be seen again."

"By the time he'd paid for the tow and the repairs to his controls," said Harris, "I should expect he wished he'd bought the nut-crackers instead."

"Wouldn't the pieces of nut-shell get into the controls?" I asked. Harris gave me an exasperated look; I can't say why.

"But we sha'n't have to worry," said George, "for we are none of us beavers."

"We soon shall be," I pointed out, "if we are forbidden to shave in space."

"Oh," said George, "I don't think it matters if it's just your daily toilet. The man I was talking of had a beard like Lord Salisbury."

"They say that soon, radio will have advanced to an extent that every craft will have one," Harris said. "Not just the big ones and the orbital stations. And they may even be able to transmit your voice rather than having to fiddle with a morse-key."

I have heard people complain about this prospect – heard them say that it will remove all the charm and wonder from space travel. For my part, it sounds a welcome development, one which can hardly fail to improve safety and deter accidents. I would happily have waited for it to be put into place, before allowing Harris and George to haul me away into orbit, but it is so easy to be wise after the event.

By the time we retired for our last night on Earth – our last night for a while, I should say – Harris and George had edited my list almost out of all recognition. There seemed no end to the amount of things which it was foolish, or inadvisable, or even illegal to carry onto a space-craft, though they might be articles one would use every day in the normal course of events.

I suppressed my urge to cavil at the manner in which they deleted items, and told myself that the shorter my list became, the easier it would make matters in the morning when we provisioned in preparation to depart for orbit. With that happy thought fixed in the fore part of my mind, I made my way to the window of my room, and arranged myself – not without some contortion – at an angle from which I could view the night sky through it.

It was a clear and chill winter night, not quite cold enough for frost, but certainly cold enough that I was glad to be in a modern hotel with equally modern, efficient heating systems.

Since they first went into operation, I had many times glanced upward and seen the orbital stations. From the ground, they were mere pinpricks of light in the dark blanket of the night sky, and were one to capture a photographic image, it would be a herculean task to distinguish the man-made star from the more traditional sort among which it sits.

No such difficulty is met, of course, when viewing them by the human eye rather than the camera's lens. Where the stars sit fixed, the stations move at a steady pace, progressing across the sky slower than a shooting star, and yet somehow giving the impression that they could go as fast as one of those, if only they could be bothered to; or perhaps if only they didn't think that to progress round the zodiac at so giddy a speed might disagree with the people on the station.

I had rather hoped to catch sight of one of them now, and to imagine that in less than a day I would be aboard one of these orbiting oases – perhaps even the very one I espied. But only the motionless stars met my gaze; and before long, I was dissuaded by the cold air from waiting about hopefully for one to track its way across the small area of sky that I could see through my window.

Consequently I consigned myself to bed, where my last conscious thoughts were to wonder however I would get any sleep without gravity to keep me from floating out from between the sheets, and waking to find my head downward and my feet pointing in the direction of Saturn.

4

Next morning I woke in a positive frame of mind. Why worry, I asked myself. George was right; dozens of ships took off for space every day – hundreds in a year – thousands, if you thought of all the different space-ports around the globe. "You're far more likely to come to grief in a railway accident," he said, "than in a space-ship crash."

Then I opened the *Times*, and read that eight souls had perished in a railway accident in Carmarthenshire.

Having made arrangements with the local stores for our requirements – they call the stores a "chandler's", as though Maplin were a sea-port and not a space-port – George led the way to the ship which was to be our home from home for the next two weeks.

The first shipyard we came to was spic and span, with a sign freshly painted, and for a moment I mentally resolved to forgive George any of his little ways for the next few days; until George marched on past the entrance to that yard, giving it no second glance.

He went on past half-a-dozen more yards, each one shabbier than the last, until Harris spoke.

"I say, George, how much further are you going to make us walk?"

"Pooh!" said George. "Don't be so impatient. After a day or two in the sphere, you'll be crying out to be able to take a stroll. The yard we want is Peckover's, just along here."

We finally turned in at the gate of Peckover's yard – the dingiest of all those we had seen – and made for the office, where George enquired after Mr. Peckover.

"Not here," said the sole occupant of the office, a very young and nervous-looking man in spectacles and too garish a tie.

George asked whether he was expected back soon, and the young man couldn't say, he was sure.

George asked whether the young man could let us have the sphere that he had reserved a week ago. The young man's features took on a look suggestive of a bilious attack, but after swallowing a couple of times, he said he supposed he could try to find the booking.

We gave our names, and the young man looked at several sheets of paper, one after another, until finally he came up with one which seemed to satisfy him.

"Capital fellow!" cried Harris. "Lead the way to it."

But the young man said he couldn't leave the office; said that Mr. Peckover would discharge him upon the spot, if word reached him that he had done so.

"Then how are we to know which one is ours?" I enquired, attempting to keep any peevish tone from my voice.

"Sixth one from the end," said the young man, and made George sign the sheet of paper in numerous places, and then produced another sheet – our flight-plan – and made him sign all over that, too. I dare say that if that young man had at that juncture handed George a deed signing over all his worldly goods and his first-born child, George would have autographed it without objection.

Finally the young man gave George a small key-ring, and an instruction manual, and we left him guarding Mr. Peckover's office with every fibre of his being.

We progressed into the yard itself, walking slowly, so that we might admire the gleaming metal and finely crafted rivets of the different vessels. Some were extravagantly large; others were scarcely the size of a coffin, if coffins were manufactured in spheres rather than whatever the proper term is for coffin-shaped. Some were round, while others were not; for all space-going craft are known as "spheres", whether or not they actually are spherical.

"Hulloa!" said Harris, stopping by the sixth craft from the end of the row. "You've done us proud here, George."

Certainly the ship we stood before was larger than most of those in the yard; a good deal larger than I had anticipated.

"Well, you see," said George with pride, "as I said, I know a man who knows a man. And he knows a couple of men, in turn, who are quite chummy with old Peckover – I think they play billiards in the evening. It isn't how much money you lay down, you see," he went on, every inch of him the experienced traveller condescending to pass hints and tips on to the novice. "It's knowing where to find a bargain, and making sure you're there at the best time to take advantage of it – and there you are!"

He underlined that final exclamation, so to speak, by trying to open the craft's door and display to us its interior. It refused to co-operate.

"Don't you have to crank it open with that wheel?" said Harris. He was right; to enter the sphere required two doors to be open, outer and inner. The arrangement is cumbersome, but it guards against any fool accidentally opening the door in space and letting all the air out

"Oh, yes, I was forgetting." George cranked the wheel forcefully, and then repeated the procedure for the inner door. Finally, he could throw the door of that craft open for us to troop inside.

"We shall be all right in here, sha'n't we, J.?" said Harris; and I sat in an armchair, and sank into it a little way, and agreed that it did seem very comfortable.

"Let's get our luggage aboard," said George. So I rose from the armchair, with a slight reluctance. I stood outside the sphere; Harris stood in the doorway; and George remained aboard. I would take a case or a box and pass it to Harris; Harris would ease it through the narrow confines of the entry-hatch, and pass it to George, who would stow it carefully where it would least be in the way.

As I turned from handing Harris the last crate but two, I found myself almost nose to nose with a tall, somewhat cadaverous gentleman. I assumed, from the close attention he was paying to us and to the ship, that this must be Mr. Peckover.

I bade him a cheery good-morning, and politely asked if he would mind stepping a few paces to the side so that I could reach George's Gladstone-bag.

He declined to do so, in a truculent manner, and demanded to know what we were doing.

Harris, from the doorway, replied that he was not an experienced astronaut, but he would call it loading baggage aboard the ship in preparation for launching, or embarkation, or whatever the proper term was.

This did nothing to soothe the cadaverous man's temper, and he stood between me and the door, which also meant between George's Gladstone-bag and the door.

"What the deuce is happening out there?" asked George, squeezing his head through the narrow gap between Harris and the edge of the entry-hatch.

"Do I not have the honour," I said, "of addressing Mr. Peckover?"

The man looked at me as though I had insulted him gravely; explained, with some force, that his name was Hannay; that he was the personal servant of Lord Freckleton; that this ship had been hired for the especial use of Lord Freckleton alone; that he was here to prepare the ship for his lordship to embark at noon; that Lord Freckleton himself was currently in conference with Mr. Peckover regarding the fitting-out of the craft, which Mr. Peckover had but lately carried out to his lordship's specification in preparation; and that the three of us were no doubt criminals, swindlers and bilks, and that he had a good mind to call a policeman and have us all put in charge.

"You mistake yourself, sir," George said, somehow finding a safe passage between the Scylla of the entry hatch and the Charybdis of Harris's waistcoat. "We three have hired this ship from Mr. Peckover ourselves, and that young shaver in the office gave us the keys and the relevant documents not twenty minutes since."

But the valet just grunted at George, and said, "If that's so, then you'll have the key to the control lock?"

"It is in my hand," said George, and held it up. The valet grunted again.

"In that case, sir," he said, emphasising the word 'sir' so that we were to understand it was spoken grudgingly and under duress, "I presume that that key will fit the lock?"

"Don't be such an ass," said George; but he went back inside, and Harris and I followed, and so did the valet.

George sat in the chair at the helm, and reached for the lock that prevents the Cavorite guidance system from becoming operative until launching-time.

"Oh," he said, after a second, and tried it again, and said "Oh," again.

"Let me try," said Harris. He snatched the key from George's hand, forced it into the lock, and twisted it, in the way he must have twisted that leaky tap which had led to us all being here, this morn. Had he been able to twist it any harder, he must have broken that key; because the lock would not operate the controls.

Then the man snatched the key from Harris's hand in turn, and gave it back to George – threw it at him, I might almost say. He took another key from his inside pocket, used that second key to open the control-lock with perfect ease, and gave George a look that made George's shoulders droop, until they slumped nearly to forty-five degrees.

"I say," I said, a thought striking me. "You don't suppose that ass in the office could have meant the sixth ship from the other end?"

The valet allowed that such an intention on the young man's part appeared highly probable, and invited us once more to take our leave from Lord Freckleton's sphere.

I am not one of those old-fashioned types who believes that the serving classes should have no rights and know their place always; I applaud the modern view which holds that all men are created equal, or very nearly so, and all walk with two feet upon the same planet, breathing the same air.

But I do think that valet might have given us a hand in offloading all our luggage from Lord Freckleton's space-ship.

The sixth vessel from the other end of the line was rather less than half the size of Lord Freckleton's. We looked at it for a moment. Then I looked at George. George did not seem to like that look I gave him; at any rate, he escaped from it by climbing into the ship, and making sure that the key would unlock its controls. I believe he may have been hoping it would not; but it did.

"I suppose," said George, "we may as well go and fetch our luggage over to this ship."

At a railway station, we would have engaged a porter; but no porters were in evidence in Peckover's yard. We trudged back and forth with our cases, which was galling, under the contented gaze of Lord Freckleton's manservant, which was infuriating.

Making our sixth or seventh hauling-trip around the shipyard, we returned to our craft to discover a fresh party upon the scene, who did much to brighten up her environs with ringlets, a pair of grey eyes, and a demure expression. George – who was the only one of us wearing headgear – raised his cricket-cap to her, and Harris casually stood in between the newcomer and the crate of brown ale, as though by doing so he would shield it from her view rather than drawing her attention to it.

The lady introduced herself as Miss Dickson, and indicating the craft next to ours, begged of us whether we thought she had found the sphere which she had hired; "for all of them do look so alike," she sighed.

"Well, Miss Dickson," said Harris after the usual pleasantries were disposed of, "the surest way to tell is to make sure that your key fits the controls. Do you wish me to check for you?"

The lady said that it was too kind of him to offer; but when he advanced upon her, she clambered into the sphere herself, and unlocked the controls without Harris's help.

"Surely," I ventured, "a young lady such as you doesn't plan to venture into orbit all by herself?"

"Oh, no," said Miss Dickson, emerging from the hatch once more. "Two dear friends of mine will accompany me – they sent me on ahead to secure the sphere, while they dealt with a few final things."

George wanted to know whether Miss Dickson's friends were also of the female variety, which is George all over; but Miss Dickson merely smiled at him and remarked that even with all the advances in society wrought by space travel, she did not believe that a mixed party in a space-craft would be viewed as decorous, any more than they would in the compartment of a railway carriage.

"Why," she added, "here are my companions now."

Two more young ladies were advancing upon us. Miss Dickson

hastened to introduce us to Miss Craddock and Miss Lexlake. Miss Lexlake in particular was a tall, willowy creation with a firmness of the eye and the jaw which made me determine to treat her with circumspection. The two newest arrivals were carrying something large and rolled-up, beneath their arms; my instinct was to offer them assistance with their burden, but there was something about Miss Lexlake that gave me pause. Certainly she and Miss Craddock seemed to bear up under the weight of it without any sign of feminine weakness; they marched straight into the ship with their load once we were all introduced, and emerged without it.

George recovered a little from his faux pas when we learned that the three ladies' itinerary was in essence identical to ours – to Selene City, upon the Moon, coming and going via whatever orbital stations seemed most suitable, and most suggestive of an entertaining visit. He became quite conversational with those three young ladies; and Harris took the opportunity to casually ease the crate of ale on board our own ship as George spoke to them.

It soon became clear that despite their tender years, this feminine trio were all experienced space travellers; and I thought it shabby of George, upon learning this, to mention that I was the only one present who had never yet been beyond the atmosphere.

Miss Dickson and Miss Craddock promptly began to reel off lists of things that I must do, must see, or must experience during my first spatial journey; and, speaking of reeling, my head soon began to.

"Ladies," I pleaded, as soon as both of them paused for breath at the same moment, "we are only going to space for two weeks. I am most grateful for your kindness, in recommending so many things to me; but if I adopted every suggestion you have made to me in the past five minutes, I should have a grey beard by the time I returned from orbit."

Miss Lexlake, who had until now refrained from adding to the torrent of advice, now spoke.

"Are you gentlemen quite sure," said she, "that you have packed your baggage aboard adequately?"

We all looked at the higgledy-piggledy stacks of cases and boxes which had lately been transferred from Lord Freckleton's ship. The more I looked at them, the more askew and inadequate they seemed.

Miss Lexlake, without waiting to be asked, marched on board our ship and took a closer look – I might almost call it a closer stare – at our worldly goods.

"What about this one?" she said, indicating a valise of George's which was wedged precariously in the pile. "Is it quite safe?"

"Oh, yes, quite safe; it's got a lock on," said George, contriving entirely to miss the thrust of Miss Lexlake's question.

Miss Lexlake eyed the luggage, and delivered herself of a deep sigh.

"Arabel!" she called through the craft's hatch. "Emily! Would you be good enough…?"

Miss Dickson and Miss Craddock joined Miss Lexlake at her call, and we three gentlemen watched in astonishment as the ladies began to take down and rearrange our baggage. I was relieved to see that none of them seemed to express outrage, or indeed any surprise at all, at the alcoholic element thereof.

"I say," said Harris, "won't you let me – "

"No need, Mr Harris," said Miss Lexlake firmly. "We sha'n't be more than a moment, and besides, there is no room for any more assistance."

Within five minutes, those three young ladies had re-packed our entire collection of impedimenta, as neatly and as precisely as any railway porter could have done it, and without the necessity to tip him for the trouble.

"My goodness," said George, "thank you very much, ladies. You are too kind."

"Perhaps we are," said Miss Lexlake, "but it would be a great shame were one of you gentlemen to have your brains dashed out by a packing-case upon launching your ship. You must remember, you see, that once beyond Earth's gravity, anything loose in the ship is apt to float around; and just because you're out of gravity and weightless, doesn't mean that inertia ceases to have an effect."

"Inertia?" Harris said.

"You know, old man," I said, eager to demonstrate the knowledge I had gleaned from my preparatory reading, and also to show that my brain was the match of the learned Miss Lexlake's. "Objects in motion remain in motion, objects at rest remain at rest. You know how when you sit in an armchair, and feel disinclined to get out of it again? That's inertia."

"That isn't quite the scientific meaning of the word," said Miss Lexlake, "but in essence you have it." She plucked a hatpin from her bonnet. "If I were to toss this pin toward Miss Craddock, you see, it would fall to the ground, because of gravity's pull. But if gravity were not to affect it – if it were plated with Cavorite, or if we had left Earth so far behind that its pull had diminished to nothing – then the pin would continue in the direction in which I had thrown it, indefinitely."

She returned the hat pin to its usual abode, rather to the relief of George, who had been eyeing it warily.

"Every moving object has inertia," went on Miss Lexlake, "including these cases. Suppose for a second that you were to turn the ship to one side. Everything on board the ship – not excluding yourselves – would experience a tendency to continue in the direction in which you had been travelling."

"You've probably experienced this," Miss Dickson chimed in helpfully, "here on Earth. When a hansom cab turns a sharp corner, you find yourself thrown to the side – if you don't see it coming and brace yourself, that is."

"And that," said Miss Lexlake, "is why you must take care to strap all your bags carefully in place – like this." She suited the action to the word, buckling the luggage compartment's leather straps firmly in place and leaving our cases peering out between them, like a convict between prison bars.

"You're most frightfully kind," I murmured. I was, indeed, grateful for the assistance provided by the ladies, but somehow I felt that the more help they gave us, the more we were put on display as inadequate duffers who had no business venturing off the surface of their own planet.

Miss Lexlake and her friends exited the ship, and as they did so, three more people arrived on the scene; a well-dressed man with a fair moustache and a salt-and-pepper tweed suit, a woman who clung to his arm so closely that it took an effort to see any of her face below the eyes thanks to her man's shoulder, and a seedy-looking fellow who looked like an undertaker's clerk. This latter gentleman came over to us with an officious air which suggested to me that here, at last, was Mr Peckover.

5

"Hey!" appeared to be Mr Peckover's manner of greeting his customers. He tucked his thumbs into his waistcoat pockets and stared at us.

"Good afternoon, Mr Peckover," ventured George.

Mr Peckover grunted, and the other man came over to join him.

"Are we going to be long?" he said. "I particularly want to get an early start."

"Not long, my lord," said Peckover, which enabled me to further deduce that the other gentleman was Lord Freckleton. "I hope I may just attend to these ladies and gentlemen?"

His lordship huffed discontentedly, and thrust his hands into his pockets, where they remained as he strolled up and down, jingling keys and coins in a musical manner.

Peckover soon ascertained that we were two parties – or 'crews' as he chose to refer to them – of three apiece; and that while the female party were well versed in space travel, we men could not make the same boast.

"All right," he said with a sigh, as though our inexperience served solely to cause him annoyance. "You ladies may launch directly, while I make final arrangements with his lordship; and you gentlemen had better wait till I'm done there, and I'll come over and eddycate you in how to fly a ship without killing yourselves – or anyone else."

He turned to leave with Lord and Lady Freckleton, but stopped and looked back at us, evidently weighing us up and finding us wanting, like a barrel arriving at St Pancras from Burton containing less than a full complement of ale.

"Don't touch anything, meantime," he said; and Miss Dickson suppressed a sound which, to a man less versed in etiquette than I, might have suggested a giggle.

"Very well," said Miss Lexlake as Peckover and the Freckletons left us; "let us prepare for launch. Unless," she added, "you gentlemen would sooner we waited for you, to make certain you're quite all right."

We all three hastened to assure her that we would be all right – more than all right – perfectly splendid, in fact.

"Good biz!" said Miss Craddock, at which use of slang Miss Dickson again suppressed merriment.

All three ladies bade us au revoir, words which Miss Lexlake made it clear were not chosen thoughtlessly. "I hope we may see you again, once we reach the orbital stations," she said with a smile. I am sure, to do her justice, that the smile was meant in a wholly friendly manner; but somehow Miss Lexlake's air of efficiency and intelligence gave it a hint of veiled menace. Hence I regret to say that I murmured some pleasantry quietly, and was quite drowned out by Harris, who took the hand of each lady in turn and wished her a safe and pleasant journey.

At which, it became Miss Craddock's turn to suppress mirth.

The ladies climbed aboard their own ship, and secured the hatch door. As we watched, the metal sphere moved; at first the merest hint of rocking, as though disturbed by a strong wind. Then it arose, slowly and steadily, with no rotational or side-to-side motion, straight up into the air, at about a walking pace – if it had been possible for anyone to walk directly upward with nothing save the air under the soles of the feet.

The sphere rose steadily until it must have been twenty feet up, and we were all tilting our heads back to look at it. At this point, it gathered speed, and by the time it was a hundred feet above us or so, it had reached the velocity of a suburban train, or a more than usually energetic cab horse. It continued to race away from us vertically, and within a minute or two, it was the merest dot in the sky overhead. My eyes were watering from the strain of tracking it; I blinked, and when I opened my eyes once more, it was gone.

Where the sphere had been, on the ground, was a circular indentation in the earth. A couple of earthworms and a slug were revealed to view; I gained the impression that they would as soon have remained hidden, but perhaps that was just the way that the slug drew in its antennae as I regarded it.

"What charming ladies they were," said George, in a rather uncertain voice, as though he were trying to persuade himself of the fact.

"They appear extremely well educated," I said, "and – ahem! – quite lacking in feminine delicacy and reticence."

"That's the modern young woman for you," Harris said. "Can you imagine those three on the Thames? Why, put them in a skiff and they could charge down a steam-launch and overturn it. It all comes of letting women have an education."

"Oh?" said George. "Aren't you going to educate your girls, then?"

"Of course I am," said Harris; "but I hope they won't turn out, any of them, like that Miss Lexlake. There were men in my college fifteen without muscles like those in her arms."

"I thought she was a charming and intelligent young lady," George said, "and as for her arms, I see no cause for complaint. If we'd left the luggage as you packed it, we should have been awash in clutter the moment we left Earth's gravity."

"I say, you chaps," I said, trying to soothe them, "I think Lord Freckleton's about to take off."

To my relief – for George can be most provoking when he has encountered a young lady who he hopes may prove susceptible to his charms – they both broke off their conversation, and turned to see the second ship launch. It took off rather less steadily than Miss Lexlake and company's vessel; it rose abruptly to thirty feet or so, hovered for some seconds, shot up to a hundred feet, hovered again, then took on a sudden motion, like a football being kicked from the penalty mark, and vanished into the sky with a faint crack of displaced air.

"I hope he doesn't overtake Miss Lexlake and bump into her," I said as it disappeared from sight.

"He might overtake her," said George, "but I'm sure he won't hit her. That's the thing about space; there's so much room up there."

"In fact," said Harris, "that's why they call it space."

I might have found this observation more amusing if the same joke had not been made, verbatim, in the preface to the "Pocket

Guide to the Moon and Orbital Stations" which sat, true to its name, in my inside pocket.

Mr Peckover came stumping over toward us, still with his thumbs tucked into his waistcoat.

"Very well," he said. I have noticed many times before that when a man opens his conversation with 'Very well', he seldom means that things are very well, or at all close to that state of bliss. "Who's going to be piloting this sphere?"

"I expect," I said cautiously, "that we all are. Not all at once, you know, but turn and turn about."

"Oh," said Peckover. He spat onto the ground, narrowly missing the slug, and eyed us with an increasingly jaundiced air. "And I don't suppose none of you have flown one of these before – what?"

"Actually, I have," George said, taking a step forward. Peckover focused his gaze upon George at my expense and Harris's. He did not seem any the less dubious, and gave a long sigh.

"Get aboard, all of you," he said, "and I'll show you how to pilot a sphere. It's easy enough when you once know the ropes," he added, with what seemed to me a quite unnecessary subtext – that it was fortunate for us that it was a simple task to learn.

Onto – or should it be into? I really don't know which is appropriate – onto the sphere we trooped, and Mr Peckover began by jerking open a panel in its inner wall.

"First of all," he said, "before you take off, every single time, you must check your oxygen. Now I know your reservoir is full, for I filled the thing myself this morning, but you mustn't ever take it for granted. To find yourself out of air midway between the Earth and the Moon – well, it's not an easy way to peg out."

"It's such a stuffy death," murmured Harris; "a beast of a death."

I gave him a warning look; for I recognised the quotation, and I wanted to be quite certain that he was not about to break into a comic song there in the sphere with Mr Peckover as an involuntary audience. You can never be quite sure that Harris is not going to essay a comic song, even though I have done my best in a previous forum to warn the world and Harris against his doing so.

Peckover showed us how to determine whether the oxygen supply was adequate and properly working, and a dozen other things which he said were essential to our safety and well-being while we were off the surface of our dear home planet.

Finally he cranked the door closed, unlocked the controls, and invited George to be seated at them.

"You remember how to do this?" he said cautiously.

"Of course," said George. "All the Cavorite slats are interconnected, aren't they? So the controls work just like the tiller of a boat."

With which George patted the controls affectionately. He must have caught them at an angle, for the next thing I knew, I felt a jerk, and the left-hand side of the sphere abruptly shot upwards, depositing Harris and myself in a heap on the right-hand side.

Two seconds later, George's body landed on top of both of us with what a more melodramatic writer than I might have called a sickening thud, but which I shall simply describe as an unwelcome impact. George is not what one would call portly, but he is well-built and muscular. I remember reading in a patent medicine leaflet that muscle weighs more than fat; at that instant, I would have sworn that George was constructed entirely of muscles, save perhaps for his fat head.

Peckover – I don't know why – seemed to have half been expecting such a mishap, and by means of a firm grip on his chair, escaped joining the tangle of limbs. He reached out to the controls and eased the tiller back to its starting position. George rolled off Harris, and I rolled off George, and Harris passed George his cap back with an expression that made words unnecessary.

"That," said Peckover, "is how not to launch a Cavorite sphere."

"I say," remarked George, "look at this, you fellows."

We joined him at one of the windows, and to my considerable astonishment, I saw nothing save blue sky above and below us. By craning my neck and looking down as far as I could, I found I could see the land below; the North Sea (grey rather than blue), fields divided into neat squares and oblongs by hedges, and a small moving dot which I deduced, from the fact that it was moving along a thin line, must be one of the London, Tilbury and Southend Railway's steam trains. It was a most disconcerting feeling, and yet at the same time exhilarating.

"We aren't weightless," I said.

"You aren't far enough from the Earth to be weightless," said Peckover. "We aren't even a quarter of a mile up. I'm going to take us back down, and we shall try launching again."

He guided us gently back to our starting point and invited George to take the pilot's seat once more, which he did – somewhat more circumspectly, this time. Harris and I held onto the various handles with which the interior of the sphere was provided, and which made it look a little like a globular version of an underground railway carriage.

I looked at the luggage, and uttered silent thanks for the efficient re-packing which Miss Lexlake and her friends had performed upon it.

On his second attempt, George managed to make the vessel rise in the air on a more even keel – if I may say that of a ship which entirely lacks a keel – and guide it around in a circular direction at a height of some quarter of a mile. Harris ventured to let go of his handle and come and look over his shoulder; I was worried for a moment – I know that I cannot abide anyone looking over my shoulder when I'm engaged in any task whatsoever – but no further mishaps occurred.

"Do you want a spin at the controls, Harris?" George enquired, now sounding quite genial.

Harris said that he supposed there had to be a first time; and George got out of the captain's chair – being very careful not to touch the controls – and made way for Harris.

Harris initially placed his hands on the controls with the reticence of a man touching an electric stove-top which may or may not be red hot. The ship did not so much as quiver, and he gave Peckover an enquiring look.

"She won't move, sir," said Peckover, "not less'n you tell her to. See, she's in equilibrium at the moment."

"Equilibrium? Isn't that a mineral water?" said Harris. George gave a knowing chuckle. I could pardon Harris his question, myself, for if there are two things in this universe of which Harris is utterly ignorant, one is the laws of physics and the other is mineral water.

"He means, you ass," said George, "that the gravitic shields are engaged to just such an extent that they balance the force of gravity on the sphere and cancel it out. That's how we come to be standing still in the air."

Harris took a suspicious look out of one window, where we had a good view of a small, fleecy cloud at some distance.

"That cloud is moving," he objected to George.

"That cloud," said Peckover, "is made of water vapour and has very little mass. It moves upon the breeze. This ship – " he gave the wall next to the window an affectionate thump, which made Harris look alarmed for a second – "is made of metal. It would take a much stronger wind than this to blow it around the sky."

Thus reassured, Harris finally consented to be shown the controls, and to learn how to adjust the angle of the Cavorite plates such that they cancelled out gravity to a greater or a lesser extent. Harris is not a man to worry himself about anything unduly, and within ten minutes, he had acquired the ability to make the sphere dodge about the sky like a bagatelle ball.

"Extraordinary," he said, "how easy it is, once you grow used to it. Come over, do, J., and give it a try."

I took over the pilot's seat and looked at the controls.

Once, as a child, I persuaded a railwayman to allow me to step onto the footplate of a locomotive engine – a treat which fulfilled an urge I had cherished since the first time I experienced the delights of the railway train. The engine-driver started to explain what each and every control did; and once my initial delight had worn off somewhat, I was alarmed to discover that there were hundreds of the things, and by the time the driver had reached the conclusion of his tour round the footplate, I could not remember a single one of his explanations. Neither could I tell you any of them to this day – except the steam-whistle, which he allowed me to sound, and then gave me a piece of cotton-waste upon which to wipe my hands. I kept that piece of cotton-waste as a treasured souvenir for half of my childhood.

Perhaps it was merely the passage of years, but the controls of that sphere appeared very much less complex than those of the steam train. The sphere was surrounded all over with a great many small and wafer-thin plates of Cavorite, which is impervious to the force of gravity. I believe that the scientists are still engaged in trying to puzzle out how this can be so; given that they cannot even reach a mutually agreeable conclusion as to whether gravity is a constant, a variable power, a wave, or something entirely sui generis with no similarity to any other force of nature – well, I suspect that they may be at their studies for some considerable time yet; especially since the scientific departments of our great Universities are increasingly in receipt of funding from industry to encourage their research. I am no scientist; but I am enough of one to know that if an early answer to this conundrum be found, then the funding from industry will no doubt cease, as being no longer required; and consequently the mysteries of gravitics seem to me likely to remain mysteries for a while.

Such were the thoughts in my mind as I took my seat at the controls of the sphere.

Peckover patiently showed me how I might, by means of adjusting the angle of the Cavorite panels, increase or decrease the force of gravity on one side or other of the ship.

"I beg your pardon," I said to him, "but can one really refer to this ship as having 'sides' when it is, to all intents, spherical?"

"Of course it has sides," interjected George; "the inside and the outside." And he laughed heartily.

Mr Peckover, who did not laugh, explained that it was the convention that the pilot of the sphere faced for'ard, and to his left and right were port and starboard, respectively.

The mention of 'port and starboard' set me a-shudder. I am not inexperienced in boats and ships; but just as Coleridge could never remember the fate of Kubla Khan after the visitor from Porlock drove it from his head, I have tremendous worry in remembering which of 'port' and 'starboard' relates to 'left' and which to 'right'. This is of trivial import when reading a naval-themed work by Captain Marryat, or even when sculling up the Thames; but in the present setting it appeared rather more vital.

As a very young man, when I first encountered the joys of boating, I was taken out on the water by a slightly older friend called Crompton. Crompton was the sort of fellow who knew everything – had done everything – had travelled everywhere – and found nothing more delightful than to share his knowledge and wisdom with a young shaver such as I.

"Take that rope and get ready to untie it," said Crompton as we went aboard.

"Which rope?" I asked; for we were tied up to two bollards, each secured by a different painter. "The left one, or the right one?"

Crompton smiled knowingly at me. "My dear J., pray don't let any seaman hear you talking like that, or they'll know you immediately for a complete and utter land-lubber. On the water, we talk not of left and right, but of port and starboard."

"I see," said I, not seeing. "And which is which?"

Crompton's smile broadened. "It may seem perplexing at first; but I know a little trick, by using which you'll always be able to remember. Port," he said, "is a kind of wine; and to drink wine is all right – wouldn't you say?"

I had little more experience of wine than of sailing; but somehow I felt disinclined to admit as much to Crompton. "Oh, yes, rather," I said.

"Why, there you are! Port is right. Just remember that maxim, and you'll never struggle to recall it in the future."

I was foolish enough to take Crompton at his word, and it was only afterwards that I learned that port is left, in nautical parlance. But by this time, Crompton's aide-memoire had driven its way firmly into my memory; and now, whenever I need to remind myself of my ports and starboard on the water, or in space, you may perhaps hear me mutter to myself, "Port is all right, but Crompton was all wrong, so port is left."

There are a dozen easier and more accurate ways of remembering it, I am certain; but the memory of that day and of Crompton's easy assuredness are fixed in my brain, like a mile-stone rooted deep in the earth, and I can no more dislodge them than Sisyphus could roll his rock up the hill without it tumbling back down. The human mind is a wonderfully illogical construction.

Fortunately for me, the controls of the sphere were constructed along more logical lines. Once I had rid myself of the preconception that they would bear any resemblance to the tiller of a boat, or the reins of a horse, I soon gathered the principle that to extend the Cavorite flaps on one quarter – or side – of the ship was to decrease gravity on that side, and hence to make it rise; and once that was plain to me, I soon learned how to control the sphere's progress with a more delicate touch, which could be achieved by altering the angle of any one flap rather than the whole set of them on one side. The default control steers them all together, but finer work is easy to master with a little practice; and though I say it who shouldn't, I fancy that after a few minutes, Mr Peckover seemed very well pleased with my progress.

"Just take her back down," he said, "and I shall alight, and leave you gentlemen to start your journey proper."

He sat with his hands ready to take over the controls from me had I made a bosh of descending back to Earth; but the sphere was quite content to come down at a steady and gentle pace, and when it finally touched the surface once more, it didn't bounce more than once. Harris complained that his teeth had come together sharply with the force of touch-down and that he had almost bitten his tongue; but when has Harris ever been satisfied with any man's steering of any craft upon land, sea or air, save for his own?

6

Mr Peckover having departed, we three were left to our own devices.

"I suppose," said George, "we should make a start, if we are to reach an orbital station by tonight."

"Are we to make for Oakapple Orbital?" I asked, mentally consulting Baedeker.

"Half a mo.," said Harris. "You mean there is some risk that we won't make it tonight?"

"Well," George said, "remember that the further away from Earth we progress, the less effect upon our ship the controls will have. It's something called the inverse square law."

As I have already narrated, Harris is no physicist, and he just grunted.

"Very well," he said. "Then the quicker we launch the better."

"There are hammocks aboard for sleeping," I reminded him.

"Have you seen those hammocks? Hammocks," said Harris with a jaundiced air, "into which one has to tie oneself, to prevent oneself floating away in the night, are not my idea of a peaceful night's sleep."

"Don't be such a wet blanket, Harris," said George. "It's all part of the fun of a trip into space."

Harris asked George pointedly whether he had slept strapped into a hammock on his previous trip in a space sphere; to which George replied in the negative, and reminded Harris that that voyage had lasted but two hours.

"You see!" said Harris. "I never knew a fellow like you for blathering about matters you've no experience of. Upon my word, I've half a mind to go home."

I reminded Harris of the crates of beer in our baggage, and of the joys awaiting on the orbital stations of night-clubs and gaming-halls and restaurants; and with a sigh of long suffering Harris was persuaded to remain aboard sphere.

We re-sealed the hatch, and checked the air and water supplies, and ran through the list of vital checks which Mr Peckover had impressed upon us must be performed at the start of each and every voyage; and then we were off – off at last – off into the atmosphere, and beyond it.

George took the controls for the launch, and we rose from the planetary surface with admirable smoothness. I admired the view through the window of the Earth below, and tried to decide whether we were receding from the Earth, or it from us.

Harris, meantime, was fiddling with the luggage straps, with the intent of removing the first crate of ale from the neatly stacked cases.

"You'd better be quick about it if you're going to drink beer," said George, looking over his shoulder at Harris. "Once we leave Earth's gravity you won't be able to."

Harris paused in the very act of wielding a patent bottle-opener, and rubbed one ear with his free hand.

"I swear I must be going deaf, George," he said. "I almost fancied I heard you say that we couldn't drink beer outside Earth's gravity."

"That's just what I did say," said George.

Harris advanced upon George with a wild expression on his face.

"Why, for heaven's sake? Do they have some kind of licensing statute in orbit, that forbids you to drink alcohol?"

"Oh," George said casually, "the law in question is a dashed sight harder to get around than the licensing laws; it's the jolly old laws of physics that shall be vexing us, soon."

I joined Harris next to George.

"What law may this be, then?" I could recall nothing of this in the guide books with which I had prepared myself.

George took his hands off the controls and plucked the bottle and its opener from Harris's grasp; Harris gave a little gasp and tried to cling onto them, but he was too slow – which goes to show how deeply affected he must have been by this turn of events.

"Watch this," said George. He plied the opener, and the cap of the bottle popped free and tinkled to the floor of the sphere. George lifted the bottle to his lips and drank with relish.

"We watched it," I said. "What were we meant to derive from it?"

"What happens when you open a bottle of beer?"

"I drink it," said Harris.

"Before that?"

"I don't usually let much time pass between opening and drinking it," said Harris.

George sighed in exasperation. "Imagine you're in an hotel on Earth, and you ask for a beer. It comes to you in a pint glass, with a head upon it. Do you follow me?"

Harris looked at George as though he suspected some verbal trickery. "Yes."

"Where is the head?"

"On the beer."

"Exactly. At the top of the beer. Beer," said George, sounding more and more like a professor addressing a rabble of not particularly bright undergraduates, "is produced by the fermentation of yeast, which gives as a by-product dioxide of carbon – a gas. That gas rises to the surface of beer upon Earth, and forms a head."

"And why shouldn't it?"

"Do use your own head, Harris, won't you? The head appears at the top of beer because the dioxide is lighter than the liquid. But that's under gravity. If you were to pour a beer in space, firstly you wouldn't be able to get it into the glass, and secondly, the head wouldn't form on the top. You'd have a little globe of beer, floating around the cabin like a balloon, with the head on the outside, like pastry round a beef Wellington."

"I'd heard talk," I said, "of beer having specific gravity, but I didn't realise that beer was specific to gravity."

I thought this a rather clever witticism, especially for one made up on the spur of the moment; but Harris gave me a savage look, and told me that this was no laughing matter.

"Do you mean," he said to George, "that once we leave Earth's gravity, we cannot safely or enjoyably quaff any of that beer which J. so thoughtfully stocked us with?"

"I mean exactly that, old man. Until we get to the Moon, anyway, when we shall have gravity once more."

"In that case," Harris said, "bring this ship to a stop upon the instant, I entreat you."

George being occupied with the bottle he had already opened, Harris took it upon himself to adjust the controls so that the ship was balanced between gravity and immunity to gravity – in other words, we were holding steady like a sailing ship at anchor, except that no anchor was required. This was fortunate, as the chain it would have needed to reach the ground would have taken up most of the space inside the sphere, even wound up.

"I thought," said George, decorously wiping his lips, "that you wanted to get to Oakapple Orbital without any delay."

"That," said Harris, "was before you told me we were forbidden beer en route." And he retrieved his patent bottle-opener from George, and took another bottle, and opened it for himself.

I hate to feel left out when my friends are enjoying themselves, even if it involves the sacrifice of sobriety and clean living; so I opened myself a bottle, too, and we let the ship hang there while we proved to our own satisfaction that we were still, for the moment at least, safely inside our planet's gravitical pull.

We were not quite certain of the fact after one bottle each, however, and so we thought it prudent to repeat the experiment, for the sake of certainty.

At this point, I found myself moved to compose verse:
"Drinking beer
Outside the atmosphere
Is never a good idea,
I fear."

"Jolly good, J.," said George. "But you'd better write it down if you want to remember it tomorrow."

Harris, at this juncture, burst out into a sudden explosion of laughter. I was surprised that it should take even Harris so long to see the wry amusement in my impromptu ditty; but it turned out he had not even been listening to me recite it.

"What on earth do you find so hilarious, then, Harris?" asked George.

"Last night," Harris explained, "on my way to Maplin, I found myself sharing a railway carriage with a dreadful man in a three-shilling hat and pimples all over his chivvy, and a woman of whom I need say no more, than that she looked exactly the sort of woman who would attach herself to such a man."

George and I began to make vague noises of commiseration, but Harris overrode us.

"They were talking – I couldn't help but overhear 'em – about a Temperance Society outing they were going to attend, up into orbit; they're probably somewhere up here at this very moment. George, you said it was carbon dioxide that made beer go peculiar in orbit?"

"Yes, but what would that matter to a Temperance Society?"

"Why," chortled Harris, "these Temperance beanfeasts are famous for bringing along terrifying amounts of lemonade, and ginger-beer, and – what the dickens is the name of that thing that sounds as though it should be a rat-poison? Phosphodone, that's right; and all of those beastly slops are chock-full of carbon dioxide, enough to give any decent man indigestion and palpitations; and – and just think of a ship full of Temperance types with crate upon crate of this dreadful stuff, and they can't open 'em or enjoy 'em or feel superior to us beer-drinkers with 'em or anything!"

"That's all very well," I said, "but at the end of the day, while in orbit, we are no better off than they, are we? We're both denied a favourite beverage to which we had been looking forward, before our departure from Earth's gravity."

Harris laughed in triumph – I might almost say he cackled.

"That's what you think, J.! We shall be all right, even when we do find ourselves without gravity and without ale."

He pointed to another crate, neatly and securely stacked, courtesy of Miss Lexlake and her pals.

"We've got whisky!"

Since Harris had reminded us of the existence aboard of whisky, it seemed appropriate to use a little of it to toast our departure from the Earth's surface; and so we marked the occasion.

"Oh, dash it," said Harris after a while.

"What's wrong, old man?"

"I think," he said, "the sun's setting."

I peered out of the window. A sunset from up above ground level is a peculiar thing, and not at all akin to the experience of it down below.

The first thing I noticed was that some nearby clouds were turning deep orange. To measure distances in the sky is no easy matter, for one has no fixed point of reference, save for one's self, to work from. But I should have said that these clouds were less than a mile distant from us, both horizontally and vertically.

Looking further into the distance, I espied the sunset itself, approaching us as we hung in the sky, a line of shadow advancing over the surface of the planet below. On the other side of the terminator, light faded into darkness, and I could observe a few stars in the sky, as well as the occasional glow from this or that city on the dark side of the sunset line.

I think that it was at about this point that I first realised how spectacular were the sights I was likely to see upon this journey. I felt a warmth somewhere inside me – I do not say that the whisky was not in part responsible – and I almost felt impelled to share with Harris and George the nature of this epiphany. Indeed, it was only the thought of the laugh with which Harris would surely greet such an announcement from me that made me hesitate – at first.

I was still staring through the window – I fancy that I was trying to decide whether a particular gleam of light below, on the Continental coast, was Dunkerque, or The Hague, or what – when another light, very much nearer, caught my attention. It was aloft at our level, and it was approaching us at some speed.

My first thought was that it was a meteor, and that we were about to be knocked out of the sky and killed. A moment's reflection sufficed to tell me that this theory was bunk, for the light was moving far more slowly than any meteor. Furthermore, there was a kind of artificial quality about the light it emitted which led me to deduce that it was no natural article, but a man-made one.

"Look, you chaps," I said, "I think there's another sphere overhauling us – just yonder."

By the time George and Harris had joined me, it had approached closer yet, and now was plainly another space-vessel.

"Surely he's not going to collide with us?" ventured Harris.

But as it loomed up, so it slackened in speed, until it came to a stop no more than fifty feet from us. Then a blue light began to glow from it.

"Oh, corks," said George. "That means it's the police, I think."

"Have they come for you, old fellow?" Harris enquired sociably. "Don't worry. We'll conceal you somewhere."

I don't like to imply that Harris's judgment was clouded for any reason, but there was certainly no nook or cranny aboard our ship that would have hidden anything larger than quite a small kitten.

"Don't be an ass," said George curtly.

"Well, you are the only one of us who's been up here before and had the opportunity to commit an offence," pointed out Harris. "Did you moor your sphere next to a 'No Trespassing' notice board? You make a point of doing that on the river."

"Firstly," said George, "that hobby horse belongs to J., not to me; and secondly, they don't have boards like that in orbit."

"Thirdly," I said, "you two stop squabbling. Look, he's coming over."

The double-hatch on the side of the police vessel had opened, to permit the exit of a figure resembling nothing so much as Bibendum, the Michelin tyres mascot. He held onto the handle by the hatch with one hand; in the other –

"Is he holding a gun?" said George.

"It look uncommonly like one," said I.

7

We all three stared through the atmospherium porthole in dismay.

"I heard once," said Harris, "about a gang of bandits on the Wyoming frontier who disguised themselves as lawmen so as to rob stage-coaches. They would pretend to be the real article and stop the coach, in order to search for contraband; and then they would shoot the passengers and make off with all their valuables."

Still clinging onto the handrail with one arm, the diving-suited figure raised the other one, until the gun – if gun it were – pointed in our exact direction.

"George," said Harris in a choked voice, "can you unlock the controls and get us away from here, pronto?"

"Not a chance, Harris. He'd pot us before we could move an inch."

As George spoke, the weapon discharged. Something of metal caught the rays of the setting sun, and flashed as it shot toward us. The whole of our sphere reverberated with a dull clang.

George peered out of the window at an angle. "Of course," he said ruefully. "What chumps we are. It's a grappling rope, and he's snagged it round us."

The stranger secured the other end of his device to his own ship, then swung hand over hand towards us. Had he released his grip, he would have fallen to certain death on the ground far below, but he progressed with no more sign of nerves than would a monkey swinging from tree to tree in the jungle, until he disappeared from our window-limited view, and we knew he must have reached the surface of our ship.

One of the electric needles on our controls began to move across its dial, like a railway telegraph.

"He's in our hatch," said George. He plucked his cap from his head and quickly straightened his hair, before replacing it.

The needle crawled up to the other end of the dial, and a second clang sounded out – this one plainly coming from the inner door of our hatch.

"I suppose we must open it," I said.

Harris sighed, and spun the wheel that operated the hatch controls. There was a gentle hiss of air – again reminiscent of a sound one might hear on a railway – and the hatch swung open. There stood Officer Bibendum.

He stepped inside, and with a twist first one way then the other, removed the diver's helmet from his space-suit, revealing himself to be pink-cheeked, moustachioed, black-haired, and irascible in nature. At least, the first three were incontrovertible; the fourth one, while some surmise was involved, seemed a very fair bet, given the scornful look he turned upon us. I wished fervently that Harris had not left the whisky bottle sitting in the middle of our control panel.

"Good hevening, gentlemen," he said, emphasising the word 'gentlemen' just sufficiently that we could all see that he didn't mean it.

"Good evening, constable," I ventured. "Can we be of assistance?"

"Hassistance, my foot," snorted the policeman, which suggested that my choice of conversational gambit had been a poor one.

"Is there a problem, constable...?" George hazarded, giving the question an upward tone at the end. George has had many encounters with police constables in his career, some of them on more friendly terms than others, and he has often told me that it is always a good move to ascertain their name – if possible, before they arrest you – because he thinks it "makes it so much harder for them to be beastly if you make them treat you as an acquaintance."

"Nuttall," said the policeman. "Constable Nuttall of the Hatmospheric and Horbital Link. And I must ask you gentlemen – " again he emphasised that word quite unpleasantly – "to give me a hexplanation for your presence here."

"We are making our way," said Harris, "from Maplin to Oakapple Orbital. Merely that, and nothing more."

Constable Nuttall was perhaps not a reader of the late, great Poe;

at any rate, he snorted, and said something to himself that sounded sceptical.

"We are, indeed," I said, feeling it my duty to back up George in the presence of the law, as indeed I had done many times before in our youth.

"Ho," said Nuttall. "And if that's so, p'raps you would like to hexplain why you're a-dangling 'ere in the hatmosphere, with night coming on, and not so much as a single light displayed habout your sphere. Do I really need to remind you of the provisions of the Spatial Travel and Cargo Hact, 1899?"

We all three of us said nothing; but if the look on my face matched those I saw on the expressions of Harris and George, I fear that we needed no words to express to the champion of the law our utter ignorance of that Act of Parliament.

"Which you're sitting 'ere," Nuttall said ponderously, "hobstructing of the way and causing a danger to hother shipping, contrary to section 44 of the Hact. Neither are you displaying lights hupon your craft as specified by section 49 of the Hact."

We began to burble profuse apologies for the error of our ways, and to promise that if only Constable Nuttall would overlook our sins, we should no longer cause our sphere to hover motionless in the middle of a shipping lane, and would festoon it with more lights than the Trocadero on a winter night.

I saw Harris slip his hand into his pocket, and shook my head in his direction in the hope that he might observe my hint; for your average London bobby may be persuaded to turn a blind eye to a trifling infringement of the law for half-a-crown, but the doughty men of the A.O.L. are not so easily bought and sold.

Nuttall advanced to the centre of the sphere, and cast a cold eye upon our control panel. The one thing more prominent than the whisky bottle sitting among the controls, was the level of the amber fluid contained within it, which was certainly nearer to the bottom of the bottle than to the neck thereof.

To my relief, he passed no remark upon the whisky, but instead reached out and turned a switch from one setting to another.

"Oh, I say," George murmured, with a gesture to the window.

A certain gleam from all sides of the casement suggested that the exterior of our sphere was now illuminated.

"Your ship, gentlemen," said Nuttall, "is now lit up in haccordance with section 49 of the Hact."

"Awfully kind of you," Harris simpered. "And we promise to be on our way immediately you leave us – don't we, chaps?"

We so promised. But Nuttall took no steps to return to his own vessel.

"I dare say you'd like to," the constable remarked, eyeing each of us in turn with a jaundiced air.

"Oh, officer," I said with my most disarming manner, "surely you can't intend to detain us just for infringing one regulation?"

"Two regulations," quoth the arm of the law.

"...two regulations. But now you've corrected us, and there's no danger at all that we'll err in that way again – isn't that so, you men?"

Harris and George both vowed once more to adhere to the least and littlest paragraph of the law as regards space travel and space-faring vessels. But the constable yet remained unmoved.

"You see, sirs," he said (I breathed a mental sigh of relief that we were no longer "gentlemen"), "we in the A.O.L. sometimes are given notice that wanted criminals are thought to be hentering into our jurisdiction, and this being so, we make it our business to scrutinise hanyone resembling the description of such wanted criminals with hextreme care and thoroughness."

He rocked back on his heels contemplatively, then forward again, and went on.

"And in the current hinstance, we have it on Scotland Yard's hauthority that three notorious rogues and confidence-men have been seen making for Maplin, with the presumed hintent of hobtaining a sphere and departing from there, into what one might term, our manor. Three rogues," he repeated, "of an age and hoverall description not dissimilar to yours."

"Harris," said George jocularly, "have you been robbing banks again?"

The constabulary gentleman gave George another look.

"It's all right," said George. "I'm a banker myself – at least, I work in a bank."

"He calls it work," remarked Harris pointedly.

"Hupon further hinspection of this ship and its contents," PC Nuttall said, rising above the petty witticisms of George and Harris, "it becomes hevident to me that you gents are not the suspicious characters I thought you might be. Haccordingly I shall take my leave of you. But," he added with a stern look, "I hexpect you to himmediately raise your ship to the five mile limit before you turn in for the rest which you hevidently need."

His eye wandered once again to the whisky bottle, in a kind of meaningful way.

We all assured him once again that we should uplift our ship to well beyond that mark with the promptitude of a racehorse approaching the finishing-post, and he appeared mollified.

"Then I bid you good-hevening, sirs," he said, and retrieving his helmet, he re-attached it to the neck of his protective suit, and stepped back into the airlock.

George opened the outer door, and we watched him glide back to his own vessel, winding in the grapple-rope as he went.

"Well," I said, "better lift us higher up, George."

George put his hands on the controls, and turned the Cavorite blinds to an increased angle. By now it was fully dark outside, and looking out of the window gave little assistance in judging our speed and direction of motion; but a gentle pressure upon my feet confirmed to me that we were travelling upward.

"We might have been in trouble, there. I thought that police fellow was uncommonly sensible," said Harris.

"I thought George was uncommonly sensible," said I. "I still remember that time you had been celebrating your birthday, George, and tried to pinch a bobby's helmet in Great Lovejoy Street. I had to bail you out from West End Central police-station. Lord alone knows where you'd have been dragged off to up here, if you'd pulled the same trick."

"I couldn't," objected George. "He wasn't wearing a helmet. Well, not the traditional pointy sort with the silver doo-dah on top."

Harris laughed. "If you'd stolen his space helmet he could hardly have taken us anywhere."

"I say," I interjected. "Is it just my fancy, or am I becoming lighter on my feet?"

Harris, who as I may have remarked before takes the largest size in waistcoats of we three, bounced on his heels, just as PC Nuttall had done a few minutes beforehand.

"Crumbs," he exclaimed. "I think old J. is right for once. Upon my word, I feel five years younger."

"We are beginning to escape Earth's gravity," said George cheerfully.

I crossed to a window, and peered through it in a downward direction. Just as our vessel was in darkness, so the planet below was also dark, in the main; but over to one side, I could see the sunset-line crossing the Earth's surface, giving an effect uncannily similar to the sight of the crescent moon from Earth.

Turning my attention upward, I looked for the Moon. I could not see it, and for a foolish moment I was seized by a fear that we had gone horribly off course due to the whisky, and were going to miss the Moon and drift off into space, or plunge into the Sun.

Something of this unreasoned worry must have shown in my face, because Harris came over to me with a solicitous air and asked "What's the matter, J., old chap? Is the lessened gravity getting to your tummy?"

I do wish he had not said that. I have remarked on previous occasions upon mal de mer, and my experiences with that peculiar and distressing syndrome. A medical fellow I know informs me that sea-sickness is all down to the little tubes of one's middle ear, which contain liquid rather like a builder's spirit-level, and give to the brain the awareness of whether or not it is aslant or on an even keel.

I personally find that my own two eyes give me that information perfectly adequately, without having to call in another sensory organ entirely, which it seems to me should focus its concern upon hearing, rather than arrogating to itself another task which is already well in hand. It is as if a brick-layer, building a house, should suddenly discover another workman interposing himself by the wall and starting to clap bricks down, when all the time he should be doing his own job of erecting scaffolding, or dealing with the installation of the gas-piping.

Such a state of affairs can only lead to chaos in the construction department; and by the same token, having one's ears shove their oar into a man's balance instead of leaving it to his eyes, leads inevitably to queasiness and unwelcome sensations amidships – a term which in the current instance may be taken either literally or figuratively.

Up until the second when Harris made that remark, I was feeling fresh and invigorated at the growing sensation of lightness about my body. The moment he spoke, and reminded me of the presence within me of a digestive system, and the presence within that of certain quantities of beer and whisky, the whole space-vessel seemed to switch from rising smoothly and steadily, to lurching about the sky like a spavined cab-horse.

"George," I said, "can't you make this thing fly a spot steadier?"

"I am in perfect control," said George coldly, "and I couldn't give you a smoother ride for a pension. Harris – I appeal to you to back me up."

"George does seem to have the controls well in hand," said Harris. "But I say, George, you might ease off a little. Poor old J. is getting the colly-wobbles, I fancy."

I might have explained that the only reason for my initial worry was that I had not been able to see the moon from our window; but it seemed a lot of effort to go to just to clarify a trivial point. Besides, a mere moment of thought reminded me that we were still within the upper limits of Earth's atmosphere. It was no cause for concern that I could not spot the moon above me yet, any more than a railway traveller should fear to board a train at Paddington just because he cannot look down the line and espy Bristol in the distance.

"I tell you what," said George. "We're well above the five mile limit that that policeman warned us of. Let's anchor here for the night – so to speak – while we still have some gravity to keep us in our hammocks, and then we can resume in the morning and head for Oakapple Orbital."

"That's a splendid idea," said Harris, and I made the proposal nem. con. by means of an affirmative and wordless grunt, which seemed to be a little safer than opening my mouth to actually speak.

George brought the controls back to the point where the upward thrust of air, rendered weightless below the craft's Cavorite slats, balanced exactly the force of gravity on the ship from beneath, and there we hovered, in Earth's upper atmosphere. My internal workings resumed their normal unobtrusive function. I lifted one foot tentatively, and replaced it on the deck; then I essayed a gentle upward bound. I returned to my starting point, but I rose higher, and sank more slowly, than would have been the case on Earth's surface.

"Right-o," said George, lifting his hands from the controls and locking them down – no doubt he worried that that clumsy ass Harris might bump into them, in this lower gravity, and send us racing off in any direction. "Shall we sling the hammocks?"

I was about to suggest taking it easy for a spell, with a pipe and a comfortable chair, but then I recalled that the most comfortable chair on board was not a patch upon the armchair I had so briefly occupied on Lord Freckleton's ship, and that my pipe, and all our pipes, were five miles or more below us on Earth's surface. For a few moments, I once more began to consider this expedition a tom-fool affair, and that we were all perfect asses for having ventured upon it.

But George was full of beans still, and had already hopped out of the pilot's seat and over to the locker where the hammocks were stowed.

I was quite prepared to learn that the hammocks were of some complex design which required a qualification in civil engineering or in architecture to instal properly. I have had experience of hammocks during boating trips before now, and some of them have been confoundedly complicated, to the point where I would curse aloud as I tried to unravel them, and vow never more to have anything to do with so beastly a contraption.

I will say, though, that the hammocks aboard Mr Peckover's space-ship were some of the easiest to put up that I have ever encountered. Even Harris didn't make a botch of it, which only goes to show how the science of hammock design must have advanced in leaps and bounds over the past few years.

Then when we had them all three untangled and fixed securely to the mooring pegs on the wall, I was equally ready for an argument to arise over who should sleep in which one.

I was about to lay claim to the lowest one of the three, but George spoke first, and said he rather fancied sleeping in the uppermost one.

He must have seen the looks of surprise on the faces of Harris and myself, for he proceeded to bend his knees and spring upward. He caught the edge of the topmost hammock, and with a heave, bundled himself over the side and into it. George may be the youngest of us, but even so, that leap displayed a level of athleticism I had not seen him display since his days as a wing three-quarter for the Old Meltonians – and that was quite ten years ago.

He sat there with his legs swinging, and what I should have called an impertinent expression had I seen it upon the face of a man whom I did not regard as a bosom friend.

"Oh, don't stand there looking like two cats at a queen," he said. "It's easy enough in this gravity."

Harris rather tentatively took hold of the edge of the middle hammock, and vaulted upward. He overdid it a little, and came within an ace of hitting the small of George's back with the top of his head, before he hauled himself to safety.

All of this made me quite content to choose the lowest hammock, into and out of which I could climb without needing to hop up and down in low gravity.

The question of sleeping accommodation thus being resolved, we emerged once more from our hammocks and determined to dine as well as we could, in the unusual circumstances.

8

The athletic Miss Lexlake had stowed our baggage so securely, leaving almost no space between one case and another, that we had cause to be grateful for the low gravity as we tried to extract our boxes of provisions; but eventually we hauled the main food-hamper out into the open, and opened it up, and made a very adequate supper out of bread and cheese, and cold ham, and pickled onions, and another bottle of beer apiece — for we all knew that upon the morrow, we should leave Earth's gravitational pull entirely, and the beer (as we had previously discussed) would then be a forbidden pleasure. By unspoken but mutual consent, we left the remainder of the whisky in reserve for zero-gravity.

"Would any of you men like dessert to conclude?" I asked, reaching into the hamper and holding up a can of preserved peaches. "These are packed in syrup, and somehow I don't think it would be a good idea to open them without gravity."

"I wouldn't say no," George said. "Always assuming, that is, that you have some means of opening the dashed things."

"Yes," said Harris. "I assume you have brought a tin-opener, this time?"

It does seem hard that George and Harris should keep reminding me at every opportunity of the one occasion — years ago, it was, now — when we could not break into a tin. It was not even because I had forgotten the tin-opener, either; it had just become misplaced. And it was hardly my fault that George and Harris took it on themselves to attack it by unorthodox methods and hurt themselves. But that is human nature; one's friends never recall the countless times when you have backed them up, and helped them in a tight spot, and stood them drinks, but only those where you happen to have let them down in a trifling kind of a way.

Happily, on this occasion, the tin-opener was where it belonged, and the peaches opened as easily as if they had been a daisy greeting the morning sun; and our repast was concluded to our entire satisfaction.

Harris tipped up the open tin of peaches, and let the final drops of the juice therein drain directly into his mouth.

"What do we do with the tin?" he asked. "It's got sharp edges, and we don't want it to float about the place when we lose gravity. Someone might get hurt."

"We can simply toss it out of the airlock," I said, and got to my feet to perform that task.

"Hold on," said George, as I was about to open the inner hatch. "You will keep thinking this is a boat on water, J. Remember we aren't yet out of the Earth's pull. If we were to jettison any rubbish now, it would go straight down for five miles, and as likely as not hit some poor fellow on the head and kill him."

"But once we are in orbit?" Harris asked.

"Oh," said George, "that would be all right."

"Are you sure?" I said. "I know space is vast in extent, and so forth; but can it be in order to leave empty tins of peaches to float about round the planet, and get in the way?"

"Perhaps," suggested Harris, "if we threw it in the right direction, it would end up falling into the Sun."

"Would that risk damage to the Sun?" I asked.

"I don't suppose so," said George, "but I doubt we need worry. I know you're only thinking of the scenery, you men, but space isn't like a beach after a Bank-Holiday crowd has pic-nicked upon it. Thousands of ships have chucked their rubbish into it since space travel began, but do you see any of it out there?"

He looked out of the window at the blackness of space, with stars twinkling here and there like currants in a slice of more than usually dark Christmas pudding. I had to admit that I could see no sign of any foreign objects.

"Space," said George sagely, "is simply a huge dust-bin, and it's nowhere near full yet."

So we carefully set the empty tin back inside the hamper for the time being, and turned in for the night.

Hammocks are peculiar devices. They were (I suppose) first designed for use aboard ships at sea, but a ship at sea is the least comfortable place for one to essay sleeping in one.

The very best place to enjoy a hammock is in a shady garden on a hot summer afternoon, when you can tie it between two trees and settle down in it to partake of the sun without the necessity to move much (or at all), and let the rest of the world go by.

I am delighted to be able to report that a hammock on board a space-sphere in partial gravity is almost as comfortable as that, once you grow accustomed to the slight feeling of wrongness that comes with your body weighing less than it has for many years past.

Or perhaps it was the whisky.

At any rate, when I awoke daylight once more flooded our craft, mixing with snores from Harris in the hammock above me. I removed myself from close proximity to the latter, the better to enjoy the former, and looked once more through our window.

Below us lay our home planet, a remarkable sight indeed. From five miles up, I had expected the planet to be a small, featureless ball, brown or green in colour.

In actual fact, it filled almost the whole of the window. For my readers who have not experienced the sight, I suggest taking a soccer ball and bringing it up to your face, until it touches your nose.

I had read up on the solar system before my trip into its nearer reaches, and been impressed by how much larger than the Earth is the Sun, and similarly the huge planets of Jupiter and beyond. Compared to these, our globe is modest indeed; and yet compared to the puny size of a single human being, how immense the Earth is!

The planetary sphere loomed, to the exclusion of everything else. White whirls of cloud occupied much of the view; but where they permitted, I could see browns and greens, and the bright vivid hue of the ocean, as blue as a Bristol blue-glass bottle. Attuning my focus to the horizon and squinting a little, I could distinctly observe that its line was uneven rather than regular, and concluded that I was seeing hills and vales.

So pleasing to the eye was this vista, that I remained for quite two minutes by the window enjoying it, before I bethought me of my companions. It seemed to me that to miss this moment would be a crime; so I took the stick that slides into the hoops on top of the wicker food-hamper to keep the lid down, and used it to prod both Harris and George into wakefulness.

Harris was a little testy, and said something about how he wasn't going to get out of bed with no hot breakfast to greet him; but when George accidentally kicked him in the ribs on the way down from the top hammock, Harris groaned in resignation and came forth, and once he was upright and had seen the view beneath us, even he admitted that it was worth a guinea a box.

Rather than dine on bread and cold cuts, we all agreed that we should press straight on into orbit proper, and make for Oakapple Station, where we could eat in rather more elaborate style than was possible aboard our sphere.

George opened a drawer that was set near the controls, and took out a plump volume that rather resembled the smaller brother of a Bradshaw railway timetable. This, I learned, was a guide to the positions of all the orbital stations, relative to one another and to the Earth.

"That looks complicated," said Harris.

"Oh, punk," said George. "It's easy enough. Pass me the sextant."

I looked at Harris, and Harris looked at me; and George looked around at both of us.

"Come on, you asses," he said. "I need the sextant to know what course to steer."

"What's a sextant?" Harris asked.

It was a crumb of comfort, if only a small one, to know that although my knowledge of sextants was infinitesimal, Harris's was evidently still more lacking.

"What's a sextant?" George hooted. "You pair of dummies! A sextant — well — a sextant is — is a device for taking views of the stars."

"Like a telescope?" Harris said, which seemed to make George angrier still.

"No, you blithering buffoon, not like a telescope. A sextant is quite different."

"How?" I asked.

"Well, you put a telescope to your eye, while a sextant you put... Oh, I can't be bothered explaining the simplest of things to you nincompoops. I must say," George snorted, "that if I were going to space for the first time, I should have taken jolly good care that I knew a few things about how to get around safely, once you are up there."

For a moment I considered passing George my copy of the Young Person's Guide to the Orbital Stations, but I feared he might have responded to it in a negative manner.

"Oh, do stop staring at me like a pair of owls," George sighed, "and help me find the sextant."

And so we set to looking for that sextant. The hunt was not rendered any easier by the fact that neither Harris or I had the least idea of what the item we were searching for might look like.

We turned out all the drawers aboard that vessel; we searched every nook and cranny; we looked under the chairs, and inside the air-lock, and in every place we could imagine a sextant to be concealed, as well as a good many where we couldn't. Finally George lost his head and started to pull all the boxes and cases, which Miss Lexlake had packed away so carefully, out of the storage area. Of course the sextant was not among them, or behind them; and he tried to push them all back, and they wouldn't fit, and he kicked the food-hamper, thinking it wouldn't hurt him because of the low gravity, and thus he was reminded of the fact that objects in low gravity have less weight, but retain their original mass. I was well aware of this — it was covered very adequately in the Young Person's Guide — but it did not seem quite the time to give George a lecture on elementary orbital science, not while he was hopping on one foot and holding the other, and cursing in pain.

"Is this your sextant, which has been sitting here in plain sight all along?" asked Harris, picking up from the upper part of the control panel a metal contraption that looked as though it had been filched from the interior workings of a grandfather clock.

George stopped cursing for a second, to examine it.

"I dare say it is," he admitted.

He took it from Harris, and turned it over and over in his hands. Then he put it down and picked the book up, and looked at the first few pages, and then at the last few pages.

"Of all the damn' fool things!" he exclaimed. "What reputable shipyard allows a fellow to hire a space-vessel, without including instructions on how to work a sextant? It's most provoking," he concluded, like Humpty Dumpty in Alice.

I tried to recall what I knew about sextants. It was very little in the first place, and what small amount I did know, I had forgotten. I took hold of the device. It had an eye-piece, and a mirror, and many other elements.

Several parts proved, upon inspection, to move, or slide, or otherwise permit of being adjusted. But to me, the entirety of it was a perfect mystery.

Harris took it from me, and held it to his eye.

"I said that it wasn't a telescope," George growled.

"Then why," demanded Harris in hurt tones, "has it got an eye-piece?"

George snatched it from Harris, and put his eye to it.

"It does seem to."

"Perhaps," I suggested, "it's a telescope and a sextant all in one — like one of those pen-knives that comes with a corkscrew and a pair of scissors attached, and a thing for getting stones out of horses' hooves."

George gave me a sceptical look, but I don't believe he quite dared to contradict my suggestion.

"Very well," he said. "We must take especial care, of course, not to point it at the sun, or we'll blind ourselves."

"I shall assuredly not do so," I said, "but if not at the sun, then at what do we point it?"

George tossed the sextant back to me and picked up the book once more.

After much trial and error we found a way of using the sextant — I don't say it was the correct way, mind, or that any sailor who watched us and our struggles with that sextant would not have had a dozen fits at the way we abused the poor instrument — but eventually we came up with a course which satisfied George; or, at least, made him say he was satisfied. I do not know whether, in his heart of hearts, George was fully confident in that course; but I do know that by the time he said he was, I was very aware that I had not yet breakfasted, and I know George to be a chap who likes to lay down a solid foundation in the morning (so to speak), to see him through the day.

And so we set off for orbit. The higher we rose from Earth, the more gravity relinquished its grip upon us, like the elderly aunt of our youth who will insist on clasping you close to her, but who then boards her train and concludes her visit.

"How much longer shall we be, George?" I asked after a little while.

"Oh! A quarter of an hour, I expect."

Twenty minutes passed, and I found that if I pushed down with both feet, I rose alarmingly into mid-air, and did not return to the deck.

"Where the dickens is that station?" Harris demanded.

George frowned, and looked out of first one window and then another.

"It's that confounded sextant," he said. "Fancy making one with a telescope attached. It's small wonder that it didn't work properly. A tool should be just that — one tool — not a dozen different things at once."

"So we're lost in space," concluded Harris.

"Don't blame me," retorted George. "You didn't help getting us here, to speak of."

"I didn't know," said Harris, "that I was going to need to qualify as an able-seaman before setting foot on this rotten hulk. Wherever can that station be?"

"The trouble is that they move," George said mournfully.

"We move," I pointed out. "We just need to move in the right direction."

Harris picked up the sextant — gingerly, as though it were an anarchist's infernal device — and George studied the book of orbital schedules suspiciously. Feeling that there was little I could do to assist, I began to practice moving about the sphere in the absence of gravity.

I soon established that flapping one's arms like wings was of no use, and that the forceful exhalation of a lungful of air also did little to propel me about. The knack, I discovered, was to brace one's feet or hands against the floor or wall of the sphere, and push off, like launching a boat. I also soon learned that once in motion, as Isaac Newton so ably predicted, I remained in motion, with no way in evidence to arrest my progress; and I found this out by colliding with Harris from behind. I shouted a warning; but Harris merely begged me to "shut up for a moment, while I'm working this sextant". The next sound he uttered was a yelp as I bumped into the back of his neck.

I regret to say that he turned around and gave me a violent shove, whereat I retreated the way I had approached, involuntarily; what time Harris also found himself in motion, proving for the second time in a minute what a jolly clever man Isaac Newton was, and collided with the picnic hamper, which had somehow begun to hover amidships.

"Do stop making such a racket, you men," pleaded George. "You've made me lose my place in these confounded tide-tables again."

I brought myself to a halt by grasping a handle, and since it happened to be next to a window, looked out of it while I regained my bearings. The picnic hamper came drifting back in my direction. I fended it off, as gently as I could, and it started to travel toward Harris once again.

"I say!" I called out in a moment. "I think I see the orbital station."

For indeed, outside the ship, I distinctly observed a dot against the blackness of infinity that was larger than a star, and moved against them.

"Where?" Harris shouted. He was adrift in the middle of the sphere, and had no footholds against which to push. Finally the hamper came back within his reach on its return journey; he grabbed that hamper and tossed it violently in a rearward direction, which propelled him forward and over to the window where I was clinging to the rail. With Harris's usual lack of foresight, this also sent the hamper, which – if I may say so without indelicacy – weighed less than Harris, into forceful motion; and it might have careered all over the place, but by good luck it shot backward into the hammocks, and got tangled up there.

Harris and I clung to the hand-grips by that window as though our lives depended on it, and shouted out commands to George; and George brought our sphere about, and tacked it this way and that in the general approximation of our instructions, until the station was close enough to display its shape to us.

Most of the orbital stations are built to a similar design; they are as though one were to take a gas-jet's tube and bend it back upon itself until it forms a complete ring, and then weld struts from one side of the ring to the other to maintain its annular shape. Upon our approaching within range, men in protective suits began to swarm out from hatches, and they propelled themselves over to us, and wound ropes around us, and hauled us in to dock. This is necessary, because the stations rotate like a merry-go-round, in order that centrifugal force may provide those inside with a facsimile of gravity, and I dare say that most people would find it beyond their powers to bring a sphere in to dock in those circumstances.

At least, I am certain that George would.

They tied us safely to the station's outside, and we began to go round and around in time with the rotation of the artificial satellite. Finally they attached a kind of flexible tube from the hatch of our ship, to an equivalent hatch on the station, and we were free to enter.

"There! We did it," said Harris, throwing open the inner door of our hatch. "I never doubted for a second that we would."

"I never doubted for a second, either," said George, replacing the fat book of schedules in its drawer and closing it firmly.

We passed through the tube, and the station's hatch, and found ourselves — once more upon our feet — inside the station, and facing a handsome young lady who beamed at the three of us indiscriminately.

"God damn and blast," she said in honeyed tones — that, at any rate, was what it sounded to our English ears as though she had said.

The resourceful young lady must have seen the blank looks upon our faces, for she spoke again, this time in our own tongue.

"Good morning and welcome to New Bornholm."

"George, you prize ass," said Harris wrathfully, "you've brought us to the wrong station."

9

There is some dispute among nations with regard to the space beyond Earth's atmosphere. When Professor Cavor's wonderful invention was first made public, it immediately became clear that any nation, or even any private individual, with the means to either buy or manufacture Cavorite, could venture into orbit without much in the way of ceremony.

The Professor being an Englishman, Westminster originally attempted to stake a claim upon the whole of the ether; but it very soon grew obvious, not least when Cavor's own opinions – regarding which he was not reticent – were aired, that it would be perfectly futile for us to persist in such a claim, which it was impossible to enforce or to police. It is possible to establish custom-posts at every road that crosses a border between nations, and even (if one were foolish enough and prepared to throw away enough money) to build a fence or wall connecting every one of those custom-posts, in order to prevent unauthorised travellers from passing between sovereign territories; but you can't erect a barbed-wire fence around an entire planet.

Some attorneys – especially American ones – began to bring lawsuits under the principle of ancient lights, or some such, in which the plaintiff would plead that because they owned a patch of land, they also had rights extending in a sort of wedge to the centre of the Earth below that land, and in an ever-expanding slice of the sky and stars above it. But the courts tossed out all such suits, not least because – as we had just found out, in our misadventures with the sextant – the Earth rotates about its axis, and passes around the Sun in its orbit. Thus a litigant who could claim in his writ one day that the Moon – or part of the Moon – lay above his farmstead in Connecticut, would find by the time that his case came on, that the Moon had stolen away from him, and was now (if one accepted his argument) the property of an Australian swagman, or a Chinese mandarin.

And so the Treaty of Folkestone was soon passed by all the major nations of the world, which declared all of the void beyond Earth's atmosphere terra nullius – an area, owned by no man or nation, into which anybody might pass freely.

This philanthropically intended maxim works very well for space. It does not, of course, work so well once one reaches the Moon, or another planet, and even now the courts are once more busy determining procedure for staking claim to the soil of other worlds; for, especially where that soil contains valuable ores or minerals, a certain hotness tends to arise, just as it did in the days of the American frontier gold-rushes, and lawlessness is rife.

After the last signature had been inscribed at Folkestone, it did not take long before the value became clear of establishing orbiting oases where travellers could obtain food, water, air and rest. Naturally, it also became evident that once a man has food, water, air and rest, he will inevitably begin to look about him for entertainment and pleasure; and so the orbital stations very soon took on a role that was not merely functional, and became what we know them as today – destinations in their own right, rather than mere way-stations like an old coaching inn.

The question of which station was the first is a vexed one; the British began to build theirs first, the Brazilians completed theirs first, and the Americans contrived to open theirs to travellers one day before the Brazilian station flung its doors wide (so to speak; one can't fling a station's doors wide in reality, of course, for the air would all get out and the occupants be suffocated.)

Some of the stations were built by the governments of great nations; others have been constructed by large companies and magnates of business as private enterprises; and some, even, by single individuals. The German governmental station, named in honour of the late Chancellor Bismarck, lays proud claim to being the largest orbital station; but we had decided, while making our plans, that it would not feature on our itinerary. We were all agreed that a station manned and run by the German state would be little more than an extension of that state in orbit; and George said that he did not relish the thought of being fined for walking the wrong way round the station, or for inadvertently hanging his washing out in the incorrect order.

Oakapple Station, on the other hand, is a British station; but the British government had no hand in its construction, and precious little in its daily routine. It was planned and built by a simple Welshman, by name Gareth Oakes. Oakes, seizing upon an opportunity to change his metier from digging coal out of the Rhondda valley to digging minerals out of the Moon, chanced to "make it big", as the Americans say; and with the small fortune thus amassed, he set about building Oakapple Station, which served to transform his small fortune into a larger one. I have heard it said that Oakes was offered a title by the Prime Minister, but that he had respectfully declined it, saying he had neither the manners nor the interest to take a seat in the House of Lords, and that he much preferred to leave politics to those better qualified than he.

Personally I wonder whether our politicians truly are better qualified to run the country than Mr Oakes; but that is by-the-bye.

At any rate, we three found ourselves now upon the Danish station rather than upon Oakapple, as we had fondly imagined we should be. George was all for taking off again, and hunting down Oakapple's whereabouts; but Harris and I persuaded him to at least stay for a meal, Harris making the cogent point that at least, upon a Danish station, we should find some decent bacon. I am pleased to advise that this was yet another occasion where Harris was proven correct. I can't think what must be coming over the man in his middle age.

After an interlude where conversation was replaced almost wholly by the sound of three men munching, I pushed my plate away contentedly and regarded George.

"If we're to find Oakapple," I said, "I think it would be well-advised for us to take instruction in the use of that wretched sextant."

George snorted, and said that he knew perfectly well how to navigate using a sextant; but after both Harris and I gave him a reproachful look, he wilted somewhat, and consented to "refresh his memory a little" on the subject.

Once we had paid for three repasts – at a cost many times what we should have shelled out for them on Earth, for the cost of shipping supplies to orbit is not a small one even with Cavorite's aid – we set out in search of succour. As luck had it, at the very moment that we were departing the dining-hall, we chanced upon a Danish naval party also about to leave, all splendid in gold braid and peaked caps, who proved more than happy to allow a trio of English wayfarers to attach themselves to their number.

They couldn't allow us onto their ship, which they said was not in order since we were foreign nationals; but the navigator went aboard and fetched his own sextant, and explained the proper use of it to us. The eye-piece, we learned, was an integral part of the machine, and not as I had supposed an ill-advised attempt to make it serve the function of a telescope as well as its true sextantly duty.

Our memories thus refreshed – as we allowed George to call it – we were able to return to our own ship, to pay the Danes a docking-fee the amount of which gave Harris cause to make a sharp intake of breath, and to once more embark ourselves into emptiness.

George took the controls once again, while Harris and I both took careful grip of hand-holds, and having consulted the sextant and the book full of numbers, we were cast off.

In order to avoid the risk of one colliding with another, all the orbital stations travel at the same height from the earth's surface, and maintain a minimum distance between one and another. The effect of this upon the traveller is that if he docks at one station, it is a matter of comparative simplicity for him to reach any other; he needs only to stay in the same plane of orbit and direct his vessel either forward or backward, as required, and the next station will soon hove into view. The Spanish station is always the next in a clockwise direction from the Danish one, for example, and one of the American ones next, and so on. The stations remain in the same order relative to one another, just as if they were railway stations rather than artificial moons. I almost wonder that they do not attach rails from one to another, and institute an orbital railway service between them; but perhaps there are good reasons known to science why this helpful development cannot be made.

Our hearts seemed light as the sphere whirled along its path – in a spiritual sense, I mean, rather than merely being physically weightless. It seemed no time at all before we saw a second station grow from a dot in the distance to a huge construction that filled half the window; George tacked carefully around it, and we continued our flight. A few minutes later, we repeated the procedure a second time, and then a third.

The third station was not yet completed, and we could see men in protective suits drifting here and there around its bulk like tugs around a Transatlantic liner, bolting and welding and riveting. They say that the work is dangerous to those engaged upon it, and that the pay they receive reflects that risk; which is why the stations are constructed upon the planet's surface, as much as is feasible, and lifted into place with Cavorite, and only then are the workers called in to carry out whatever final additions are required to make it ready for the travelling public's use.

I am glad I am not an orbital construction worker; for even if the pay outweighed the danger attached to the job a dozen times over, I cannot think that there is much in orbit to expend it upon.

"Next stop, Oakapple Orbital," said George cheerfully as we left the construction crew in our wake.

We found it scarcely surprising that there was much scurry and bustle in the immediate vicinity of Oakapple Orbital; after all, it is one of the best known of its kind, and hence one of the most frequented. As we approached, there were many small constructions hanging in the void, like buoys around a harbour, and they bore gaudy advertising signs; some familiar to us from Earth (such as those puffing soap – for men must wash in orbit just as elsewhere), others for goods or services specific to the region; space-sphere repair and maintenance, suppliers of air ("James & Myers' Alpine Air: As Pure As The Mountains"), and so on.

But as we came closer to the huge station itself, these slogans and pictures all faded to nothing by comparison.

Oakapple Orbital, as is well known, carries the station's name painted onto its exterior in letters that can be seen for miles. I have never seen the point of this, for large as those letters are, by the time one sees them from a space vessel, one is already far closer to Oakapple than to any other station. But there is apparently value in being able to claim that your station's name plate can be seen from the Earth's surface – even if to make it out clearly requires use of the Earl of Rosse's huge telescope.

Harris and I watched the station approach, expecting at every moment to see those enormous letters rotate into our view and confirm to us that here, at last, was our first planned destination in orbit.

But as George manoeuvred us toward docking distance, and Oakapple rotated, what came into view was not the station's name.

"Whatever does that say?" asked Harris, pressing his nose to the atmospherium-glass of the window like a small boy outside a confectioner's shop.

"It ends with an N," I said, "so it can't be Oakapple Orbital after all."

"I tell you it is," George said irately. "Perhaps the sign reads 'Oakapple Orbital Station'?"

"Not in any drawing or photograph of it that I have ever seen," I replied. "George, you tremendous dunce, you've brought us to the wrong station a second time."

"I think," said Harris hesitantly, "that it says 'Women'."

"Surely," I said, "that can't be an advertisement, even here in orbit."

George muttered something about how he should be so lucky; but we drew closer, and the station continued to revolve until the whole legend could be discerned.

"Gracious mercy," exclaimed Harris as we read the enormous letters.

Now that we were so close to Oakapple, we could see here and there fragments of the proper sign painted on the surface, giving its name. But over that name had been stretched a huge sheet of canvas, well secured with ropes to the station itself; and upon that canvas these words had been painted in heavy black letters –

VOTES FOR WOMEN.

"You don't suppose...?" George murmured.

"Suffragists," said Harris, with a disapproving air.

"You don't approve of votes for women?" I said. Ethelbertha is not herself a member of any women's suffrage organisation – at least, if she is, she has not confessed it to her husband – but she has more than once remarked to me that she can see no good reason why women are denied the vote, especially since men continue to make such a tremendous shambles of running the nation. And even had I been disposed to introduce strife into our wedded bliss, I would have found it hard to argue this last point.

"Confounded nonsense," said Harris. "Women don't have the brains for politics – it's a proven fact. Can you imagine what a pass we should come to if women were allowed to stand as parliamentary candidates? At Prime Minister's Questions we should see members asking advice on the latest fashion in hats, or exchanging gossip about their favourite novelettes."

"I'm not so sure that that wouldn't be an improvement on some of the things that do take place in Parliament," I ventured. But Harris was well under way now.

"No, J., it's sheer twaddle. If we give women the vote we shall end up under petticoat rule and the country will descend into utter chaos. We shall become the world's laughing stock, and the Empire will fall into fragments. It was a mistake to allow them into the universities; I said at the time that this was the thin end of the wedge, and so it has been, too. Gilbert and Sullivan got it just right. If I run into the woman who erected that ludicrous sign when we dock at the Station, I shall tell her to her face what I think of her and her confounded antics." Harris clapped his hands together as he finished that statement, as though to shake the dust of feminism from them.

"Well," said George, "you're welcome to do as you choose, old man; but have you thought of the likelihood that the women who placed that sign there, are very likely to be Miss Lexlake and her friends?"

Harris spluttered in a way that suggested he had not considered that likelihood.

But it is always the devil's own hard work to dissuade Harris of an opinion, once he has formed it.

"Stuff!" he cried, then added, "And nonsense. There must be dozens of women in space at the moment. Any one of them could have been behind this preposterous gesture."

"More than one, I think," I said, as I gauged the dimensions of the painted canvas.

George steered us closer to the station.

"Well, at least one," he said.

"Of course it was at least one," Harris said. "Really, George –"

"Because," said George, "I can see her. I believe she's chained herself to it."

Harris's mouth fell open, and an oath escaped through it. He tried to stride over to George, but forgot that he was weightless, so that for two seconds his legs described wild circles, like a man whose bicycle chain has just snapped unexpectedly. Then, remembering himself, he pushed off the wall over to George and snatched up the sextant, staring down the eyepiece in the direction of the station.

"It is Miss Lexlake," he said in a kind of choke. "And she has."

10

It came as no surprise to us that Oakapple did not begin to bristle with dock workers to bring us safely in to the station. We were almost an hour sitting there. It might have been a tedious experience, save for the fact that we were presented with seats a short distance only from the unfolding drama. George locked the controls, and we all three of us clustered in a row at the window to watch.

A little clump of suited figures were bustling around Miss Lexlake. Every now and again, one of them would bend and touch his suit's helmet to that of hers. The conjunction appeared to the untutored eye hardly delicate, but I had read in the reliable Guide to the Orbital Stations of the trick – almost as old as space travel itself – of speaking to another person in a space-suit by touching helmets, so that the vibrations of one's voice are transmitted as sound by that contact.

"I suppose," said Harris, "that they need to cut her loose and have gone for a suitable implement."

But time still passed, and though the figures continued to swarm about Miss Lexlake, none of them seemed to take any action to free her from her bonds. The lady herself sat in patient pose, as calmly as though she were on a bench in Hyde Park, with the rays of the sun catching the brightly painted colours of her suit – green, white and violet.

Finally, some more dockers arrived and hauled us in, then connected us hatch to hatch. As they did so, Miss Lexlake appeared still to be in situ.

As soon as our craft was linked by a flexible tube to Oakapple, George flung open the hatch and hastened onto the station. Harris and I followed. After only a few hours' weightlessness, it already felt quite peculiar to be able to walk with a semblance of normality.

No doubt George felt it, too; but he was too busy to complain about it. He sought out the first crew member of Oakapple station that he could see, and demanded the full particulars of how Miss

Lexlake and her sign came to be so firmly attached to the station's exterior.

That crew member went and fetched another crew member, who went and fetched another, while all the time we were all – especially George – hopping from frustration. George told them each, several times apiece, and in various forms of language, that we were acquainted with Miss Lexlake and concerned for her well-being.

Finally a large man with an even larger moustache – the sort one should not shave off in the absence of gravity – appeared on the scene. He wore the uniform of authority; a beadle, they call them on Oakapple. George once more sang his plaintive song, and at long last found an ear willing to comprehend. The latest arrival, who gave his name as Neville, explained the position.

"A certain young lady," he said, "engaged one of the station's beadles in conversation, and while distracted, another young lady – the one whom you observed – this young lady made her way, without authority, to the exterior of the station; and before we were even aware of her action, she had secured her – ahem! – banner to the station's outer shell, and secured her – ahem! – herself also, in such a fashion that were any man to try to sever her shackles, he must also inevitably cut the air-pipe of her vacuum-suit, and that would, of course, have consequences; consequences I need hardly go into."

I was rather glad he had not gone into them.

"But, dash it," George protested, "if she isn't freed and brought back inside, her air will run out anyway, and – and – "

"And there would be consequences then, too," Harris added. I believe he thought he was being helpful.

"This had occurred to us," said Neville.

He pulled out a little notebook from a pocket, and began to take down details with a stub of pencil. I looked at my watch. The second hand seemed to be rotating with a nasty, indecent haste.

"Mr Neville," I suggested, "would it be of any avail if one of us were to put on a protective suit, and venture outside to try to reason with the lady?"

"Two of us," said George instantly.

Harris said nothing; but I fancied that I could deduce from his expression which two of us would be the volunteers.

"At this juncture," said Neville, looking up sharply from his notes, "we are frankly at a loss, and no suggestion is to be dismissed without consideration."

He regarded me uneasily, and the thought occurred that he was as concerned about my safety – and presumably George's – as he was about Miss Lexlake's.

But finally he gave a nod. "Dyer!" he called, and another uniformed beadle stepped forward.

"Get these three gentlemen into suits. They are acquainted with the lady outside and it may be they can reason with her. Quickly, man, quickly – there's no time to lose."

For a second Harris looked startled; but rather than show the white feather and excuse himself, he kept quiet, and allowed himself to be enlisted into the rescue party alongside me and George.

I have never ventured into the depths of the ocean, and – assuming always that George is not scizcd by another of his insane ideas about suitable venues for a holiday – I never shall. Consequently I had never been inside a protective suit before; Mr Peckover had given us some brief instructions upon their use in an emergency, and I was pretty much resigned to having to don one when we reached the Moon, at least; but the thought of making my suited debut in the vacuum of space, rather than on the Moon where I should at least have a proper surface beneath my feet and a horizon to which to refer, would have filled me with terror had the entire affair not taken place in jig time.

Dyer and a couple of other Oakapple workers took George, Harris and myself, and before we knew a thing, we were being grasped like three sacks of potatoes by market porters, and bundled into a suit each. I do not say that we could have donned the suits ourselves more quickly, without their assistance; but there was something undignified about the whole procedure. A brief, wild thought came to me that the egregious Dyer would never, ever have succeeded in the post of gentleman's valet; and that thought led in turn to my recollecting Lord Freckleton's valet, and wondering to what extent he helped his lordship into his space-suit, should he require to wear one.

But there was no time for random fancies; Dyer secured my suit firmly about my body, thrust the helmet into my hands – I grasped it with no more conscious thought than a new-born infant clutching its mother's hand – and then the three of us were hustled to a hatch, where another suited figure awaited us, helm under arm.

"Neville tells me you're going outside to reason with the madwoman," he said, with a frown that betrayed his own opinion of our chances of success. "You know how to talk between suits, in a vacuum?"

George did, and I did. Harris did not. I have never once known Harris to be able to contribute decisive knowledge at a moment of crisis.

With a sigh, the man by the hatch snatched Harris's helmet and clapped it over his head, securing it deftly, before completing his own attire by means of his own helmet, and touching it to Harris's.

Quite what he said to Harris I do not know, for neither George nor I could hear more than a muffled buzz. But he must have been satisfied with Harris's response, for he gestured to us to fasten our own helmets, then checked them to ensure they were air-tight.

Once we were encased in our suits to his satisfaction, he spun the wheel to open the inner hatch, like Captain Ahab bringing his ship about to pursue the white whale, and bustled us into the hatch, where he joined us. The inner door swung closed – slowly, but with a kind of inexorability that I did not altogether like. Finally the outer hatch was operated, and the air inside with us puffed away into space, leaving us in vacuum.

Our suits all swelled up immediately like a man with mumps, which served to make our appearance more grotesque yet. I think it is the helmet that leads to this strange effect. It blocks your view of a man's face. Already, before we even passed through the outer hatch, I found myself fighting to tell which of the suited figures beside me was George and which Harris.

Of course, real space-farmers decorate their suits in distinctive fashion, like jockeys on Earth, each with their own unique design and color. Some are true works of art. I have seen their wonderful stylings mocked upon more than one occasion as gaudy, and as demonstrative of how those who choose to make a living away from the Earth's surface are all lacking in taste and discretion – this, more often than not, from someone who would see nothing to look twice at in a military dress uniform, or a man dressed in fox-hunting pink (despite this last hue being in fact scarlet). The truth is that in space, it may be a matter of life and death to be able to identify another man by his suit in an instant. Space-farers may be daring; some would even say reckless; but few of them would risk throwing away their own life by carelessness, and those who do tend to serve, in the main, as an exponent of Mr. Darwin's celebrated theory of the survival of the fittest.

Even had he not possessed a painted suit, I would have had no difficulty in identifying the Oakapple man – his name, by the by, I later discovered to be Souter – for he swung straight out of the exit and onto the external surface of the station, where he belayed himself to a railing, and then carried out the same procedure for us. Feeling fractionally more secure now that I was – supposedly – unable to tumble off the station and drift away into the void, I climbed hand over hand along the rope, and in a few moments, there we were – standing on the outer surface of Oakapple Orbital.

Had the purpose of our excursion been for pleasure, I dare say that we should all have thought it a jolly experience and a fine spectacle. The Sun was a fiery ball of light in one direction; the Moon a scarcely less obvious landmark, looming at us out of the night; while largest still, the Earth itself sat like a plump monarch on a throne, master of all it surveyed.

For a moment I was rather taken aback by the fact that – from where we were standing – the Earth was above us, and the Moon below. Reason told me that my feet should be pointing toward the Earth's surface. My feet, I discovered that day, are a confounded pair of reactionaries, and disinclined to accede to a change of circumstances. They have spent five-and-thirty years at the bottom-most extremity of my body, in contact with the Earth, and now they seemed to cry out in protest at the unfamiliar angle I was asking them to adopt.

I should have liked to take some time thoroughly to adapt myself and my expectations to the peculiar surroundings; but I knew well enough that time was fleeting and that even seconds might be of the essence. I could only push all concerns and worries away from me, trust in Souter to attend to my welfare, and focus my own thoughts on Miss Lexlake and how best to approach her.

The station's surface curved gently away from me to left and right; by turning (and I had to turn my whole body, for if I turned my head alone as I would have on Earth, I found myself looking only at the inside of my own helmet) I could see it recede into the distance in a regular arc, and join up with itself at the furthest point from me. Inside that tube of metal was air, and life, and other people, and I am quite sure that all of us would sooner have been on the other side of the metal where we stood.

But there was no use in fretting. Souter lifted one swollen arm, and pointed; and hand over hand, handhold by handhold, footstep by footstep, we made our way across the surface of Oakapple, beetles crawling round a tree-trunk, until Miss Lexlake and her banner were in sight.

Souter beckoned us to touch helmets, which we did, as best we could.

"I shall stay here," he said, "while you address the lady – there she is – just by yonder pipe-work."

Miss Lexlake's suit, as I have said, was itself distinctively painted, and she was sitting as we had seen her before, calm and still, like Britannia on a penny-piece daring the waves to splash her majestic feet.

George raised a hand, to signal that he would make first approach. George, I was a little envious to see, was taking to space as though he had been treading vacuum since his cradle; he swarmed up from rail to rail like a monkey up a tree. I followed as quickly as I dared – which I expect was fairly slowly; but in that strange and alien setting, time seemed to lose meaning, and I could not for the life of me tell you with confidence whether it took me one minute or five to reach the lady.

By the time I pulled myself up on the last handle, George was already alongside Miss Lexlake, and his helmet was pressed to hers. She had not altered her position, or indeed given any outward sign that she was aware of his presence. For a moment the wild surmise struck me that she had somehow escaped from her suit and left it there, empty, to guard her placard.

But when I touched my helmet to hers, on the opposite side from George, I heard with adequate clarity George's familiar voice, in the middle of a sentence:

"–don't allow yourself to be freed, and come inside, your air will all be used up, and then – then –"

"Then I shall die," Miss Lexlake said in a calmer and more relaxed tone than I would ever have been able to muster, were I in her place.

"My dear madam," George said – I could almost hear him splutter with surprise – "surely you can't be so determined to make away with yourself?"

"Believe me," said Miss Lexlake, "I do not crave death; but the refusal of male politicians to listen to our cry for justice has weighed heavily upon my heart, as well as the hearts of other women. Should I die a martyr here in space, as I am resigned to, then at least it will show the males of England – and other nations – that women are not the weakling fools they think us. I face my end like a true Briton, for a cause I know is just and fair, and in the expectation that my martyrdom will lead to the success of our movement."

I may not have recalled every word of that remarkable statement with accuracy; but such was the gist of what she said, and I could not help but be moved by her quiet eloquence and her determination.

"Miss Lexlake," George said – even via third-hand sound vibrations from his helmet through the lady's to mine, I could hear the plaintive note in his voice – "surely your friends and family will be devastated to learn of your fate. It isn't too late to think of them and to rethink your decision to do away with yourself like this. I beseech you to reconsider – do!"

"My family," said the incipient martyr, "will not miss me; my father will consider himself well rid of a foolish girl with ideas above her station. He will devote his attention to my brothers, as he always has in any event. And my friends – most of them are with me in the suffragist movement, and I feel certain that all of them would not only applaud my chosen course, but adopt it themselves if they believed it would lead to our eventual triumph."

"Including Miss Craddock and Miss Dickson?" said George.

"They are fully aware of my actions. We left Earth together with this end in mind."

"Has it not occurred to you that if you will not turn aside from your plan, your friends will surely be arrested for aiding and abetting in a suicide?" George asked. I thought this rather shrewd of him.

But it cut no ice with the lady. "We have discussed the possibility," she said, "and they are willing to run the risk for the cause. You shall not dissuade me, I am afraid, and you may as well return to the safety of the station."

George stood upright, breaking contact between helmets, and placed his hands on his hips – insofar as one can do so in a spacesuit where one's hips are separated from one's hands by a cushion of air as well as the suit itself. He was plainly at a loss, and I took it upon myself to carry on where George had left off.

"Good-afternoon, Miss Lexlake," I began, and instantly felt no end of an ass for my formality in the circumstances. However, she took my greeting in her stride and wished me a good afternoon in return. I believe she almost went on to say that she hoped she saw me well. We could have expended the remainder of her air in polite formalities, but I reminded myself of the need for urgent steps.

"I hope you'll forgive me for interfering," I said, "when we have been but lately introduced; but I must echo what George here says. No matter how just your cause, it would be nothing short of a tragedy to sacrifice your life for it."

"A tragedy?" Miss Lexlake repeated. "Hamlet is a tragedy, and it has lived three hundred years past its author's death. If by my own single sacrifice I can obtain justice for every English woman, then I give my life gladly. I believe your presence here is the result of genuine concern for me, rather than a simple male desire to meddle; but you shall not dissuade me."

I was reminded disconcertingly of how hard it is to argue with Ethelbertha when she has once made up her mind. If she has decided that we shall dine upon leg of mutton next Tuesday, then all suggestions of any other dish are perfectly futile. How much energy I had expended pointlessly in such debates – and how much more crucial a situation I now found myself in!

"Miss Lexlake," I went on, my thoughts galloping as I tried to form a forceful argument in so alien a place and so short a time, "I know I have not had the opportunity to come to know you well; but it is plain to me that you are a most remarkable and intelligent woman – "

"That you think an intelligent woman is remarkable," said Miss Lexlake, "speaks volumes."

"I beg your pardon – I didn't mean it in that sense. What I was trying to suggest, was that a young lady of your calibre surely has a great deal to offer to the cause of votes for women – a cause which I myself view with the greatest sympathy." Which was true, for Miss Lexlake's willingness to make the ultimate sacrifice for the suffrage movement had made a deep impression upon me. "By sacrificing yourself, you will deny the movement the benefit of your mind and your energy in the future. Can you not reconsider?"

She was silent for a moment, but I could see her face through the glass of her helmet, and by her reaction I knew that I had managed to find a chink in her armour; though whether or not it was large enough to turn to my advantage, I was less certain.

"No," she said. "Your words are honeyed, and they touch me; but I have come thus far, and the end of my race is in sight. I will not turn from the proper course now, so close to my goal."

George bent down and tried to talk to her; then Harris came up and pushed George aside, and took his own turn at convincing her; but none of us could sway her.

We were pretty much at our wits' end, if not beyond them, when I caught something moving out of the corner of my eye.

A space-vessel was approaching the station; a vessel far larger, far grander, than our own, eclipsing even Lord Freckleton's in its size and splendour. As it glided closer to Oakapple, a swarm of figures in suits welled up from what seemed like every hatch, hastening to dock it.

Souter appeared alongside us in a trice, looking agitated.

"What news?" I said, forgetting myself for a moment. Touching my helmet to his, I repeated the question.

"That ship," he said, "belongs to Mr. Oakes himself, and if he finds this situation going on here at Oakapple – why, I don't know what he might do. You gentlemen had better come back inside," he added sorrowfully, "if you can't get the lady to see sense."

11

Souter assisted us back inside, and once the ante-chamber to the hatch had been refilled with air, we removed our helmets once more. I was mightily glad to do so; but the fact that we had failed, all three of us, to prevail upon Miss Lexlake not to sacrifice her life, weighed heavily upon me. After all (I said to myself) I had spoken nothing but the truth when I had attempted to persuade her not to. She was just what I had told her to her face; a most remarkable and courageous woman.

We had been so determined to become the heroes of the hour – so certain that we should escort Celia Lexlake back to air and safety, to the cheers and relief of all Oakapple. And we had failed; we had failed utterly.

Souter hurried away as soon as the inner hatch could be opened, and left us there. I hoped that Neville or Dyer might appear to take charge of us, and even to soothe our amour propre by telling us that we had done all any human being could have done, if not more. But nobody came; we three were left by the hatch, holding our helmets and crestfallen.

For a while we none of us said anything; I don't believe any of us felt like speaking. I know I did not. Finally George sighed, and said, "What a rotten sell."

"Does anyone know how much air she had in her suit?" Harris asked tentatively.

None of us did, which only served to make us further downcast still. Somehow it seemed inevitable that our uncertainty could only lead to one conclusion – that Miss Lexlake had only minutes of air left, if that, and that she might even now be expiring from its absence, on the other side of a cold metal barrier from us.

"They say drowning is quite a peaceful way to peg out," I ventured; "once you stop struggling, that is."

Both George and Harris turned upon me and chided me without mercy.

"Of all the things to say, J.!" snapped Harris. "Bless my soul, sometimes I think you were born altogether lacking in good taste – and I say that as a friend."

"If you've nothing more helpful to contribute than that," George went on, "you might as well keep your silly cake-hole shut. Poor Miss Lexlake – whatever will her friends say?"

"They already know about her," I told George. "She said as much to me, just now. They are all adherents to the cause of women's suffrage. I dare say any of them might have done the same."

"Wait!" Harris called out, as George was about to dismiss me with another sneer. "I've an idea!"

Both George and I pushed forward against Harris in our eagerness, and made him bump the back of his head on the metal wall next to the hatch.

"Confound it," he gasped, "can't you leave a man to explain?"

"If you had just detailed your plan," I said, "instead of announcing it like a herald going before a king, we might already be acting upon it."

"Why," Harris said, "Miss Dickson and Miss Craddock. Where are they? They are surely on the station somewhere. If we could find them – and persuade them to reason with Miss Lexlake themselves – maybe their words would be more persuasive than ours, coming from intimate friends – "

"What makes you think we could persuade them," said George tartly, "when we couldn't sway Miss Lexlake?"

This seemed to me a cogent point; but Harris simply said to George, "I'm waiting for your better idea."

And George had to admit that he had none.

"Quick, then," I said. "We must find Neville, or Dyer – someone who can tell us where the other ladies might be."

And so, clad still from neck to foot in our vacuum-suits, we rushed away to search. We soon learned that it was quicker to abandon our helmets for the nonce and to have both hands free, for the gravity which the station generated by its rotation was not sufficient to enable us to walk in our normal fashion, and it proved easiest to make progress partly with long, loping strides and partly by pulling ourselves along by our hands on the ubiquitous handrails and holds.

Somehow we found ourselves in the main concourse or promenade of Oakapple. There was a bustle and a chatter about the area; I am not sure whether the people there knew the entirety of what was transpiring outside the station, but it seemed certain that they had at least an inkling that all was not well, and the sudden appearance among their midst of three tired, panting men in vacuum suits stirred up their worry still further.

Of course, this made them get in our way and cluster around us, and ask us questions we could hardly hear (even the ones which were in English, which was by no means all of them), and had no time to answer anyway; and I am afraid to say that we forgot ourselves somewhat and invited several of them to depart from our presence, rather curtly. I like to think that I can retain always the repose that stamps the cast of Vere de Vere; but I challenge any fellow reading this to imagine himself in our situation and to claim with frankness that he could have done so.

No beadles were to be seen – I suppose they were all otherwise occupied in the crisis. And though we searched every face we saw, none of them belonged to Miss Craddock or to Miss Dickson. For all we knew, the beadles had already taken them into custody and confined them in who knew what wretched brig or cell Oakapple used in such cases. Once more I had cause to curse the Pocket Guide to the Orbital Stations, which had been silent on the subject of incarceration – though I surmised that there must be some kind of imprisonment available, rather than wrong-doers simply being tossed through a hatch and left to float off into infinity.

Finally we escaped from the main promenade, and found ourselves in a corridor which seemed to be for the use of restaurant staff, going by the odours of boiled cabbage and potatoes that drifted through it. Emerging at the other end of the passage, we saw a sign pointing us to the MAIN DOCKING AREA, and for lack of any better plan, followed its instructions.

Within a few minutes we found ourselves back almost at our starting point.

Harris groaned, and leaned against the wall.

"I'm sorry, you men, but I'm beastly tired. I thought you were meant to be invigorated by space travel," he went on, ill-humour in his voice, "but I feel as if I'd run up the Wrekin and back down."

For perhaps ten seconds, Harris enjoyed that slump against the wall. Then he found himself violently propelled forward, and had cause to be grateful for the low gravity, as he fell slowly enough to catch himself on his own hands.

The reason for this sudden development was that Harris had been leaning on a hatch, and that the hatch had suddenly sprung open, giving him an unexpected shove.

Well, I say 'unexpected'; but that was nothing compared to the next startling development, which was that through the hatch stepped two figures – both in suits, both lacking helmets; one a bantam of a man whose head came no higher than any of our shoulders, and the other an inch or two taller, in a suit painted in violet, green and white – Miss Celia Lexlake herself, and no other.

12

It was immediately obvious that we were recognised, for Miss Lexlake flushed a becoming shade of pink upon seeing us.

I was the first to recover the power of speech.

"Miss Lexlake," I stammered, "this is an unforeseen pleasure."

Which may sound a weak conversational overture now I come to relate the story, but I don't suppose there is a single book of etiquette that could have provided me with a fully appropriate greeting in those singular circumstances.

"Gentlemen," said Miss Lexlake, hesitantly; she said no more, but coloured deeper still, which gave me the scanty comfort of knowing that she too was at a loss for the proper words.

The small man who had accompanied her filled the awkward silence.

"You are acquainted with this lady?" he said in curt tones.

Even so short a sentence sufficed to display to us a strong Welsh accent in his voice, and I realised that this must be none other than Gareth Oakes himself.

"After a fashion," George prevaricated.

"Were you behind her – hr'mm – her unorthodox actions today?"

We all three hastened to deny any involvement at all.

Oakes snorted. "I might have known it," he said. "I suppose you are all opposed to the introduction of votes for women?"

"I never really thought much about the subject," said Harris, once more displaying that when a ticklish situation besets us, Harris may be depended upon to think of absolutely the worst thing possible to say, and to say it.

Fortunately Miss Lexlake recovered her wits swiftly enough to explain to Oakes what role we had played, in brief; and though her explanation was short, it sufficed to mollify Gareth Oakes to an extent.

"I suggest," he said, "that we all of us adjourn to my private sitting-room, where we can review the present position like civilised people. I'm sure that I, for one, don't know half of what has been happening on Oakapple today."

We all of us expressed assent to this superlative idea, and were led through various locked and barred doors bearing warnings of the direst nature against those who would pass through them unbidden, until we found ourselves in an amply spaced, pleasantly decorated chamber where we were all happy enough to be seated in comfortable chairs, to sip refreshing liquids, and to explain to one another the recent course of events as seen from everyone's particular viewpoint.

Before we had reached very far in these explanations, the door opened once more to admit Mr. Neville, Mr. Souter – who was carrying our jackets and paraphernalia which we had set aside in our haste to reach Miss Lexlake – and Mr. Dyer, ushering with him Miss Dickson and Miss Craddock.

"Emily, dearest!" Miss Lexlake carolled. "And Arabel! I thought never to have seen your darling faces again."

She sprang from her chair with the force of a hurricane, and embraced both her friends.

I shall not attempt to reproduce every aspect of the conversation that took place in Mr Oakes' sitting-room, not least because throughout much of it two or more people were talking at once, and human type-setting, I fear, has not yet reached the level of development which would be required to give anybody who did not witness it directly the experience of being there. Permit me to compose a summary:

Miss Lexlake and her friends – who were together with her in her plot, as we had correctly surmised – had by devious means distracted a beadle, allowing Miss Craddock and Miss Lexlake to exit through the hatch he was supposed to be supervising, while Miss Dickson held his attention. Having unfurled and secured their VOTES FOR WOMEN banner, Miss Craddock had proceeded to help Miss Lexlake secure herself to the station by a chain which intertwined with her air-pipe.

It transpired that the Stoic calm with which Miss Lexlake had remained in her chosen position while first the beadles, and then we three men, had tried to talk her around, was due not so much to extraordinary self-control on her part, but because she feared that if she moved too much, the chains might snag her air-pipe and present her with a demise even more premature than the one for which she was prepared.

"I was quite ready to die out there for my cause," she said blithely, "but I did want to see what everyone would do in the face of my protest. Certainly," she said, "I expected men to intervene; but I was more surprised to encounter you three gentlemen again, and particularly to be subjected to such impassioned pleading on your part."

George positively simpered at this compliment, and even Harris rubbed his moustache and muttered something about how no decent fellow could have acted otherwise.

"But however did you come to leave your post, Celia, my dear?" Miss Dickson cried. "You were so staunch in your resolve!"

"Not that we aren't delighted to see you again," said Miss Craddock; "but – "

"Mr. Oakes succeeded where Mr. Harris and his friends failed," said Miss Lexlake. Seeing us look crestfallen, she hastened to add, "Through no fault of their own. It was providential indeed that Mr. Oakes should have arrived when he did, for I had scarcely half an hour's air supply remaining."

All eyes turned upon Gareth Oakes.

"I see no need to make a song and dance out of it," said Oakes in his pleasant Welsh burr. "When I saw the banner which you ladies had plastered over my station, and when I once got to wag my jaw with the lady who had placed it there, I realised that there was nothing else I could do as a decent man."

"But what did you do?" Miss Craddock's curiosity was evidently growing at such a rate that she could barely contain it.

"Why," said Oakes, "I said to the lady that so far as I was concerned, there was but one person who taught me all I know about everything save mining – and she was no dunce even at that, for she'd been a pit worker as a girl, before they put an end to such things – and that was my mother, Lord rest her soul! I gave Miss

Lexlake, here, my solemn vow that if she would abandon her protest and consent to return to safety, I would allow that banner to fly from Oakapple Orbital Station for so long as I'm master of the place; and it remains in place yet, don't it, Neville?"

"So it does, Mr Oakes, so it does," confirmed Neville.

"And there that banner flies," Oakes said, thumping his hand gently upon his coffee table for emphasis and coming perilously near to spilling the drink upon it, "until such time as Parlyment sees a grain of sense and all adults in the nation are granted the franchise. And I told Neville here what I'll tell him again – that I absolutely decline to bring any charges against Miss Lexlake and her fearless companions; and furthermore I hope they will feel free to remain here as my guests, free of any room-charge or docking-fee, for so long as they may choose."

Miss Craddock's face was a picture; a pretty picture, yes – but a picture.

"Emily," said Miss Lexlake, "I acted as I thought best, and I hope you'll forgive me if you think I made the wrong decision; but Mr Oakes seemed sincere, and – well – this kind gentleman, J. here, was so persuasive about how the suffrage movement would benefit from my continued presence among it – "

It was, I confess, my turn to blush at this point; thankfully Harris dug me in the ribs, which I believe he meant as a gesture of friendship, but which so startled me that I was temporarily unable to find any words.

Mr. Oakes smiled. He had a thin and rather pinched face, and a smile did not seem to come to it very easily; but smile he did.

"I understand that you told Miss Lexlake that she is a remarkable woman," he said to me, and I had to admit that I had doubtless said something of the sort.

"Aye, well, and so she is; and so long as Britain can produce ladies such as her, I reckon we'll be safe and well."

Oakes rose from his seat and began to stroll between us. His eyes were dark and shrewd. He certainly looked very much like what I knew him to have begun his career as – a Welsh coal-miner; but there was something about him which betrayed him as being something much more special than a mere hewer of coal. As I watched him, I came to the conclusion that here was a man who, had he not ventured into the sky and there made his fortune, would have made it in some other way, or at least achieved fame by some means.

He continued to dominate the conversation as we discussed the political balance of the suffrage movement, and how women might best achieve their goal in winning the vote. It is perhaps the most telling compliment that I can pay to Oakes's remarkable personality that none of our distaff companions, not even Miss Lexlake, sought to take issue with him upon his pronouncements. I had privately wondered whether his overt support for their cause betokened nothing more than enlightened self-interest and the pressing necessity to avoid the publicity which would have ensued, had Celia Lexlake martyred herself as per plan. But the more I listened to him, the more it became clear that he took a genuine interest in women's suffrage, from the viewpoint of an ally; and since Miss Lexlake and her friends appeared content to accept him as one, I was myself happy to be guided by their acceptance.

A long and interesting discussion, which I found most informative, was concluded only by Oakes suggesting delicately that Miss Lexlake might be weary after the exertions of her day. Though obviously a scion of no noble stock, Oakes had evidently taken the time to learn polished manners – another point which made him rise in my esteem. Miss Lexlake apparently thought so too. She admitted that she was feeling somewhat run down and that a rest would be welcome; I mused to myself that most women would be quite prostrated at the very idea of performing half of the deeds to Miss Lexlake's name that day. Certainly I myself was also weary, and I caught George out of the corner of my eye stifling a yawn.

And so the party broke up, with young Dyer escorting Harris, George and myself to quarters which were allocated to us upon Oakes' command.

"I can't say how long I shall be here for," said Oakes as we departed. "There are many calls upon my time on the Earth and the Moon as well as here; but I hope to see you all again before you depart from Oakapple, if circumstances permit."

We all alike responded that it would be a pleasure to do so.

We reached our quarters – a small but quite adequate room apiece, which was more than we had expected to be accommodated in upon the station – and George, in an excess of either generosity or exhaustion, tipped Dyer half a crown, which seemed to more than satisfy him.

The guest rooms on Oakapple Orbital – or at least, those in which we found ourselves now – were connected by a door to the room either side, which could either be locked or left unlocked depending on the constitution and numbers of a party. I happened to have the central room of our three, with George to my left and Harris to my right, and consequently after we had tended to our immediate needs and arranged our bags as required, we all gathered in my room.

"Well," I said, "this has been quite the adventure, George. I might have known that when you suggested a nice, restful trip up to space, that we should have nothing of the sort."

"Come now, J.," Harris said. "All's well that ends well, you know. And today could have ended up worse; frightfully worse, in fact."

"Ends well?" I echoed. "We have hardly begun. This is only our second night off the planet. Is it night, by the way? I have already lost track of time quite hopelessly."

I looked at my watch. It claimed that the time stood at a quarter after four, but whether this was accurate, or whether it was a.m. or p.m., or whether I had even remembered to wind the wretched timepiece, were questions far beyond my capability at that moment.

And as I reached that conclusion, George yawned again; Miss Lexlake and her companions being no longer present, he did not trouble to conceal it more than rudimentarily.

"Do you know," said Harris, "I don't care a jot whether it's night or not. I am exhausted, and you fellows are, too. We have had a most lively day, one way and another, and I wish to take this chance to sleep in an actual bed and not a confounded hammock contraption of knotted strings, that you have to tie yourself to or risk floating out. It's up to you two to decide whether you follow suit. But I am going to bed."

George answered this statement of intent with yet another yawn, so pronounced that for a moment I thought the top of his head was going to come loose; and by mutual consent, we all retired to test out the beds in our new billets.

I believe that they were more than adequately comfortable; but I cannot quite be sure, for I was so exhausted that I think I could have slept on a mattress filled with rusty nails and razor blades.

13

There is a particular kind of sleep which can only be obtained by hard physical labour; when you sink into it, you sink like a stone going into a pond, and (unlike the stone) you emerge some time later feeling much refreshed, but at the same time, less than certain whether you have slumbered for ten minutes, ten hours, or somewhere in between.

Just such a sleep was mine, in that little bedroom on Oakapple Orbital; and I duly woke from it feeling quite heartened, and with the growing conviction that space was a jolly place after all, and that George and Harris were not altogether chuckleheads for having suggested a trip there, and for dragging me along on it.

Having performed my usual toilet – if not quite in the usual manner, for like so many other things, such matters are handled differently in orbit – I smote first upon the connecting door to Harris's room, and then upon George's; and was rather disappointed to receive no response from either side.

Nothing loath, I flung both doors open wide, to discover that Harris had evidently already awoken, dressed, and gone out onto the station; whilst George was still tucked up in a muddle of blankets and sheets, snoring happily, and my banging on his door had failed to wake him, any more than knocking had awakened Duncan after his fateful encounter with Macbeth.

I decided to leave George to his slumbers, and to venture out in search of Harris.

While looking for Harris, I found a Gatti's restaurant. I tried to work out how long it had been since I had eaten a proper meal, and couldn't; which I took as evidence that I was probably in need of one, and that Harris was just as likely to be in that restaurant as he was anywhere else on Oakapple. As it turned out, he was not; but by the time I had gone inside and glanced over every table, one of Gatti's immaculately dressed waiters was at my elbow and showing me to a seat.

Even after my journey into orbit, there are still a great many things I do not know about space travel. One of them is how a restaurant can operate in the setting of an orbital station, where almost every procedure must be subtly different from its earthly counterpart. I can, however, confirm that Monsieur Gatti's restaurant on Oakapple is every bit the equal of his terrestrial franchises.

When I saw *l'addition*, I had to look at it twice. Of course, in orbit, everything from beans to bacon must be shipped up from below, and even with Professor Cavor's assistance, to do so costs money. I was engaged in hasty calculations as to whether I would need to make a swift trip to the bank which I had seen earlier on the concourse, but before I could reach a definite conclusion, the head waiter himself descended upon me and gently chided me for not making it clear that I was the guest of *le patron*, Monsieur Oakes. He plucked the bill from my fingers and retreated with it held securely in his own, and I did not see it again.

I felt better and better disposed towards my new Welsh friend.

Leaving the restaurant and returning to the promenade, I found a bank of a dozen clocks all arranged in a row, each telling a different time, and each bearing under it the name of one of the world's great cities. I checked my watch against the LONDON clock and they agreed at twenty minutes after eight in the evening; my internal sense of time was still unfathomable – I have heard other space travellers say that they, too, lost track of time easily once in orbit – but I was prepared to accept the mechanical evidence as adequate.

I walked for some minutes up and down the concourse. There were a good many retail outlets there, mainly, I learned, charging exorbitant prices to reflect Oakapple's exorbitant status. While I could have doubtless prevailed upon my position as Gareth Oakes' guest aboard the station, it seemed churlish to run that horse, so to speak, into the ground; and besides, I was still keeping an eye out for Harris. You can never trust Harris not to get into mischief at the least opportunity.

I paused to examine a stationer's, to which my attention had been drawn by a display of picture postcards. There were several striking shots of the Moon, and of Oakapple itself; there were also some less edifying cards, with pictures by Mr. Donald McGill of nubile young ladies and leering space-travellers, with jokes about Cavorite undergarments, and Orion's belt, and Uranus. These, it seemed to me, were just the kind of thing to attract Harris; but there was no sign of him thereabouts, and after a few moments the stationer started to look at me with a meaningful expression, as though to invite me to either make a purchase or move along. I moved along.

Continuing my journey around the station, I next came upon another section of it which the Young Person's Guide to the Orbital Stations had scarcely touched upon – namely, the casino.

And there it was that I found Harris, sitting cheerfully at the green baize, losing his money at chemin de fer, in between a well-dressed lady in fashionable attire and a sandy-haired fellow gloomily nursing a brandy-and-soda as though it were the last he would ever drink.

"Oh! There you are, J.," he said, pushing back his chair. "I was wondering when I should see you again. You and George were both sound asleep."

"George is, still," I said. "How long have you been frittering away your cash here?"

"I say, old man – "

"Don't you I-say-old-man me. You always lose money when you gamble; you know it perfectly well. What would your wife say?"

"She wouldn't be bothered," said Harris, so earnestly that for a moment I half believed him. "She is only vexed when I play roulette; roulette has such a way of making you stay for longer than you ought, don't you find? But they don't have roulette here, because of the gravity; only cards."

I do not personally disapprove of gambling; I have never seen the fascination in it that seizes on some men and makes them mere chattels of its siren lure. I do not mind expending a half-crown on the St Leger or the Derby, but beyond that I choose not to go.

"Anyway," said Harris, taking advantage of my momentary silence as I considered the position, "you should see the way some of the people here chuck money away. You'd think they came straight out of Brewster's Millions, the way they carry on. The worst one," he confided, dropping his voice for fear of being overheard, "is old Freckleton, whom we saw at Peckover's yard. I wouldn't care, only the blighter will keep on winning."

I looked over at the gaming table. Lord Freckleton was just gathering up a collection of chips with a satisfied expression.

As he did so, I saw two figures approaching behind him; I recognised them both, for I had also seen them at Peckover's – his wife, and his valet. The latter of these murmured a few words into Freckleton's ear, and he spoke to the croupier.

"I'm afraid I must cut and run for now," he said in a measured voice. I should not have thought that such a voice belonged to a nobleman, had I heard it without the benefit of seeing its owner; but it certainly fitted his ascetic appearance well enough.

His valet scooped up the stacks of chips by Freckleton's place at the table, and Lady Freckleton once more adopted the position in which I had first seen her, back on Earth; namely, clinging closely to his arm, as though she sought to hide herself behind him. The valet tossed a couple of chips to the croupier as a pourboire, and the trio departed.

"What's got you, J., old chap?"

Harris's voice stirred me from a reverie.

"I was just thinking about his lordship and his retinue," I said, which was true, so far as it went.

"I suppose," said Harris, "that I shan't get any peace from you to play cards?"

"You suppose correctly," I said, and Harris sighed.

"Why do we not take a stroll about the station?" I suggested. Something was niggling at the back of my mind, and whenever I tried to bring it into mental focus, it evaded my thought processes. Thoughts like that are like a kettle that will not boil, it is of no use to confront them – you must pretend to have lost all interest in them, if you wish to make tea, or to bring a stray notion into brightness and clarity.

We were passing a jeweller's store, and I was making a show of looking at the trinkets on display and being shocked by their expense, when that thought bounded into the spotlight at the forefront of my brain, and I turned to Harris.

"Harris," I said, hesitating a little for fear that my idea was beyond the bounds of preposterousness, "did you think anything odd about Freckleton, and his wife and that man of his – what was his name?

"Hannay. And no; should I have?"

"I suppose," I said quietly, as much to myself as to Harris, "that Lord Freckleton really is who he purports to be?"

Harris looked at me steadily.

"I knew it was a mistake," he said, "to let you go out of the station, chasing after Miss Lexlake. You have picked up sunstroke, that's what you have done. Come along with me and have a brandy-and-soda."

I waved away the thought of brandy-and-soda. "Do think a second, Harris, you chump, instead of assuming I must have gone potty. You remember PC Nuttall?"

"I could hardly forget him."

"Do you not recall that he was searching for three criminals who had left Earth at about the same time as we did?"

"Indeed I do, but – Oh, dash it, J., you can't mean…?"

"Lord Freckleton," I said, "or the man who calls himself Lord Freckleton, does not strike me as flawlessly polished in his manners or dress."

"Well, that means nothing," said Harris. "Neither is George – to take an example not entirely at random – and if he's a criminal mastermind, he conceals it very well indeed."

"George is not a member of the nobility," I pointed out. "Furthermore, when Hannay came up to him just now, it seemed to me very much as though Hannay was giving him orders, and not the other way about. Don't you think that odd, for a lord and his valet? And his wife kept clinging to him, as though she were scared of something."

"Perhaps," said Harris, "they are newly wed. Ladies will retain an affectionate stance toward their husband, you know, J., for weeks and weeks after they marry."

"No," I said, "there was something else about her – I can't think quite what –"

"Do you think she and Lord Freckleton are – ahem! – in an irregular relationship?"

That was not what had been niggling at my mind, but for once, I was ready to concede that Harris might have come up with a bright idea.

"I suppose that's possible," I said.

"It's more likely than Freckleton being some crook in false plumage; and in any case, J., Nuttall told us that the three criminals were men. Lord Freckleton and Hannay are of the male gender; but Lady Freckleton is another matter. I tell you what," said Harris. "Did we not pass a bookshop just back there? Yes, I thought so. Come along with me."

He took my by the arm in an avuncular but firm way, and we retraced our steps a little way, until we reached the bookshop in question. Harris turned into it; and since he still had hold of my arm, and I in turn was attached to that arm, I also turned into it.

Harris led me to the reference section, where he finally deigned to release his grip upon me.

"What have you in mind?" I asked him.

Harris, waving away the attentions of a shop assistant who came snapping at his heels, looked up and down the shelves until he found a volume of a familiar crimson hue, and pulled it from its place. He opened the book towards its centre, read for a few moments, then wordlessly passed it to me, with his forefinger marking the place.

I scanned the entry in question carefully, and once I had digested it, looked back up at Harris.

"The fact that Lord and Lady Freckleton are listed in Who's Who, and have been married for five years," I said, "is by itself no guarantee that the people we have encountered under those names are the genuine article. I dare say that Beerbohm Tree has an entry in that volume; but if I were to introduce myself to you as Mr Tree, you would be unwise to take my claim at face value."

Harris shut Who's Who with a thud and slid it back into place.

"What do you suggest? We can't consult Constable Nuttall,

can we? He could be on quite the other side of the planet, by now."

"True. But I am certain that the beadles here on Oakapple will have ways of communicating with the terrestrial police. They may even have the right to detain people here on the station; it is private property, after all. I'm not sure of the legal niceties of trespass in space – are you?"

"Absolutely not," said Harris, as though he were proud of his ignorance on the topic.

"I suggest," I said, "that we seek out that very efficient Mr Neville, and in a quiet and friendly kind of way, inform him of what we have observed."

"What *you* have observed," Harris said pointedly, which I thought mean of him.

"You don't believe I may be right?"

"You may be right," Harris said, "but equally you may be making a deuced fool of yourself. Bear in mind, old chap, that today has been an extremely long ordeal for you, as it has for all three of us, and that your critical faculties may not be at their peak."

I would dearly have loved to disagree with Harris, but I felt I could hardly do so, not least because we were still in the middle of the bookshop and the shop assistant was still hovering in our general vicinity. (I use 'hovering' figuratively, of course; the bookshop, like the rest of Oakapple, was under the rule of centrifugal force – or do I mean centipetral? – and hence of quasi-gravity).

"I believe," I said crisply, "that we should go and wake up George, who has been a slugabed too long, and consult him."

We made our way back to our quarters, to find that George was awake – after a fashion. He was sitting in his nightshirt, staring at a cup of tea as though it had delivered some mortal insult to him and he was trying to decide what retribution best fitted the crime.

"George, old man," said Harris, breezing into the room like a small hurricane, "time to rise and shine. You don't want to let your system become divorced from earthly hours just because we're up here, where sunrise and sunset don't mean what they do down below."

George merely groaned, and said that he had half a mind simply to go back to bed, and sleep through to what his timepiece said was morning.

"Less of that nonsense," I said. "We need to seek your opinion on an important matter. Your opinion is, of course, of little value; but it is the only opinion to which Harris and I have ready access, so it will have to do."

George swallowed half his tea with a shudder, and paid attention to us while we explained my theorem and Harris's scepticism of it.

George took another sip when we had finished. "It's funny you should have thought that," he said, "because something peculiar about the Freckletons did strike me, too."

"What?"

"Freckleton evidently has the desire and the money to take his valet – may his moustache fall out overnight – into space with him. I wondered to myself why Lady Freckleton didn't seem to have a maid with her, in that case."

"Good Lord," said Harris.

"Perhaps she dresses herself," I suggested.

"Perhaps, but it's odd, and when you take it together with your idea..." George pushed the remainder of his tea away, with a new resolve.

"I am going to speak to Neville," I said. "Very likely I am being a stupid, suspicious ass; but I still resent the way Hannay treated us back in Peckover's shipyard at Maplin, and if by any chance my suspicions are correct, it will give me great pleasure to drop him into hot water. Come along."

We left our quarters, intending to enter the concourse and make our way to the beadles' office. But when we approached the promenade, it was barred by a closed hatch marked NO ADMITTANCE, with guards standing by it to reinforce the ban. A few people were standing around, getting in the way, in the aimless way that folk have on Earth when a street has been barred off for a fire or a falling building.

We pushed our way forward, and found that one of the beadles was our friend Neville.

"Ah, good evening, gentlemen," he said. "I'm afraid nobody

is being admitted to the concourse at the moment."

"Why?" demanded George.

Neville coughed. "I'm sure the news will be all over the station soon enough," he said, "that the bank in the concourse has been robbed."

"I knew it," I exclaimed, incautiously. My words drew the attention of several people from the crowd at the barrier, and Neville raised one eyebrow a measured fraction of an inch.

"Do I take it that you know something about the crime?"

"Well, not exactly know," I said, "but – "

I was uncertain how much I should seek to explain to Neville in this public forum; but the beadle took in the situation instantly.

"I think," he said, "that you and your friends had best accompany me, and you can tell me what you don't exactly know somewhere that we can give one another our full attention."

He deputed another of the beadles to take charge of the barricade, and led the three of us to his own office.

It was not a large room – few rooms are large on the orbital stations, where to build them is costly and to fill them with air not cheap. His desk and chair – made mostly, like so much of the furnishings about Oakapple – was of steel, and upon the desk I saw many papers and notices of an official bent.

Apart from Neville's own chair, there were only two other seats in the room. One was already occupied, by a beefy man with a large nose, who turned towards us with an immediate air of suspicion. His nose seemed to quiver, as though he were sniffing out our sins. This, we learned, was Superintendent Veele of the A.O.L., a senior officer of that division.

"I am fortunate," said Neville, with a sidelong look at us suggesting that he felt anything but fortunate, "to have Superintendent Veele here on the station. He was sent for in order to assist with – ahem! – Miss Lexlake and the unusual situation we were placed in, with which you assisted us so generously; but by the time he reached us, the matter had already been resolved."

Veele snorted, like a sergeant-major, at the mention of Miss Lexlake; it seemed plain to me that he was awfully vexed by having arrived too late to participate in that affair, and that he was ready to take out his annoyance at the first opportunity.

Neville sat behind his desk. There was only one other free chair; Harris was the quickest to move, and secured it, while George and I sat informally upon the edge of Neville's desk, at his invitation. The metal desk-top might not have been a comfortable resting place, but the level of gravity aboard Oakapple was sufficiently low that we made shift contentedly.

"Well, Neville," said Veele in a peevish tone, "am I to arrest these rascals?"

"Not at all, Mr. Veele," said Neville. "I believe these men have some information which may assist our enquiries into the bank-robbery."

"Is that so?" said Veele. He rose from his seat and peered into first my face, then George's, then Harris's, from a distance which felt a little uncomfortable. Then he turned back to Neville. "You know," he said, "that three habitual criminals are reported to have left Earth very recently – "

"Oh," said Harris, "we know all about that."

"Do you, now?" Veele's nose quivered again. I wished silently to myself that Harris had phrased that remark in a different way.

"You see, Mr. Veele," I explained hastily, "on our way up here we encountered one of your constables – Nuttall, his name was – and he was quite content that we were not the rogues whom he sought."

"Nuttall!" grunted Veele. "That man couldn't catch a cold in a fever hospital." And he made us all give our names, and addresses, and show our papers; and when he saw George's hire-receipt from Mr. Peckover, he grew quite excited, for it seemed that the trio of criminals had left Maplin at much the same time as we had.

I feared that we were all about to be clapped in irons and have summary justice meted out unto us; but Neville, that sterling fellow, discouraged Veele, and while they were still deciding the point, the door to the beadle's office opened and there stood Gareth Oakes, with the air of a man who owns the place and can go where he likes – which of course, in this case, he was.

14

I took heart in Oakes' presence, for I was certain that we had in him an ally upon whom we could depend; and while, no doubt, Superintendent Veele's authority was such that he could have arrested us over Oakes' head, I doubted that he would wish to ride so roughly shod over the desires of the owner of Oakapple.

So indeed it proved; Oakes laughed to scorn the suggestion that we might be the dubious trio sought by the A.O.L., and told Veele, in almost so many words, to rein himself in. Veele's nose quivered like a whole tree full of leaves, but he subsided – not without several more suspicious looks at us – and I was finally able to explain my suspicions regarding the Freckleton party.

"What you say is, of course, remarkable," Neville said when I had said all I could think of to say that might support my suspicion. "But merely because it is remarkable is no cause to reject it out of hand, especially given one particular piece of information of which I assume you to be unaware."

"Go on," I said, as he paused to emphasise whatever point he was about to make.

"Only one ship departed this station," said Neville, "in between the robbery, and the news of it reaching the beadles and our being able to order that no further vessels be permitted to launch. Aboard that ship was Lord Freckleton and his party. I had, I admit," he continued a little ruefully, "discounted the possibility of them being in any way interested in the crime; but now – "

"Then the money's gone?"

From the dismay in George's voice, one might almost have thought that the stolen money might have belonged to him personally. But George, as a banker himself, seemed to take the robbery as a slight to all in the banking business. If I myself had the misfortune to be a banker, I should have been privately relieved to hear that another bank had been robbed, on the grounds that that would mean that my own bank had not been. But perhaps this is why I am not a banker.

"The money has not yet been recovered, certainly."

"What are you going to do?" I asked, before reflecting that I was likely to be given a dusty answer to a question which impinged upon the beadle's own professional business and to which I was hardly entitled to a response.

"Nothing," interjected Veele, "if he has any common sense at all. Lord Freckleton rob a bank! The idea's absurd. What's more, the robber was bearded, and Freckleton's clean-shaven." (Which I had to admit was so.)

"The question's moot," said Neville. "Since Lord Freckleton's ship has left the station, I have no legal standing with which to pursue it. My authority as head beadle, you know, is purely conferred to me by Mr. Oakes as owner of this station."

Veele looked positively exuberant, at that.

"However," went on Neville, "I have ongoing enquiries here on the station. May I suggest that we remain here pending their resolution? It shouldn't take long."

Oakes touched a bell, and a young maid duly brought in a tray of tea. The vessels from which we were to drink were more utilitarian than decorative, but that I did not much mind. I did mind that the tea somehow managed to be both strong and weak at the same time, a combination I had not previously encountered in my career as a tea drinker, but it gave me something to do with my hands while we awaited developments.

George said afterwards that it is practically impossible to get a good cup of tea in space. It is something to do with the gravity, he thought.

At last another beadle – it was Dyer – entered to update us. Firstly, he reported, following a search of Oakapple, the stolen money had not yet been found.

"Go on," said Oakes warily, and Veele took out his official notepad and pencil, licking the latter with relish.

"As you know, sir, the money that was stolen came from multiple currencies – we believe, at the present time, eleven; but translating it into pounds sterling at the current exchange rate, sir, the sum is in the vicinity of twenty-one thousand pounds."

A faint whimper escaped from George.

For a moment I was surprised by the size of the robbers' haul; but, naturally, the orbital stations are visited by so many every day, from so many different nations, that most of them possess at least one bank and bureau de change where trade is always brisk; and, of course, they must be ready to deal with every monetary request made of them as much as is possible. Since to transfer money to and from orbit as cargo is an expense which most financial institutions would take any steps to avoid, it is little surprise that they often accumulate a tidy amount of wealth in their vaults.

And now that wealth had gone – gone in the first ever orbital bank robbery! And we were in the thick of it!

"But what we did find," said Dyer, "in Number 8 gentlemen's conveniences, was this." He threw onto Neville's desk something that was jet black in colour, and bristled. For a horrid instant, I thought it must be some kind of savage creature from the Martian deserts. Closer inspection, though, proved it to be a false beard and a wig.

"So much for the description of the bank-robber we had!" growled Oakes. "We might have known that anyone can put on false whiskers."

"On the other hand," said Neville, "this lets our friend Freckleton – or whatever his name is – " (Veele snorted again.) – "back into the picture."

"I won't have it," growled Veele. "Even if we concede that Freckleton isn't Freckleton but is Bustany – a theorem of which I have the gravest doubt – Ronald Bustany and his confederates have no form for robbery at all. They're confidence tricksters, pure and simple."

Neville rubbed his chin thoughtfully, took a few paces – which was all that anyone could have taken in that room – and turned to face us again.

"I agree," he said, "that Ronald Bustany and his companions are well known to the police as confidence tricksters, fraudsters and general practitioners of sharpness. It's correct, too, that not one of them has form – I should say, has a criminal history – of robbery, either with violence or without. Truth to tell, I should have thought that Bustany would find such a thing beneath him. He isn't exactly Professor Moriarty – don't worry about such a thing, sirs – but he fancies himself something of a criminal mastermind, and it's a fact that he has more intelligence in his noggin, as well as cunning, than your average rogue.

"Now I can well believe Bustany to be capable," he went on, "of impersonating a member of the nobility and of setting up, say, a line of credit based upon that fake identity, before vanishing and leaving the true Lord Freckleton to resolve the tangle. Equally, the false Lord Freckleton would doubtless be able to hire a space-vessel on credit without much trouble. But bank robbery really isn't his normal style.

"On the other hand," he said, walking back to his starting point and once more turning, "twenty-one thousand pounds, even nowadays, is a frightful lot of money. Any criminal might find his mouth watering at the thought of twenty-one thousand pounds."

My own mouth was watering at the thought of twenty-one thousand pounds; and lest the reader fear I am being an unreliable narrator, I must assure you that I am free from criminal records and from criminal tendencies.

"Don't you agree, Mr. Veele?" said Neville; and Veele, with the worst of grace, admitted that it might be so.

"I think we can at least establish something," said Neville. He wrote something in his notebook, tore out the page and handed it to Dyer, who left the room.

"What are you up to?" barked Veele.

"Official business," said Neville, jerking his head towards us to signify that we mere mortals were not worthy of sharing in his confidence. This was a neat way of taking the wind out of Veele's sails, since Veele could hardly argue that Neville should have spoken freely in front of us without conceding that we were no longer regarded as suspects in the matter.

And so we waited, in increasing awkwardness, until Dyer returned, with a folded newspaper under one arm, and ushering in a waiflike young lady with round, nervous eyes. It was fortunate that she was of unassuming dimensions, for the office was becoming extremely cramped.

"You wished to see this person, Mr Neville? She was the maid who cleaned the Freckletons' suite last night."

Harris arose from his chair, and the maid took it nervously.

"Shall I speak to the lady, Mr. Veele? Thank you. Now," said Neville, taking the newspaper from Dyer and glancing through it, "please let me have your name."

If the room had been any larger, we would not all have been able to hear her say "Julia Clay, sir."

"You have done nothing wrong, Julia," said Neville, "so pray don't be scared. You saw and spoke to the gentleman who occupied Suite H last night?"

"Yes, sir." She sounded a little less hesitant, now.

"Very good. Now, Julia, this newspaper contains a photograph of a certain person. I am going to show you that photograph, and I should like you to tell me whether the subject of the photograph is the man in Suite H."

He folded the paper deftly, with the photograph uppermost.

"Oh, sir, I'm sorry – "

"Don't be sorry; just be honest."

"I'm sorry, but I'm certain sure it isn't him. I really don't think it looks a bit like him, though I hope I may die."

Neville dropped the paper on his desk with a satisfied expression, and we all leaned over to look at it. The man in it was a perfect stranger to me, as well.

"That settles it," he said. "The man in that photograph is Alfred Nugent Oliver Croxton, eldest son of the third Earl of Lundy. He bears the courtesy title of Lord Freckleton; the real Lord Freckleton does, I mean. And if, as I surmise, he is nothing like the man you three encountered – "

"Not in the least," we all said.

"The rascals," said Oakes, hissing his S's like a true Welshman.

"You may go, Julia," said Neville. And Julia went, with every appearance of relief.

"There we have it, gentlemen," Neville smiled. "Do you agree, Mr Veele?"

"I do not," said Veele. "That girl was terrified. She would have said anything to you to escape from the beadles. You plainly wanted her to give a certain opinion; and she gave it."

"Gentlemen, gentlemen," said Oakes soothingly. "What about the note which the bank-robber passed to the cashier? Can you not establish from the handwriting on that...?"

"It was typed," said Neville gloomily. He dug about on his desk. "Here, see. I've had my men make copies."

He passed one to Oakes, and another to Veele. I made a hopeful face at him, and he allowed me to take a third, which I studied. It was wholly typed in capitals:

KINDLY FILL THIS BAG WITH MONEY, it read. THE LARGEST DENOMINATIONS YOU HAVE. UPON NO CIRCUMSTANCES SOUND AN ALARM. I HAVE A GUN IN MY POCKET, AND I SHALL USE IT SHOULD YOU DO SO.

Harris snatched it from me, and he and George looked at it together.

"Quite formal," remarked Oakes. "And well typed."

"I'd make sure it was well typed, if I were planning a robbery like this," said Veele.

"We must take action," Neville said, and Oakes nodded firmly. "May I suggest that you follow Freckleton's ship – or rather, the ship containing the man calling himself Freckleton? Its filed flight-plan is for Selene City."

Veele was clearly running as low on patience with Neville as Neville was with Veele.

"I still don't believe," he snapped, "that Freckleton is anyone but Freckleton. You may wish to make a fool of yourself before the world by accusing a British nobleman of impersonating himself. I choose not to do so. Good day, sirs."

With which remark Superintendent Veele swept out of the room. George annexed his chair before Oakes could do so.

"Confound the man!" exclaimed Oakes – meaning Veele rather than George. "I never knew the likes of him for pig-headedness."

Neville sighed. "He's at a loss, and waspish about it, sir. Rather than concede that we beadles may have an idea about a crime here on our own station, he prefers to think we're a handful of idiots who know nothing about police and detective work."

"But you were in the Met.," said Oakes.

Neville smiled thinly. "Quite so, sir."

"I shall take action, even if Veele won't," said Oakes. "You say they filed a flight-plan for Selene City?"

"That's right, sir. Of course, if they are the bank-robbers, it may have been a false lead, but – "

"Perhaps," said Oakes, "but I'm damned if I'm going to sit around here, wasting time like a billy-goat on a spoil-heap, after that robbery. Very likely they are making for Selene City. A man can lose himself quite easily on the Moon, if he doesn't want to be found. Also, I know Sir Oswald Inkpen, the chief of police for the City, and while you as an Oakapple beadle may have no direct authority there, Neville, I can guarantee that – unlike that unspeakable clod Veele – Ossie Inkpen will at least listen to us. I'm going to take the Rhondda Cynon Taff down to Selene City, and you shall accompany me, and we'll hopefully find the truth down there about that man – Bustany, did you say he was called? Golly, what a name."

"If I were called Bustany," I remarked, "I might prefer to adopt another name in preference."

Neville looked at me sharply, and I realised too late that my words had served to remind him that we civilians were still present.

"Gentlemen," he said, "I think we should not detain you further; but I do thank you most sincerely for your assistance."

In the face of so strong a hint we could not well remain in Neville's office, and we emerged, to find that the concourse had re-opened, save for the area directly by the bank, which remained interdicted by the beadles from the prying eyes of the common people.

15

George exhaled. "Well, my saints, what a day!"

Before either Harris or I could add our own observations to that expressive opinion, a man bounded up to us, startling us all. His face was adorned by a close crop of sandy hair, and he bore a hopeful expression.

"Pardon my intrusion, gentlemen," he said, "but I could not help but observe you emerging from the beadles' quarters. May I enquire whether you are able to supply to an officer of the Press any information on today's infamous bank robbery?"

"An officer of the Press!" exclaimed Harris. "Does the Press extend its grip even up into orbit, then?"

The fellow looked quite hurt by that. "Of course we do," he said, producing his card. It proclaimed him to be Harold Eppley, accredited representative of the Orbital Herald, with headquarters and printing-office on the US station Hesperus.

"You don't sound very American," Harris said.

"I'm not very American. I'm not American at all. I am the Herald's reporter here on Oakapple, and to have some news – some actual, juicy news – rather than a dreary list of which celebrities have passed through on their route to where and in whose company – "

Mr. Eppley's eyes took on a hungry look.

"I am also a writer and journalist, after a fashion," I said, "and I know what it is to be on your beam-ends crying out for a decent chunk of copy. I am sure we can oblige this chap by telling him what we know."

"Should we?" George said. "What if he prints it, and this man Bustany gets wind of it, and it allows him to escape justice?"

"Don't be an ass, George," said Harris. "Bustany has already left the station, and won't have a chance to pick up a newspaper. You don't suppose that W. H. Smith has a stationer's floating in lunar orbit, do you?"

I could tell by the gleam in Eppley's eyes that he was absorbing all this information.

"I suggest," I said, cutting through the bickering session which I could see Harris and George were building up to, "that we retire to a convenient watering-hole, such as that little French-style estaminet over yonder, and we can discuss the matter in greater comfort, greater seclusion, and with food and drink inside us all. I don't know about you, George, but the tea Beadle Neville served us seemed to me unfit to throw at a cat for yowling."

You can always sway Harris by suggesting food and drink; and once he started reciting the dishes he thought they might serve in the restaurant, any rearguard defence from George was doomed to be swept away to ruin.

The estaminet proved both comfortable and quiet, and securing a table for four at the back of the dining area (which is to say, against the outer wall of the station, allowing one to glance through the window and watch stars pass by), we related to Mr. Eppley our experiences from our encounter with the supposed Lord Freckleton on Earth, to our interview in the beadle's office half an hour previously.

"You know," Eppley said, "I thought there was something a bit skew-whiff about Freckleton."

"Oh!" I said. "You saw him, then?"

"As I was saying, part of my duties is to detail which people of note have visited the station either to stay, or to pass through. English noblemen," Eppley said, with a curl of the lip, "are definitely people of note, to an American-owned newspaper and its audience."

Harris uttered a sudden exclamation.

"That's where I've seen you before!" he said. "You were at the same chemmy table in the casino with him, before the robbery."

"Quite right," conceded Eppley. "I don't haunt gaming-houses for their own sake, of course, but I wanted to work up a story on Lord Freckleton."

"Really?" said Harris. "You seemed to know your way about a game of chemmy all right."

Eppley smiled ruefully. "One picks up no end of strange odds and ends of knowledge," he said, "when one's a journalist."

"Wait, though," said Harris. "Freckleton... he was in the casino, with you and me almost the same time as the robbery."

"That's only to be expected," I said. "While the supposed Lord Freckleton remains in view of dozens of people in the casino, his valet goes to rob the bank, cool as a cucumber. D'you remember me remarking on how the valet came to the card-table, and practically ordered his lordship to come away with him?"

I beamed at my own cleverness in reasoning this out. I had assumed that the impersonator of Lord Freckleton must be the leader of the party; but to promote Hannay the valet to that role instead made quite as much sense to me, and furthermore, it gave me an extra reason to scorn Hannay in particular – Hannay who had been so snide and unsympathetic to us over that little misunderstanding at Maplin, a misunderstanding that might have happened to anyone.

"No," Eppley said. "I know when Freckleton left the casino, for I left only a minute or two after him. And the robbery didn't take place till nearly a quarter of an hour after that."

We agreed that, at least in theory, Lord Freckleton himself might have been the culprit, and went on with our tale; and when we concluded it with Oakes' avowed intention to pursue the thieves to Selene City, Eppley uttered a hoarse cry of despair.

"What's the matter, old fellow?" asked George solicitously. "Tummy-ache?"

"Of all the rotten, rancid, beastly, devilish luck," growled Eppley. "I ought to follow the story and chase the lot of them to Selene City, too; but I received word a few minutes ago that my sphere has failed its safety routine – what atrocious timing! – and I can't fly it until it's been repaired, which will be a day or two at least. And by then I shall be so far behind them that it won't be worth the trip. Did ever a man have such foul bad fortune?"

"I'm sure that there will be other stories," said Harris, which is a dangerous thing to say to a journalist who has just lost a scoop. Luckily for him, Eppley's response was continued gloom, rather than anything more violent.

Then Eppley slumped down in his chair, almost enough to slide right onto the floor, and sat there in a semi-supine position with his chin almost on the table. It was a pitiful sight, and it aroused a fellow feeling in me.

"You know," I said, "if you're so desperate to follow this story to the Moon..." And I looked at George and Harris in an encouraging way.

It was George who first realised at what I was hinting, of course.

"Really, J.?"

"It's not his fault that his sphere is in for maintenance," I said, "and since we're going there anyway, I'm sure we could find room for him..."

"What!" said Harris, catching up with us. "You mean, take him to the Moon with us?"

Eppley's downcast face gave a kind of twitch, and rearranged itself into the expression of a man who hardly dares hope that a way out of his troubles has suddenly presented itself.

"Are there no scheduled vessels?" said George; which was an idea I had, I admit, overlooked. But Eppley indicated a negative.

"Not for nearly twenty-four hours; and that one's the Ulysses, which is almost always fully booked inbound and outbound."

"I don't know – " began Harris.

"The paper would pay," said Eppley quickly.

George and Harris exchanged another glance.

I prefer to believe that if I were in their shoes, I should not have allowed my judgment to be swayed merely by an offer of vulgar money; but perhaps George was still feeling the financial sting of the robbery on behalf of bankers everywhere.

"Dash it," he said, "J.'s right – we were heading in that direction anyway; and besides, I don't know about you, Harris, but I'm curious to know what the end of this all may turn out to be, and this seems an excellent excuse to keep poking our noses into the affair – don't you think, J.?"

"I couldn't agree more," I said.

"Oh, very well," said Harris. "But he puts up his own hammock – upon that I insist."

It seemed clear that Eppley would have put up hammocks for a whole battleship full of sailors, if it bestowed on him a place on a vessel bound for Selene City at that moment.

"You're too good," he kept repeating, in the sort of way that a man does when he is desperate to be disagreed with. Consequently, I disagreed, and said it was a favour from one man of letters to another – that I was confident we would hardly know he was there.

"And besides," I pointed out, "Mr Eppley, I am sure, knows how to pilot a sphere; and you can't deny that none of us is a dab hand at that – not even you, George."

"In which case," said Harris, "I suppose we had better settle with the garsong here, and prepare for a speedy departure."

"In order to follow Oakes as closely as possible?" said George.

"That, and also to give me as little chance as possible to change my mind."

"There is another consideration," I said, "which in my view trumps them all; which is that once Oakes and Neville are off the station, there will remain nobody who is likely to argue with that frightful Superintendent Veele, should he once more take a fancy to arrest all three of us out of hand. Once we leave Oakapple, we shall at least be free from that risk."

Eppley began to chuckle, then turned it into a cough, and turned his expression of amusement into one of concern. "I'm sorry," he said, "it really can't be a pleasant position to be in."

"Indeed it isn't," said George. "You haven't met Veele."

"And I hope I never shall," said Eppley. "But really, it's too rich to suppose that three chaps like you could turn bank-robber."

He smiled round at each of us in turn; and I chose to take his words as reflecting upon our transparent honesty and decency, rather than thinking he meant that we would have lacked the brains or the courage to carry out such a crime.

"Then it's settled," said Harris. "Let's go and pack up our things, and make for the Moon. Will you have much in the way of baggage, Eppley?"

"Oh, hardly," said the journalist. "I shall throw a few clothes into a couple of bags, and there's my portable typewriter so I can write my story up once we get there. No more than that, unless I need to provide food and drink."

I assured him that we had ample food, and more than ample drink, which seemed to set his mind fully at ease.

16

My surmise was correct. Eppley was a safe pair of hands at the controls of our sphere, and I felt a good deal less nervous now that we had secured ourselves a competent pilot, than I had when George was at the wheel.

While we had completed our formalities for departure, Eppley had briefly vanished. Once we had all met up once again, and been cast adrift from the station and seen it dwindle into the distance behind us, he looked around and began to talk. He proved a very talkative man indeed, in point of fact; anyone whom he interviewed in his capacity of journalist must have been hard put to get a word in edgeways.

"Oakes is an hour or so behind Freckleton; and we are barely an hour behind Oakes," he said. "I learned that from one of the dockers just before we embarked. Don't think ill of me, please, for having him on my pay roll. So much of my daily routine involves news of dockings and launchings from the station. It disgusts me," he quoted, "but I do it."

George said that every man had to make a living somehow, he supposed.

"Oakes seems to take the matter very personally," said Harris, "given that it wasn't his money that was stolen."

"I don't reckon that's particularly odd," I said. "If the bank robbers make a clean getaway with the money, Oakes will be placed in a most invidious position."

"I don't think he can be liable for the loss, surely?" said George, once more looking at the issue from the banker's viewpoint.

"Probably not, but don't you see, you addlepate, that if word spreads around that to visit Oakapple Station is to invite thieves and cutpurses to steal the very clothes from off your back, Mr. Oakes' enterprise is likely to see a falling-off in trade?"

"You're right, J.," said Eppley. "I think that Gareth Oakes would go to very great lengths to secure the return of that money.

And that head beadle of his appears wholly at his beck and call."

"Oh, you mean Neville?" said Harris.

"You know the man? I'm sure that he too would dearly love the thieves to be caught. He takes his duties very seriously. Rather unbending. Doesn't like to talk to the Press, though luckily a couple of the other beadles tend to be more forthcoming."

"You have covered crime reporting before?" I asked.

"I cover everything on Oakapple. I'm our only man there, unless some other chap is passing through. It isn't much of a thieves' den. A little smuggling, the occasional inebriated rowdy tourist – nothing like this bank robbery. If I can only get a scoop on this one – a scoop is an exclusive story, you know – "

I assured him that I knew what a scoop was.

Eppley secured the controls, and turned to face us fully.

"Between you, me and the control lever," he said, "I'm desperate to get off this damn' station. It's perfectly bloody. I know every inch of the wretched place, and every one of the crew practically, and I'm bored truly out of my wits. People talk about the romance of space. Romance! Don't make me laugh. There's nothing any more romantic about Oakapple Orbital than there is about King's Cross station. They both exist to leech off unsuspecting travellers and make them pay five times the true value of everything from a toothbrush to a tub of butter. And there I am, right in the middle of the place, doing my own bit to help Oakes and people like him to fleece all comers."

Harris floated up in the air and propelled himself to the luggage compartment.

"Are we on a set course?" he said to Eppley.

"Why, yes; we should be good for hours, now, barring an emergency."

"Good," said Harris; "because you need this."

He bounced off the wall and back towards us, holding the whisky bottle.

"I knew," said Eppley, "that you were three chaps of discerning judgment and benevolent nature. I knew it as soon as I saw you. I am an excellent judge of character." And he took the bottle.

Drinking whisky, or any liquid, in the absence of gravity is a task not easily performed, even though we had lately had the opportunity to rehearse it. Glasses being – obviously – de trop in the circumstances, the only way to go about it is simply to pass the bottle back and forth. Down upon Earth, we might have felt akin to four gentlemen of the road seated upon a log; but somehow, up here away from our parent planet and her mores, it seemed more jolly than it did unhygienic – rather as one does not mind breadcrumbs, or the odd ant, at a picnic party, because 'roughing it' once in a while is such daring fun. But even the most relaxed and debauched picnic could not have provided such fun to rough it, as eating and drinking in space does.

But I was all the same glad that we would be returning to Earth, to normal gravity and customs, in a few days. One does not wish one's every meal to be a picnic.

So I could comprehend quite well why Eppley wished himself somewhere closer to home and with more scenery than just a sky full of stars.

"How did you come to be in orbit, then, Eppley?" asked George. "Did you believe all that taradiddle you were mentioning, about the romance of space?"

"No – well, perhaps a little – no, really not much at all," the journalist replied. "I – well, I don't mind you three knowing, since you've been such sports in helping me out of a hole. I wanted to be a writer, and I wrote a good deal of poetry and reviews and things at Cambridge – one does, you know; but so does every other undergrad., and it's hard to get any kind of name for yourself. I tried to get in with the literary set there, but they were a beastly fast lot, and I exhausted my money in keeping up with them, without getting anywhere. So when I came down from Cambridge, I couldn't make a living, and couldn't get taken on anywhere in publishing, and I worked for a spell in the Post Office – not selling stamps over the counter, you understand, but working with horrible ledgers and accounts – until I was fed quite up.

"Now, most of my family are terribly respectable and thought a job in the G.P.O. for life was just what I needed to clip my wings and make me lead a jolly bowler-hatted type of routine. But I've one uncle – actually he's a great-uncle – " Eppley coloured, and took the bottle back from George.

"My great-uncle," he said again after about fifteen seconds, "is Professor Joseph Cavor."

"The Cavorite chap?" cried Harris.

"He. Everyone thinks he must be frightfully well off, having invented Cavorite, but in point of fact the silly ass didn't get any legal advice about it, and went into partnership with an awfully unscrupulous fellow – Bedford, his name was – and just about the only thing my uncle got out of it all, was the honour and glory of his name being on it."

We all expressed our regret at the unfortunate outcome of the professor's hard labours.

"Fortunately," said Eppley, "he doesn't care too much for money, or for fame, except among his own cohort of scientists – and from what I understand there are few enough men in the whole world who can claim such understanding of the by-ways of physics as Professor Cavor. He lives comfortably enough in Kent with a little laboratory in his garden shed, and blackboards all over his cottage, in every room, filled with more Greek symbols and letters than Homer or Euripides ever knew, I'm sure of it. And every now and again he looks at one of the blackboards with his equations and cryptic calculations upon it, and says 'Nonsense! Fatal error! Flawed reasoning!' And then he takes a duster and wipes it all away, only to start again with what always seems to me to be exactly the same mix of letters and numbers and symbols.

"But being the inventor of Cavorite, he does hold a certain amount of sway in some areas – including the space-faring world. After all, at the end of the day, he is the fellow who made it all possible. And when I said to him once about how awfully I wanted to write for a living, he told me that he knew of a man who was planning to set up a newspaper to be published up in orbit, and did I want him to put a word in?

"I felt dreadfully ashamed of myself for using my uncle in this way, rather than making my way up the ladder by my own hard work – but I'd been struggling for two years by then without getting so much as a foot, even, upon the damn ladder.

"So my uncle pulled some strings," Eppley concluded, "and managed to wangle me this post. And I've been here six months, now, and there are some days where I don't even wish myself back in the Post Office."

He morosely pushed the bottle away from him, in Harris's direction, and Harris scooped it out of the air with adroitness as it drifted by.

"But you don't want to abandon writing?" I queried.

"Oh! No; if I could get myself attached to the Selene City Journal, though, or even a decent English paper back on Earth – then I'd be as happy as could be."

Eppley's features were of the kind that make it tricky to tell his age to within five or six years simply by looking at him; but I had quietly been calculating his age in my head, from the story he had been unfolding, and had reached the conclusion that he was not yet old enough to realise the underlying truth in the time-worn adage that the grass is always greener on the other side of the fence.

"Well!" Harris said, sending the whisky back around in my direction, "whether old Neville proves to be right about Bustany and his cronies heading for the Moon, or whether he doesn't, we can do no more either way for now, than we already have. And even if Bustany escapes justice, you will still be able to find Oakes and pump him for a story. I have the impression he may be rather easier an oyster to open up than Chief Beadle Neville."

That thought seemed to hearten our new friend – or perhaps it was the whisky. In any case, we passed the next few hours as a pleasantly cheerful gathering, exchanging stories, gossip and chatter. George re-told his tale about the man who shaved his beard in space and nearly became a maroon, and in response, Eppley related a tale, which he said he had from a man who claimed it had happened to him personally – a grizzled old Russian space-dog – about a fellow who had been on a ship where they thought the pilot had been drinking vodka, because he couldn't fly the ship straight.

The pilot denied indignantly that he had been drinking, so then they worried that something had gone wrong with one of the Cavorite components and that it was this which was dragging the ship off its course. So they checked them all, and every one was working as it ought, so they blamed the pilot again, and the pilot lost his temper, and invited the navigator to try his hand at the controls.

So the navigator tried, and he couldn't make the craft fly straight, either; and the pilot laughed, and said that the ship was obviously haunted, or possessed by an evil spirit, and was doomed; and that he hadn't touched a drop of alcohol, and wouldn't even now that he was about to die, and proved it by going to the ship's water fountain for a drink.

But when he tried to operate it, there was no water; and they found out that a small meteor had hit the ship, and punched a hole in the ship's water tank, and the water had been evaporating out into vacuum and – thanks once again to Newton – the force that was thus created was what was pushing the ship constantly off course.

So they quickly riveted a patch over the hole, and were saved after all.

"I don't believe it," said Harris."

"Oh, really, Harris – " I began, feeling this to be uncivil to a man who was, in many regards, our guest.

"I correct myself; I choose not to believe it," he said. "I have a moral objection to any story in which the day is saved by some beastly little Eric drinking water instead of good whisky."

And Eppley laughed, and said there was no offence, of course. He looked slightly uncertain on that point, but it may merely have been that he could see how little whisky there was left.

But Harris went over to the luggage again by and by, and fetched out the brandy; so that was all right.

I so far forgot my cares and worries that I consented to Eppley sitting me down in the pilot's seat and inviting me to take the controls, while he started to write up some copy on his portable typewriter; and thus it is that I can now brag, safely back in England, about the time I piloted a space-sphere on its approach to the Moon.

"Oh! It's no big thing," I would say in a saloon-bar or a coffee-parlour to the others there assembled. "You see, the whole sphere is fitted with Cavorite slats on every side, which prevent gravity from having an effect on it; and if you want to steer one way or another, you simply operate the controls which roll up the slats like a Venetian blind, and let gravity do all the rest."

When I first got back to Earth, after the conclusion of the adventure which I am presently related, I confess that I made remarks akin to this one quite frequently; and they seldom or never failed to draw an admiring audience – sometimes I was even bought a drink for my pains.

"Everyone should try a trip to space," I would say. "And it isn't even a pastime that only the rich can afford. You see, because Cavorite works by controlling gravity, and gravity is with us all the time, it is effectively a source of free energy – apart from friction and little things like that, of course."

Then one day an unpleasant little man with a cloth cap and a bristly moustache interrupted just as I reached that point.

"There ain't no such thing as free energy," he said pointedly. "And I should know, for I'm an engineer."

I hesitated a moment, and made the fatal mistake of trying to beat the enemy on his own ground, rather than declining to be drawn into an engagement.

"Oh! I don't mean free, of course; but it's still frightfully efficient and doesn't get used up like coal or oil."

"Doesn't it?" My friend the engineer pushed his cap back on his head in a truculent way. "Perhaps, then, as you know so much of Cavorite and space travel, you'd care to explain to these folk how Cavorite works."

"Cavorite? Why... it – it blocks gravity," I said, hastily recalling A Pocket Guide to the Orbital Stations, "and allows you to manoeuvre your craft around in the atmosphere, and in space."

"How's it allow that?"

"Well – that is – " I felt myself backed into a corner. "I don't exactly know, truth to tell; but after all, one doesn't need to be a veterinary surgeon to ride a horse, what?"

I thought this a neat escape; but the little engineer was not yet done.

"Right, then," he said; "and once you're up there, how do you find your way around?"

This was perilous ground for me, but there was no evading it. "Why," I said, "you take a sighting with – with a sextant; and then you refer to your book of charts and tables, and it tells you at what angle you need to travel to reach your destination."

I hoped, silently, that this would satisfy the engineer, but it plainly did not.

"And upon what do you take your sight with that there sextant?" he said.

I was lost, and I knew it; and very soon everyone else in the bar knew it also, and there was nothing else for it but for me to slink off without finishing my drink. I considered throwing myself into the Thames to drown myself, from very shame; but as I was walking down toward Blackfriars Bridge, I came across another alehouse, and decided that it would be much less worry to myself and to others if I drowned my sorrows instead of my whole self; which I proceeded to do.

I might have had a chance at holding my own with that engineer if only Eppley had been a better teacher, for after he had finished his typing, he went and fetched down the sextant, and began to try and educate the three of us in the proper use of the wretched thing; but for some reason – perhaps one of us was distracted by all the excitement, or by all the whisky – I never did manage to fathom it. To this day the use of a sextant is a matter of perfect mystery to me.

17

After I had taken my shift as pilot of the sphere, and experimented in the manipulation of the controls to make us gently drift first in one direction, then in another, I pronounced myself satisfied, and made way for Harris to take the helm.

If I have a fault – Ethelbertha says I do, but she has so much more opportunity to observe them than do others – it is my aversion to taking risks. For the entire time I was strapped into the pilot's chair, even with the experienced Eppley there at my side, I could not rid myself of the nervous fear that if I moved a control too far, or in the wrong direction, the sphere would instantly shoot off into the depths of space at maximum velocity, and the four of us would never be seen again by human eye, and be discovered as mummified corpses by some alien intelligence out in the vicinity of Vega, and be displayed in whatever equivalent that race might have to our museums, or worse still, our travelling shows.

I do not say that this is not a failing; but I contend that it is at least less undesirable than Harris's counterpart.

Harris, as may have been deduced by the observant reader, is of a bluff and hearty nature. During our venture into orbit, both George and I stood several times by the windows, and stared out into space, at the countless millions of stars all around – for once free of Earth's atmosphere, the number of stars that can be seen even with the naked eye, far less a telescope, increases very considerably. And we would think – at least I would; I can't speak for George – of eternity, and poetry, and art, and of the boundless mind of man which had brought us to this place where we could appreciate the spectacle; and be quite moved by the thought, to the extent that I might even have picked up my pencil to compose verse myself (fountain-pens, of course, work by gravity and are useless in space, not to mention leaking all over one's best suit pocket); only I didn't feel like it, while being watched by my friends.

But not Harris – not he. To Harris, the stars were fixed in the endless night to let him know that the day is over and that it is time to go home for his dinner. I don't suppose the man could name a single constellation, or tell a planet from a comet, or for that matter, from a comfit. Some men are born so; there is no poetry in their souls, and it is worse than useless to attempt to inject some there, for it is what the good book calls a seed fallen on stony ground.

A man who lacks poetry in the soul lacks also imagination; and there, I fancy, is where the problem with Harris lies.

Because a man who lacks imagination also, as often as not, lacks fear. When Harris was let loose at the controls of that ship, he simply bounced it around as we approached the Moon, as though it had been a waterborne vessel rounding Cape Horn in a stormy sea. Eppley, who did not have the advantage which George and I did of knowing Harris of old, had not been holding on to anything when Harris gave the ship its first jerk, and – inertia and low gravity being what they are – he remained in place while the vessel around him dropped abruptly downward, giving the net effect of him shooting up in the air like a Chinese rocket and bumping his head on the ceiling, then hovering above us like an angel on a Christmas card.

"Frightfully sorry, Eppley," Harris called out, as the journalist let out a squeak of commingled pain and surprise. "Just a jiffy and I'll soon bring you back down."

And of course Harris reversed the controls so that the ship shot upward, whilst Eppley once more remained in his original position; so that the effect, this time, was of him veering downward and landing with a bump on the floor.

George and I had taken the precaution of clinging to the handrails as soon as Harris sat down; but George let go with one hand, and reached out to Eppley, and managed to hook him like a child with a shrimping-net at the seaside, and pulled him upright. Eppley seized hold of the back of Harris's chair, and seemed disinclined to let go.

"Are you all right, there, old fellow?" asked Harris politely.

Eppley, breathing rather hard, assured Harris that he was perfectly well – that he had just been taken a little aback at the speed with which Harris had mastered the controls, and the confidence he had shown in throwing the sphere about the sky as he had.

"Oh, pooh," said Harris modestly; "it's nothing – really nothing. Ask George or J. here and they'll tell you all about how I can handle a boat, or a horse, or a bicycle – anything that moves, in actual fact. I jolly well knew that these space-spheres would be a piece of cake to steer, as soon as I once put my mind to it."

Eppley stammered something about how Harris had a skill to be envied.

"Every man," said Harris, "has something – one thing – that he's really good at. Take J., for instance, and his scribbling – yours too, evidently, Eppley. And George – hmm, well, I am sure George is good at something – "

I believe I heard George say something under his breath at this point; but if it was what I thought he said, it was not a statement of what George was good at.

"Anyway," Harris said, "if you truly want to reach Selene City as quickly as you can, I'm happy to try and make this crate put a little pace on."

Eppley – still clinging to the back of Harris's seat with both hands, and looking as it he wished it were Harris's neck – said that he was most grateful for the offer, but that he preferred, on the whole, to trust in his own piloting. "Bearing in mind," he said, "that if we wanted, we could arrive at the Moon doing several hundred miles per hour; but if we landed on Selene City at that speed, we wouldn't need to worry any longer about catching the bank robbers – or about anything else."

"Speaking of Selene City," I murmured, "none of us has yet had the pleasure of visiting it. Won't you tell us something about it, Eppley, while we make our way there?"

Thankfully Harris was sufficiently distracted by this suggestion to allow us to ease him out of the pilot's seat, whereupon Eppley reclaimed it swiftly and strapped himself into it in a pointed manner. He proceeded to set the sphere back on its proper Moonward course and velocity, before allowing himself to relax a little and resume his role as raconteur.

Selene City (Eppley began) is a frontier town in some ways;

but while most frontier towns spring up at random, like weeds in a flower bed, Selene does at least have the benefit of forward planning. Men had been living on the Moon for some ten years before the founding of Selene City, most of them in structures or clumps of structures of a more or less temporary nature. After all, when you have a Cavorite ship, it comes provided with most of the essentials of life, at least in the short term. You might compare it to a gypsy caravan at home – a secure and warm enough space to spend the night, which makes up in mobility what it may lack in comfort and permanence.

But there is something in the spirit of Man which compels him to seek out his own company, ever and anon. Few indeed are the misanthropes who find no pleasure at all in the company of their fellows. And it does seem hard to go from one day to the next, one week to the next, without being able to buy a loaf of bread, or a tin of tooth-paste, or the daily newspaper, far less be able to enjoy an evening at the theatre or the music hall along with an early dinner, or the promise of a late one afterward.

The first general store on the moon was founded by an American –

"That doesn't surprise me," said George.

"I wouldn't mind Americans being so pushful," said Harris, "if they didn't always have so much to be pushful about."

Anyway (resumed Eppley), this American fellow – by name Percy Mace – had the bright idea of buying a number of railroad passenger coaches, which he was able to obtain cheap, due to Cavorite already having its effect upon other forms of travel.

"Do you want them to be delivered?" they asked Mace.

"Not a bit of it! Leave them where they are," said Mace, "and I'll collect them myself."

And Mace had those railroad cars fitted with Cavorite, and chained them all together, and attached them to a sphere, like the locomotive of a train; and up through the atmosphere he lifted them, and through space, as far as the Mare Imbrium on the Moon, where he set them all down and arranged them accordingly, and made them air-tight; and miners and prospectors came from all over the Moon to buy supplies at Percy Mace's settlement, which very soon became known as Maceburg – whether in the natural course of events, or by Mace's own agency; opinions differ on the point.

"Maceburg is still there, of course," Eppley said, "and so is old Mace – for he says he is perfectly happy there on the moon and sees no reason to go back down again, not at his age, which must be sixty now if he's a day. It may be the oldest town on the Moon, but it's not the largest, not any more; Selene City holds that honour."

George asked whether Eppley had ever met Mace.

"I cannot say that I have," said Eppley. "He is something of a character, they say. I understand that Gareth Oakes is an old friend of his; for you know, Oakes originally made his fortune as a lunar miner, and before he made his strike, he was just another one of the hundreds of Welsh coal miners who found work hard to come by after Cavorite came along and upset so much of the economy."

I was still a young man at the time, but I well remembered the exodus from South Wales and from the north-east of England that followed Professor Cavor's invention. Whole streets – sometimes whole mining villages – lay deserted and bare, their former occupants having decamped to the Moon to seek mineral wealth there. Married men took their wives, and even their children, with them. The entire affair was an unregulated free-for-all which was only ended, in part, by the Building 41 disaster, where an air leak claimed the lives of over twenty children as well as a few adults in an impromptu and unlicensed day nursery. After that, of course, the government stepped in and ensured that no similar disaster could ever occur again – or, at least (so some cynics remarked), if it did occur again, at least it would happen under the aegis of a Government licence.

Many of the miners, like their predecessors in '49 of whom the song tells, found scant or no success in their quest for a fortune, and sooner or later returned to Earth, or else died there on the moon and left their bodies there beneath an alien soil. Nowadays, the Moon has a planned and structured burial ground; but in those pioneer days no such luxury existed, and to this day, it is possible to stumble upon a pitiful little mound, with a cross made of steel struts lashed together, bearing perhaps a scrawled note of what poor soul lies beneath it, and often with the decedent's helmet or boots set to stand guard beside the impromptu memorial.

Upon the airless Moon, of course, no rain falls and no corrosion takes place, so the metal elements of the grave marker will remain as fresh as the day they were placed there, unless disturbed. I suppose that one day, the whole of both the Earth and the Moon will be covered by buildings in one huge mass, the planet and its satellite becoming hardly more than one enormous ants' nest; and when progress brings us that day, both the country churchyards of the Earth and the lonely little monuments of the Moon will be swept away and forgotten. I cannot help but look forward to that day with mixed feelings. I am all for progress; I am all for science and advancement making one's daily routine easier and less a cause for worry and fretfulness; but it is fatally easy to sweep away the good old things along with the bad old ones – and once they are gone, of course, they are gone. There is no bringing back the Hanging Gardens of Babylon, or the Library of Alexandria, now; and in a hundred years' time, I dare say, we shall find antiquarians mourning the loss of Victoria station, or of Collins' Music Hall, and declaring that the fine old buildings of those days will never again see their equal – just as nowadays, we still find people who bemoan the losses to architecture of the Great Fire of London, or of the 'urban renewal' practitioners who have cleansed London of so many of its slums.

I sometimes think I should like to see those who grumble and cavil about the loss of those slums, taken up and forced to live in one for a few months; but there! It is human nature to complain about whatever can be found to complain about, and if there is nothing, to invent something to be the subject of complaint.

But enough of this; I should relate what Eppley went on, now, to tell us about Selene City and her history.

The city is formed of a vast dome upon the Moon's surface, in the region known to astronomers as the Bay of Rainbows. The expense of construction was borne equally by six great nations: the United States of America, France, Russia, Germany, the dual monarchy of

Austria with Hungary – and of course, Great Britain. It remains, to this point, the only lunar settlement to have been constructed by the terrestrial nations, rather than by private enterprise or by mere happenstance. I believe that the diplomatic negotiations which had to be carried on to permit it to come into existence were both long and intense; certainly I remember one particular English daily newspaper, whose proprietor had taken against the idea, speaking out at great and repetitive length against the whole enterprise, and warning that economic ruin would surely be our lot if this crazy scheme were allowed to persist.

I have often noticed – and when I mentioned it, Eppley said as much also – that newspapers always seem to sell more when they are foretelling gloom and despondency ahead, than they are when all on the horizon is calm and rosy, and the world is turning cheerfully with no cause for worry. And yet, everyone whose opinion I have sought on the issue says that they never get enough good news – can never find a crumb of it when they need cheering up – and that they simply cannot abide the endless rounds of despair and misery that the papers usually bring. It is a mystery that is beyond me to solve, and if someone ever does come up with the explanation to this riddle, I venture to say that he will make himself a name as great as that of Professor Cavor.

Selene City was constructed by men from all six of its founding nations, and more besides. Eppley said that one of his fellow-journalists had been there during the construction, and that you never saw such a Tower of Babel – every earthly language, every hue of human skin, was there. Fortunately, though not without its setbacks, the project was completed to within a very small variance of its originally planned time and expense; for which we have to thank, not only the doughty construction workers and navvies, but also the designer, Hugo Langlois.

Architecture, those who practice it like to claim, is a science, and they may be justified in their claim. But when building huge structures upon the lunar surface is concerned, architecture and science must of necessity go hand in hand; the architect must make a structure comfortable to inhabit, while the scientist must also make it safe from the hundreds of risks that are peculiar to making one's abode off the surface of the Earth.

When a designer for Selene City was first sought, the parent nations of the new metropolis had expected dozens of interested parties to descend upon them with blueprints and plaintive cries. It proved otherwise. I suppose that with the wisdom of hindsight, one can understand the reason for their reticence; to make a great leap in the annals of your chosen industry can bring you fame and laurels, not to mention financial reward, but upon the other hand, the downfall of Sir Thomas Bouch – which came fast upon the heels of the downfall of his celebrated Tay Bridge – had occurred not many years previously, and no doubt caused some candidates to hesitate before submitting a proposal for review.

Hugo Langlois was not a renowned figure in the world of architecture, or outside it. A shy young man from the Channel Islands, as a youngster he had travelled to Australia, and seen the great mines in the deserts there, where many of the mining crew live underground, in holes that began as part of the mine workings, but in which (it was soon realised) it was possible to escape the fierce heat of the daytime sun.

When Langlois's design for Selene City was submitted, there was a great deal of scorn poured upon it for the underlying basis of the thing. For Langlois, inspired by the Australian mines, had based his plan upon the principle that the majority of his city should be underground, protected from the heat of the sun and the cold of the night upon the lunar surface, with only the topmost level of the city exposed to view from above.

Furthermore, Langlois had considered – unlike those who built most of our earthly cities – the question of expansion over time. In an eloquently written addendum to his submission, he had argued that if human colonisation of the Moon had a future, it was vital to address this point; and this he did by showing how, if it should be required, Selene City could expand below the ground – not only horizontally, but vertically.

For the Moon, though it has a core of molten metal just as the Earth does – or so say scientists, at least – can only claim a much smaller one than its parent planet does; or in other words, one can dig a lot further into the surface of the Moon (given the right tools and sufficient patience) than one can into the Earth. Consequently, Langlois argued, it should be possible for Selene City to develop in all directions, save perhaps upward. Most terrestrial cities are essentially built on a two-dimensional model, notwithstanding the occasional tall building jutting up, or underground railway beneath. Langlois saw Selene City as primarily a spherical model, rather than a flat one.

For a while, few people took Langlois's design seriously; but every other scheme submitted for the new city had flaws or drawbacks – if any one of the six participant nations expressed a liking for one, there was sure to be another one which considered it an abomination and refused to countenance even considering it for the final blueprint. And somehow, though other plans fell by the wayside, Langlois's was never quite rejected out of hand; and as time continued to pass and it became of more pressing importance for a design to be mutually selected, in the end the lot fell upon Langlois almost because nobody could find any other schema to which all six nations would agree.

It has not yet been necessary for Selene City to expand, for it is not yet filled to its original capacity; but it is growing steadily, and within ten years its inhabitants will need to take up their spades and start to dig – either sideways, or downward. But for now, it is that most peculiar thing, almost unknown to human civilisation; a metropolis containing far fewer people than it was designed to hold, not because of a decline in population, but because the population has not yet reached the city in sufficient numbers.

And this was our destination – not only the four of us, but also for Oakes and Neville's party. Whether it had also been the bank robbers' destination, only time would tell.

As we sped closer to the Moon, the satellite began to swell in our windows ahead, like a balloon being inflated by one breath after another. George swung hand over hand up to the window, and squinted through it, first with his naked eyes, then using the viewpiece of the sextant.

"Are you trying to see Selene City?" Eppley asked from the controls.

"I was hoping to."

"You won't see it yet, any more than you could make out London from Oakapple. Even the largest city is far too small to be spotted from orbit like that. They used to say that the only human structure visible from space would be the Great Wall of China, but when we finally got up there, it turned out to be nonsense; you can't see that, either."

George retired, disappointed. But the Moon grew ever closer; tiny craters turned into larger ones as we drew near, and what had seemed to be merely insignificant dots or freckles upon the lunar surface resolved themselves into small but definite craters in their own right.

One such caught my eye and I remarked upon its distinctiveness; rather than being worn and irregular at the edges, like many of the larger craters, this one was perfectly round and distinct to the point of sharpness. Indeed, looking at it, I was seized by the fancy that if we were to land there, we should find the edge of the crater as fine as a razor-blade.

I mentioned this fancy aloud, to scorn from Harris; but Eppley drew my attention to another characteristic of this crater, which I had not yet considered.

"Do you see," he said, "how that crater's edge bisects the edge of the larger crater, next to it, there?"

We did; it was hard to miss.

"Well," said Eppley, "that's how we can be sure that the smaller crater is a more recent formation than the larger one; where two craters bisect, the newer crater's wall is always the one to interrupt the elder one's. It couldn't be any other way, when you come to think about it."

We thought about it, and the truth of his statement became obvious, though I doubt I should ever have realised it myself without his prompting.

"Does that happen often?" George asked. "One crater forming on top of another, so to speak?"

By way of answer, Eppley removed his right hand from the controls, and gestured to the Moon through the sphere's window.

"See for yourself," he said.

I started at one side of the huge white globe that was swelling to fill our entire frontmost aspect, and before my eyes had travelled a quarter of the way across it, I had found a dozen places where one crater's wall crossed another.

"No wonder," said Harris, "that they used to say the moon was made of Swiss cheese. It's all over holes."

"And that was before the miners got to work on it," added George.

"Do they know," I asked, "what the cause of them is?"

"Oh, you juggins," said Harris, "everyone knows that. They're volcanos. Or rather, they were. It's as Eppley here was telling us just now. The Moon is smaller than the Earth, and has a smaller hot core inside; so while we still have volcanoes which erupt molten rock, all the Moon's volcanoes have grown as extinct as that mountain in Iceland that Jules Verne sent his chaps down, on their way to the earth's centre."

"Are you sure?" George said. "I could have sworn I read an article, once, in the Strand or somewhere, which claimed that the craters were the result of hundreds and thousands of meteoric impacts."

"Maybe you did," said Harris, "but that doesn't mean the article was correct and factual. The Sherlock Holmes stories come out in the Strand, and Mrs. Nesbit's, too; but that doesn't mean that Holmes and Watson are real people, or that the Psammead is. If the moon's craters are all caused by impact damage, why don't we have such craters on Earth, too? We make a bigger target, so if anything, there should be even more of them."

"There's that crater in Arizona – " I began.

"I jolly well knew you would bring that up," Harris said. "That crater in Arizona is just that; a crater. One crater. It isn't in the same league as what we see at this moment, up there. The Moon's surface looks like the target in a gunnery range which has had hundreds of live rounds fired at it without being changed."

"I suppose," I said, refusing to allow Harris to cow me into silence, "that you may have a point. But the Moon has so many craters – might it even be possible that both theories are correct? That some of them are created by impacts, and some by vulcanism?"

"For what it's worth," Eppley said, "that's old Cavor's theory. He believes there are too many holes in the Moon for any one thing to be the cause of all of them. But Cavor is a physicist, of course, not a geologist – or, I should say, a selenologist."

"It's an interesting question," mused George. "I don't suppose there is any way of determining the correct answer, beyond doubt. But fortunately it makes no matter when it comes to practical terms."

"You may say that," Eppley pointed out, "but it is of rather more than theoretical concern to the citizens living in Selene City or Maceburg. I suspect that they would be most interested to know whether they need worry about a rock falling from space and smashing them into atoms, or whether they need only fear an eruption from below blowing them all into eternity."

Harris looked up at the Moon again. "I don't think they would know much about it," he said, "if either of those things were to happen."

Fortunately neither of them happened as we drew closer to Selene City, and Eppley brought us in to the moon's surface.

18

One thing of which there is plenty on the Moon is space. Even more than America, there is ample room for expansion there; and this is one of the many things which Langlois took into account, when planning Selene City.

The landing-port for Selene, like that of London, is outside the city itself by some distance. But where in London, the construction of the spaceport at Maplin required the sacrifice of a great deal of farm land and many houses, even despite much of the port being built upon land reclaimed from the Thames estuary, with Selene, all that needed to be done was to roughly flatten a patch of the lunar surface a mile or two beyond the dome, to paint the flattened land with markings indicating to incoming ships where to dock, and to construct ancillary buildings – the customs warehouse, the dockers' quarters, and suchlike. There is also, as at Maplin, a railway station; but rather than a prosaic steam train of the London, Tilbury and Southend Railway which deposits the traveller in a cramped terminus at the edge of the Square Mile, Selene's spaceport is connected to its parent city by a wonder of modern engineering – a railway as different from the "Long, Tired and Slow" as a woollen mill's machinery is different from a pair of knitting needles.

The trains run upon the atmospheric principle. It may seem peculiar that this is so, given that the Moon lacks all but the most imperceptible traces of atmosphere; but by a stroke of delicious irony, an atmospheric railway has never yet been made to work properly on the earth, whilst on the moon, it runs as smoothly as butter going onto bread. No less a figure than the great Brunel attempted a railway propelled by this means, and failed – almost the only failure that the man knew throughout his distinguished career. Alas! He died without the least idea (I presume) that man would ever set foot upon the Moon – far less run atmospheric trains there; did not live to see his vision, which failed on Earth, finally vindicated upon its satellite.

The docking procedure at Selene involved more formality than had our arrival at Oakapple, but not very much more. We gave our names, which were checked against the documents we had aboard that had been counter-signed by the beadles at Oakapple; but since none of us had been asked to prove our identity either upon arrival at Oakapple, or upon our departure therefrom, I could not see that the procedure of checking served very much purpose. I also thought to myself that these lax procedures here away from the Earth must serve to make the lives of criminals such as Bustany very much easier.

Perhaps, I thought – especially after the news broke upon Earth of the robbery at Oakapple – steps might soon be taken to tighten up procedures on the Moon, and upon the orbital stations. Whether this will assist in the prevention of crime, or only serve to annoy the innocent traveller and delay him – well, I do not seek to be a prophet in that regard.

But for now, we were waved through within a few minutes.

Harris began to head for the train, but Eppley bade him pause a moment, while he carefully scanned the whole area of the port from the windows of the customs shed.

"As I thought," he said. "There's Oakes's personal ship, the Rhondda Cynon Taff."

Harris made to thump Eppley on the back, thinking he was choking, but Eppley dodged.

"It is Welsh," he explained hastily. "I forget quite what it means, I'm afraid. The only Welsh I know is a phrase Oakes taught me once. He said it meant 'good morning', but I found out later that it means something rather obscene about the English."

I had already decided that I liked Oakes, but my estimation of him now rose by another notch. I am English myself, of course, but one of the things that makes our country great is that – most often – we can take a jest against us in good part.

"I don't suppose," Eppley went on, "that any of you can recall what Lord Freckleton's ship – I beg your pardon, I should say Bustany's – looked like, or what design it was manufactured to...?"

Eppley was quite right; we could not. That it was larger than our own ship, we all three recalled well; that it had a comfortable armchair upon the main deck, I remembered with absolute clarity – I could even have described the pattern of its covering, had Eppley wished to know it; but for some reason he seemed to be vexed by my offer, rather than pleased.

"Ah, well," he said, "I am sure we shall soon learn whether or not he is on the moon. Shall we head to Selene City itself?"

We all assented, and made our way toward the station. If I had to be a railway porter, I should certainly prefer to be one in Selene City, with its lower gravity, than in London. But no porters were evident, and we had to place our cases upon the train ourselves.

As we did so, we immediately encountered familiar faces.

For there in the carriage, sitting in a row like three brightly coloured birds upon a telegraph wire, were Miss Lexlake, Miss Dickson, and Miss Craddock.

George was bareheaded on this occasion, so could not jerk off his cricket-cap as he had upon his first meeting with the ladies; but he made up for this by bowing most politely and telling the trio that this was a most unexpected pleasure – and I suppose, in fairness to George, this was not only good etiquette, but the actual truth. For none of us had had time to think the barest thought of Miss Lexlake and her friends after we had parted ways in Oakley's sitting-room.

I hastened to follow up George's good work by bowing myself – although bowing does not come so easily to me nowadays as it once did, I can still perform it creditably, which is more than one can say for Harris – and beginning to introduce them to Eppley.

"Thank you," said Miss Lexlake with some coolness, "but we have already made this gentleman's acquaintance."

Eppley coughed, and said something indistinct about how he hoped their previous encounter with him had been a pleasant one – which I could immediately see was evidence of a very hopeful nature on his part.

Miss Lexlake addressed us, her voice as clear as Eppley's had been faint.

"This man," she said, "following the conclusion of our protest upon Oakapple Station, sought to speak with me as a journalist – as a member of the politically and socially biased Press. I advised him, with full politeness, that our experiences with the newspapers have not been positive, and that consequently we prefer to confine our encounters with journalists to the staff of our own suffragist journal."

"If he had taken 'no' for an answer like a decent man," said Miss Craddock, taking up as Miss Lexlake paused for breath, "I am sure we would have borne him no ill will. But instead, he sought out the maids and the hall-porters and everyone who had encountered us, and offered them inducements – financial inducements – if they would, as he vulgarly put it, 'spill the beans about' – what was the phrase, Arabel?"

Miss Dickson chimed in on cue. "If they would 'spill the beans about those three suffragette cranks'. The maid whom he approached very properly declined his offer – I should say, his bribe – and informed us instead. Miss Lexlake was only dissuaded by Emily and myself with the greatest difficulty from seeking him out and boxing his ears."

Eppley took a step back. The contempt in Miss Lexlake's eyes suggested that boxing the journalist's ears was not necessarily a dish to be removed from the menu of the day.

"And now," Miss Craddock said, "we encounter him here again – in the company of you three, whom we had thought to be correct and upstanding gentlemen."

I thought it best to explain to the ladies, before the situation deteriorated further, the story of how Eppley had come to be our fellow traveller, and why he had hastened to the Moon at such short notice. We very soon learned that they knew nothing of the robbery, for they had departed from Oakapple some hours before it took place; rather than travelling directly from Oakapple to Selene City, they had detoured via another orbital station where Miss Dickson wished most particularly to visit a well-known hairdresser and to obtain a "space bob".

"Except," she said ruefully, "that Mademoiselle Adele has grown so popular, that one has to book an appointment with her now for weeks in advance; and by the time she has a space in her schedule, I shall long since be back on Earth. And so I must retain my present style of coiffure, at least for the present."

"I too would have liked to visit her," said Miss Lexlake.

"Didn't you think to book in advance?" said Harris.

"If you recall," said Miss Lexlake, "I was not expecting to have had any further use for a hairdresser after I arrived at Oakapple."

That silenced Harris. George spoke up, and assured Miss Dickson that her current ringlets were thoroughly charming; which was true, in my estimation, but although the compliment appeared to flatter Miss Dickson, it also brought the fierce look out in Miss Lexlake's eyes of which I had already made a mental note to take good care.

"A bank robbery! Up here!" Miss Craddock exclaimed. "I never heard of such a thing. And this explains this reporter's presence with you?"

Eppley simpered a little, and said that he was only a fellow with a job to do, trying to do it as best he could.

I think that if it had been left to Miss Lexlake, Eppley would still have been given the marble eye and the go-by; but the other two young ladies were so excited at the news of the robbery, and pressed Eppley so hard to share with them all that he knew of the crime, that she relented and allowed us four mere males to seat ourselves opposite the ladies – for the carriages on the Selene City train are not arranged in compartments, like the familiar trains back at home, but with a long corridor at the centre and seats along either side, allowing one to walk from end to end of the train if desired. Furthermore, there is but one class of travel; I am happy to relate that we were comfortable enough as the train began to move, and the strangeness of the train's composition served only to render the whole trip more strange and alluring to all of us.

George took from his pocket the photographic copy of the bank robber's note, and to his evident satisfaction, caused a flurry of interest. Eppley made to seize it from him when he realised what it was, but retreated in the face of the flashing eye of Miss Craddock, who took it and read it, while Eppley tried in vain to catch a view of it; she passed it to Miss Dickson; and she in turn to Miss Lexlake.

The rails run from the spaceport, through a notch in a low row of foothills which separate the main city from the port and mean that one cannot be seen directly from the other. As it crests the saddle between two of the hills, it turns a little to the side to take the easiest path out of the range, and at that point, Selene City comes into the traveller's view.

We gasped – all of us gasped, male and female alike; and all of us crowded over to marvel at the spectacle, Miss Lexlake tucking the photograph into her bag out of the way.

I did not make the sound for effect, as one sometimes does; I was genuinely taken aback, and I believe the same could be said for all of us. For there is no Earthly experience that I know of which can compare in any way to the first sight, from the lunar surface, of Selene City and its overarching dome.

The dome itself is not a single smooth surface; to produce and manufacture such a thing would have been difficult enough anywhere on Earth, let alone on the Moon. Instead, the dome consists of a myriad small triangles, so arranged that they fit one alongside another, and angled just so. The result is that what the Selene City dwellers call a dome is really not quite the shape of a dome; but the difference is so insignificant that only the most dedicated pedant would quibble at calling it a dome.

But for us, as we took our first sight of it, the effect of the countless triangles which made up the overall shape was to reflect the rays of the Sun; first from one, then from another, as the train moved and the angle between us, the dome, and the sun altered. It was as good as a firework exhibit, and even Eppley – the only one of us to whom this view was not a new one – looked on in admiration. I can well believe that one would never grow weary of that spectacle.

But the train sped on its way, and the dome grew nearer, until the rails led us down onto the plain upon which Selene City is built; and then we dived into a tunnel, but a tunnel far better lighted and cleaner than the sooty holes one sometimes encounters on Earthly railways. Of course, the Selene City train does not produce soot or smoke, which can only help to maintain this standard of cleanliness.

When we drew into the terminal platform, that too was as spic and span as though every inch of it had been scrubbed with care that morning. There was no difficulty in alighting from the train – for the entire railway is enclosed within a protective covering, from the port to the city, and filled with air, so that even in the event of a breakdown, the train may be evacuated in safety without the need to dress all the passengers up in vacuum suits.

George gallantly assisted the ladies from the train while Harris and Eppley went in search of a porter. Feeling a little superfluous, I looked up and down the platform, admiring the gleaming tiles and the general air of neatness – tidy, without any feeling of excess or antiseptic nature. If only, I thought to myself, the London Underground railways could look like this!

The arrivals hall, no less than the train, displayed a level of cleanliness and of modernity which did not so much attract the eye, as strike it a violent blow. I stared around me, taking it all in, while Harris and Eppley went to attend to the baggage; Eppley being no stranger to such wonders, and Harris, as I have established, being at best indifferent to the things.

Behind me, the railway platform, and behind that in turn, the surface of the moon – stark, jagged, and real in a manner which defies description to anyone who has not experienced it with their own two eyes. Not only Harris and George have subsequently agreed with me upon this; I have yet to encounter another member of the race homo sapiens who has gazed upon the moon's surface and found a way of describing it which adequately conveys its qualities.

To some extent, the spectacular sight is down to the fact that the moon has been colonised for scarce ten years, following upon countless millennia of stillness, silence and stasis. No human touch, till now, to mar its peace, no human tool to gouge marks into it; simply the astonishing mountains, the peaceful plains below them, and all overlaid with the eerie feeling which puts a gentle hand upon one's shoulder and murmurs, "I say, old chap, you do realise that the rest of the human race is two hundred thousand miles and more away from you?"

The mountain peaks of the moon display themselves in a sharper focus than any upon the Earth; the sunlight reflects from the surface of the plains inside the craters with a fierceness unknown to merely earthly gleamings. The absence of atmosphere, of course, explains these. The surface of the Moon, when under full glare of the Sun, is hotter than a griddle under a steak – this is why space-suits require to insulate the wearer from heat as well as from cold.

A baking hot day, in a city at home on Earth, is a trying ordeal. The scents of decay and filth jump up, as though given extra pep by the heat, and assault the nose; and when one tries to peer at anything in the distance, heat-haze blurs it from the sight, until one can scarcely tell a blue 'bus from a red one, and you risk finding yourself boarding one for Kensington instead of Holloway or vice versa. On the moon, there are no horses to befoul the streets, no rats to drag rubbish to and fro – and no atmosphere to shimmer in the heat and distract the eye. I'm fortunate to possess sound and clear vision, and the peaks at the horizon seemed just as pin-sharp in focus as my own hand before me. All these observations seemed to join forces at once, and to underline with a heavy stroke the fact that I stood upon a world not my own – a world for which nature had not fitted me, or my companions; a world where only the artifice of my fellow human beings stood between my frail body and death – death so sudden that one would barely have time to exclaim "What the deuce?" before the lungs were robbed of their final breath.

Already, of course, mining companies and chemical conglomerates have staked their claims on our satellite, and within a decade or two, I have no doubt, the moon will be as well-trodden as the former virgin deserts and outback of Australia. I have heard educated people discuss the means by which the Moon may be tamed, conquered, cabined, cribb'd, confined. If they gain their way, the surface of the Moon will become as well-trod as the streets of Birmingham, and no more exciting. It will have an atmosphere, like the Earth; it will have a population, like the Earth, and industry, like the Earth, and crime and dirt and decay, like the Earth. I have even heard it said that Mars and the other planets might be treated likewise.

No doubt the march of science must go on, as it has always; but to think of the whole of the solar system consisting of no more than a string of identical beads, every one a newer and smaller Earth with all its flaws and disappointments, saddens me.

But for now, here I stood, light upon my feet, with wonder in my heart, and visions in my eye.

"Where the dickens are Harris and Eppley with that porter?" burst out George.

As though by magic, George's exclamation brought those two fellows into sight. They were not accompanied by a porter; instead, between them they were trundling a long, thin kind of luggage-trolley, with steel frame and rubber wheels, piled high with the baggage of seven travellers – Harris, George, myself, Eppley, and the three young ladies. The trolley was large and sturdy, and furthermore, gravity was at a discount, being only at lunar levels; but even so, the cases and boxes teetered this way and that alarmingly as they pushed it along, and the discontented look upon Harris's face was not pleasant to behold. He must have realised this himself, for upon espying our lady companions, he composed himself, dismissed his scowl, and replaced it with a smile – a wooden one, it is true, but a smile nonetheless.

The thought suddenly struck me that Harris's smile was the only wooden thing within sight. Metal, and atmospherium-glass, and rubber, there were a-plenty, all about us; but all the things one might have expected to be fashioned out of wood, from the luggage-trolley to the customs-desks near at hand, boasted no wooden element at all. It served to add to the alien and unnatural character of our surroundings; the timbre, so to speak, lacked timber.

"There isn't a porter to be had," exclaimed Harris. "What kind of way is this to run a planet?"

"A satellite," interjected Miss Lexlake. Harris – not accustomed to being thus interrupted by a feminine voice, even one belonging to the most radical and advanced owner – spluttered.

"You see," said Eppley, "the position on the Moon is the reverse of how things are on Earth – 'down yonder', they often call it here. On Earth, you find a dozen people chasing every vacant situation. Here, there is far more work than there are people to do it. I don't suppose there's a single porter employed on the whole railway. The Moon," he concluded, patting the trolley meaningfully, "encourages you to be self-sufficient."

Harris emitted a grunt. "I think things work very well as they are 'down yonder'," he said, emphasising the last two words to flag up his repetition of Eppley's phrase.

"Well, you would, wouldn't you?" Miss Lexlake spoke once more. "On Earth – is the fashionable phrase, here, really 'down yonder'?" (Eppley nodded) " – down yonder, everything is still arranged so's to focus all the wealth and power and respect in the hands of men. That," she went on, "will not always be the case – will it?"

Miss Dickson and Miss Craddock vigorously assented.

"Around us, here," she continued, "we are seeing society run upon more sensible terms; society where every member, be they man or woman, has the opportunity to do a job of work to which they're best fitted, and to be paid a good salary for doing it. And if that means having to push one's own luggage on a trolley – well! So be it!"

I thought, but was too polite – or possibly too hesitant – to mention, that Harris's trolley contained not only his own baggage, but also Miss Lexlake's.

"I expect," Miss Craddock smiled, "that you miss all the familiar fixtures and fittings of Earth – wooden chairs, hansom-cabs drawn by horses, steam trains?"

I was alarmed by the ease with which she had read my thoughts, for a second, until I realised that she was addressing Harris rather than myself.

"I don't suppose there's a single horse on the moon," said George.

"Horses," said Miss Craddock, "require feeding, and stabling, and clearing-up of... ahem!... what they leave in their wake, and veterinary surgeons. And steam trains require coal; and whence,

Mr Harris, is coal derived? Where does it come from?"

"Wales," said Harris, without stopping to think.

"From coal mines," said Miss Craddock, crushingly. "There is no coal on the moon, and no coal mines. Therefore, there are no steam trains."

I could not fault her logic, and judging by the way he wilted, neither could Harris.

"Oil can also produce steam," said Eppley. "But electricity is the thing, nowadays. The underground railways of London use it, after all."

"The tuppenny tube!" grumbled Harris, sotto voce. "It lacks all charm."

"If one must choose between charm – granting always that one may so describe a device which infernally belches smoke and cinders – and utility," said Miss Lexlake, even more forcefully than Miss Craddock, "then give me, I pray, utility upon every occasion. Now," she went on, before Harris could utter another word, "are we not here upon important business?" She twirled the strap of her capacious reticule between her hands, and Harris swallowed, as though the strap had been his own neck.

Eppley strode up to one of the metal customs-desks. A brief conversation took place; and I think I saw something green and folding change hands, although Eppley acted with such speed and subtlety that I couldn't be certain.

"Oakes is here, as we know," he said, returning to us. "The customs chap said that he expected him to dine at the New Pagani. Let's get rid of our bags at the left-luggage office, and see if we're in time to catch him there. If not, I suppose we must go straight to the police headquarters. I want to be on the spot when they run in Bustany."

19

Eppley seemed revitalised, now that we were on the Moon, and full of the pep and hustle which befitted the reporter for an American-owned newspaper. We all trundled over to deposit our baggage at his suggestion; Eppley extracted a faithful promise from the commissionaire that he would handle his typewriter and the rest of his luggage with utmost care. We gentlemen surrendered all our cases, and the ladies kept only their handbags. As soon as we had received our tickets, he led us off in jig time to the restaurant that had been mentioned.

Just as we were approaching the entrance to that establishment, we saw Oakes and Neville emerging, at a gentle speed compared to the pace we were making, indicative of having dined well. Upon catching sight of us, Oakes hailed us, and expressed himself delighted to see us. He seemed, perhaps, a little less delighted at the presence of Eppley than of the rest of our party; but perhaps, I thought, he was not in the mood to have a journalist around his neck taking down notes on everything he did. Such is the price paid for fame and success.

"We are just on our way to the police headquarters," he said. "I'll wake up old Ossie Inkpen and get a view-halloo for Bustany and Co. sounded. We shall get to the bottom of this affair, look you, one way or another."

"Are you engaged presently?" said Neville. "You gentlemen were most helpful on Oakapple with regard to Bustany, and more than likely, you may be so again."

We assured Neville that we would happily accompany him and Oakes to the police station. Not only was it our natural desire to help the forces of law and order, but if it could be established beyond doubt that Bustany's group were behind the bank robbery, then we would have nothing more to fear from Superintendent Veele.

"But the ladies," Oakes said. "I don't wish to leave them all alone here – "

"We are quite capable of taking care of ourselves," said Miss Lexlake, and I believed her; "but I'll admit that we are curious. Mr. Harris and his friends have been telling us all about the robbery."

"Let's all of us go," suggested Eppley brightly.

Oakes gave him an old-fashioned look. "I expect you want to be there so you can get a scoop for your rotten old newspaper. Well, I suppose that's your job; and you may as well be there to see matters develop, rather than picking up rumour and gossip at third-hand as you journalist types so often do."

Eppley absorbed this accusation with evident equanimity. I am enough of a journalist myself to know that one of the first things a fellow learns who takes up writing for papers or periodicals, is how to take scorn from the public upon the chin without flinching.

It was no great distance to the police station. I continued to admire the surroundings, as we went, and compared once again in my mind the hyper-modern buildings of Selene City to their equivalent on Earth, to the advantage of the former.

Arriving at the police office, Oakes, in the vanguard, strode straight inside and up to the counter, where he asked the constable on duty for Sir Oswald Inkpen. The constable, taken aback, sent for the sergeant, who sent for the inspector, who sent for the chief inspector; who appeared from the depths of the station, brushing crumbs from his waistcoat and wearing an irate expression, which vanished as soon as he saw Oakes.

"Ah, Gorman," said Oakes. "Is Sir Oswald to be had?"

"I'm sorry, Mr. Oakes, but he's in Farsideville at present," said Gorman. "I'm the senior officer here, just at the moment."

"Then I'm afraid I have a job for you," said Oakes – who did not seem afraid in the least. "Have you heard about the bank robbery on my station?"

Gorman said he had – said a message had been sent through the station's Morse-operator, and it had been relayed to every police station on the moon.

"Excellent," said Oakes. "Now, Neville here – you know Neville, my head beadle – and I have cause to believe that the robber and his confederates are here in Selene City at this moment. These gentlemen here have rendered much assistance, and will, I understand, serve as witnesses if required."

George simpered, and Harris puffed out his chest self-importantly, as Neville and Oakes explained the situation in detail to Chief Inspector Gorman, while Gorman's sergeant took down copious notes. The ladies listened with fascination, while Eppley adopted a nonchalant and inconspicuous position at the back of our group – also taking down notes.

"I think," said Gorman when we had all given him as much information as we could muster, "that we shall need to interview this Lord Freckleton, or Mr. Bustany – as the case may be."

"He might be anywhere in the city," said Oakes, "or even out of it, by now."

"Maybe," said Gorman. "But either Lord Freckleton is who he claims to be, in which case he will be booked into a classy hotel; or he's Bustany pretending to be Lord Freckleton, and doesn't know we're onto him, and in that case, he'll still be booked into a classy hotel. Sergeant Loftus, round up a few constables, and do the rounds of the hotels. Start with Keegan's and the Selene Savoy; if you draw a blank at those, work your way down the scale. And, wait a tick – don't let them know we're onto them. If they're kosher, they'll raise the deuce of a stink, and if they are fake goods, that will just tip them off."

The sergeant departed, and Gorman showed us into a kind of waiting-room behind the scenes, where we seated ourselves. We made a certain amount of desultory small-talk, but none of us seemed inclined to chatter much. We felt, all of us, that we were close to the end of our quest; and I, at least, found myself veering from hoping that Lord Freckleton would be able to prove he was the true owner of that title, in which case I would be overwhelmed by embarrassment, to hoping that he would be unmasked as a fraud, in which case I would have to look on as the trickster met his Waterloo, and was arrested and handcuffed and all that kind of fearful procedure. That seemed barely preferable, if at all. I concluded that – not for the first time – I had landed myself in a position where no outcome appeared pleasant, and – not for the first time – I mentally cursed those asses Harris and George for talking me into leaving the planet of my birth.

My thoughts ran on in this gloomy fashion until I heard a commotion – what Shakespeare might have called an alarum – outside: and then, in came Sergeant Loftus, with a satisfied smile under his moustache, and a bevy of constables behind him, surrounding Lord Freckleton, Lady Freckleton, and Hannay the valet – all of them appearing most awfully peeved.

"My lord – my lady," said Gorman, rising to his feet with the utmost respect and politeness, "thank you for attending. I do regret having to trouble you in this way."

"I should jolly well think you should," said Freckleton, giving Gorman a disdainful look. "Perhaps you'll be good enough to tell us why we have been practically dragged out of our hotel, under the eyes of half the Moon?"

"Well, you see," said Gorman, "it's like this. Earlier today – My God, Bustany, look out!"

Lord Freckleton whirled around sharply. Within a second, he realised his error; but a second was all Gorman had needed. Chagrin spread over the faces of the three impostors.

"As I thought," said Gorman. "Ronald Bustany, I presume? You and your pals have clocked up quite a list of offences." He looked at Bustany's dismayed companions. "Let me see – you, I take it," he said to 'Hannay', "are in fact Patrick Townsend. But who is your companion?"

"Find out, copper," said the false Lady Freckleton, tilting her head back and looking Gorman in the eye from her full height. It's easy to be wise after the event, of course, but now that she was revealed as a fake, I realised that her whole attitude reminded me, more than anything else, of a noblewoman as depicted upon a London stage, rather than one in reality. Of course, I should admit that I have little experience of the actual nobility, if rather a decent amount of the stage.

"Mr. Gorman," said Miss Lexlake, rising to her feet, "may I interject here?"

"Certainly," said Gorman in puzzlement, "if you think it's relevant – "

"I'm not sure how orthodox I should be, or what the proper police procedure is in these circumstances," said Miss Lexlake, "but – well!"

With that last word, she stepped up to the ersatz Lady Freckleton, and with a swift movement, grasped her by the hair.

I gasped, and I'm pretty certain most of the rest of the room also did. "Lady Freckleton" definitely did; but it was a gasp of surprise, or perhaps of indignation; not of pain.

And her coiffure came away cleanly in Miss Lexlake's grasp, revealing a second layer beneath - a close crop of mouse-coloured hair.

"Bless my soul!" exclaimed Harris. "It's a female impersonator."

"I prefer to be addressed as 'she', not 'it'." The unmasked impostor's voice remained as feminine as before, but now it seemed somehow incongruous.

"Quite so," said Miss Lexlake, in calm tones. "I crave your forgiveness... madam?"

The former Lady Freckleton nodded curtly in response to the honorific.

"I have no axe to grind against you, or anyone like you," said Miss Lexlake. "But you appear to have been involved in a highly criminal enterprise, and – well, it seemed the quickest way to establish the facts of the matter."

By now, Gorman had regained enough composure to peer closely at the face of the third impostor. "I take it that I address Mr. Jeremy Marsh?"

"That is the name upon my official papers, and I suppose it's the name you will be booking me under." Marsh turned to Miss Lexlake. "Go on, tell me – how did you clock me?"

"I'm not sure I would have," said Miss Lexlake, "if I hadn't been told that the party of tricksters we sought consisted of three men.

You pass frightfully well, if I may be so frank. We of the women's suffrage movement have some experience in these matters, you see."

"Ah! I twig, now," said Marsh. The words came out, now, in a wholly different fashion than before; lower in pitch, and with the refined accent vanished as though it had never been. In its place came a voice less redolent of St. James' and more of... well, I don't know, for I am no phonetics expert; but I would have said, if pressed, that it savoured more of Holloway, or perhaps even Hornsey.

"Never mind that now," said Gorman. "Take these rogues into custody – all three of them."

Bustany, the smaller of the two men – the erstwhile Lord Freckleton – spoke up.

"Let me say," he said, in an uneven voice, "that Judith here is all but blameless in this affair. All that she did, she did under my influence."

"Shush, shush," said Marsh. Rather to my surprise, everybody shushed, allowing Marsh to continue.

Marsh looked around the room meeting the eyes of each one of us in turn. They were pale grey, and held a piercing quality that made me uncomfortable. Harris cleared his throat; George shifted from one foot to the other. I had the most unnerving feeling that we, who had expected to judge this uncertainly gendered criminal, were instead being judged.

The only person present who seemed able to speak was Miss Lexlake.

"Well," she said, "we have shushed. I presume, ma'am, that you have something to say?"

Marsh seemed to take courage from Miss Lexlake's style of address.

"Very well. I do, indeed." Marsh spoke slowly but steadily, choosing each word with care, like someone carefully slotting together the pieces of a jig-saw puzzle. "You are all of you – I beg your pardon; most of you – " (this with a slight curtsey to Miss Lexlake) "thinking scornful thoughts of me; thinking that I am a freak of nature – a grotesque – a gangrel wretch unfit to hold a place in civilised society."

"Oh, indeed I don't," exclaimed Miss Dickson, then clapped her hand over her mouth, bolting the stable door after the horses, so to speak, had fled.

Marsh smiled thinly. "Those few who do not scorn me, pity me instead. That is an improvement, but do forgive me, won't you, if I say that to me, that is not much preferable? I, and those like me – not to mention those close to me," (here Marsh took the hand of Bustany and squeezed it slightly), "do not crave pity, any more than we think ourselves apt targets for scorn. You see – I am a human being, am I not?"

Oakes rubbed his chin, with a faint rasping sound, and gave a slow nod, as though he had sought a way to argue the point, and found none.

"Well, then," Marsh carried on, "can you blame me, a human being, for wishing to be treated with the respect and dignity that any human being owes another? And I receive it not. In almost the whole world, my brother and sister uranists are persecuted, scorned, even tried and imprisoned. Is it any wonder, then, that so many of us – having been rendered outlaws by our very natures – decide that we may as well be hanged for a sheep as for a goat, and fall into criminal ways and companionship? Can you be surprised that, to take myself as an example, I am tempted to masquerade as a noblewoman – to take unto myself that respected role in our society which is so constantly denied me?"

Silence followed this question. After a few seconds, Marsh nodded.

"I see that I've made some impression upon you. I hope that the seed I've planted in your minds may germinate. For the tide, you see, is turning. The day will come, depend upon it, when those such as I, who love in an unconventional way, will find ourselves scarcely worthy of remark – "

Gorman finally found his voice again.

"That fine talk is all very well," he said; "but I still need to take you and your friends in charge, Mr. Marsh."

"Of course you do," sighed Marsh. "No doubt you think it the height of impertinence for me to impersonate a member of the

English nobility; no doubt the law must take its course, and punish me for so heinous a sin."

"Oh, there's that," said Gorman grimly. "But you know full well that a much more serious offence lies against your name. You will find yourself facing a far greater penalty of law for your robbery of the bank on Oakapple Orbital Station, and you'll oblige me by coming along quietly, so that I may formally charge you with that."

"What?"

Marsh's calm facade was shivered to atoms in an instant.

"You heard him," said Neville.

"Have you lost your mind, copper?" growled Bustany.

"Rob a bank? What nonsense!" chimed in Townsend, the supposed valet.

"You shall not pin this upon us!" Marsh's voice had descended from its measured, feminine tones to a low and menacing snarl. "Impersonation and fraud – I'll grant 'em to you; but to rob a bank?"

"That will be for the courts to decide," said Gorman; but it was plain that the reaction which his words had evinced from Marsh, Bustany and Townsend had made an impression upon him. It had upon me. Their astonishment seemed very genuine to me.

"What the... the... the dickens," Marsh said, plainly teetering on the brink of using an expression much less ladylike, "would we want to go robbing a bank for? We had all the money we wanted, while we were borrowing the guises of Lord and Lady Freckleton. You're a peeler – go, take your fat head back to Earth, and look up our records at Scotland Yard. If you find any kind of robbery, or the faintest suspicion of it, attaching to any of us, you can take my tits and use them as footballs."

And to underline this offer, Marsh reached inside her décolleté, extracted something that resembled a small bag filled with rice, and threw it at Gorman's feet, with the air of one who, mortally offended, challenges their offender to a duel. Miss Craddock gasped, and I regret to report that Miss Dickson giggled for a moment before stifling the sound.

Gorman prodded the rice-bag with his toe, in a thoughtful sort of way.

"What's more," added Bustany, "where do you think we've stashed the boodle from this robbery you accuse us of, eh?"

"Good point," said Marsh. "Do you want to search me?"

The expression on Gorman's face suggested that the reply to that was in the negative.

"Ye gods."

Eppley had been sitting so quietly that we had all but forgotten that he was there, until he spoke. He wrote something in his notebook with a frown, then underlined it so savagely that the point of his pencil snapped.

"I don't suppose you can put that in your story," said George, looking at the rice-bag as it lay forlorn.

I have no desire to prolong my record of this painful scene. Suffice it to say that a search of the trio of tricksters' hotel rooms revealed no stolen money; although the manager of Keegan's Hotel, upon hearing the news of Lord and Lady Freckleton's true identity, let out a string of oaths from which, Sergeant Loftus said with satisfaction, he learned three cuss-words quite unknown to him hitherto. Neither did it seem likely to Gorman and his men, or indeed to Neville and Oakes, that they might have somehow concealed the loot somewhere about Selene City.

"Just imagine," Harris grumbled, "what that bounder Veele will say when he hears this news. I don't fancy our chances at his hands, if we go back to Oakapple now."

"Or even pass it by," said George. "Remember, those ships of the A.O.L. come equipped with grapples."

"I'm very sorry, gentlemen," said Oakes. "I really thought we had the robbers in the palm of our hand, there. Look here – I dare say we could all do with a good night's rest."

(Night, on the Moon, is of course a relative thing; the days last a full month. But Selene City, and the other lunar bases, adopt the terrestrial clock, and call it night when the clock says night, no matter though the sun may still be overhead.)

And Oakes, crestfallen at the failure to catch the bank-robber though he was, insisted on putting all of us up in Keegan's Hotel at his own expense, and sending for our bags from the left-luggage office, and treating us to supper. The three ladies shared two rooms between them, and Eppley was quartered with us in a pair of rooms connected as a suite – the very quarters, in fact, which Bustany, Marsh and Townsend had so lately vacated.

"That," said Oakes, as Eppley left to see to the retrieval of the baggage, "will at least mean that the hotel isn't done out of the night's rental by those rogues."

The supper was as good as one might expect, at a hotel with the reputation of Keegan's; but somehow I don't think that any of us enjoyed it very much.

20

"Shall we go out and sight-see?" asked George after it.

"I'm blessed if I want to, quite frankly," I said. "Tomorrow, perhaps. I have had quite enough excitement for now. I feel as though I haven't had a chance to sit down and catch my breath since we took off in that confounded space-capsule."

And Harris gave his opinion silently by marching up to our rooms.

When we got there, Eppley threw himself down into an armchair – a gesture which is a good deal less satisfying under the lesser gravity which prevails upon the moon.

"The worst of all this," he grumbled, "is that I shall have to write my whole story again. I thought I had a scoop."

"Scoop of the evening," murmured Harris. "Beautiful, beautiful scoop."

Eppley was plainly not in the mood to best appreciate puns. "Oh, do stow it," he grunted, "and make yourself useful by shoving that table over."

Harris moved the table over to the armchair. Eppley sat forward, and reached for his little portable typewriter. He removed its cover, and jerked out the sheet of paper half-covered with type which sat wrapped around its roller.

"J.," he said, crumpling the paper into a ball, "be a good fellow and pass me a blank page. There's half a ream in my folio-case, just there."

I opened the case and supplied Eppley with a clean sheet of foolscap in exchange for the discarded one, and shot the latter into the wastebasket – or tried to. Of course, I forgot yet again to take lunar gravity into account, and missed my mark by feet. As Eppley's typewriter keys began to click and clack, George picked up the surplus sheet, and idly flattening it out, scanned it.

My eyes were focused on Eppley – as I've remarked elsewhere, there are few simple pleasures so enjoyable as watching someone else work when one has no work to occupy oneself – but after a moment, I caught out of the corner of my eye a frown forming on George's face. George, being the cheerful and uncomplicated soul he is, seldom has recourse to expressions such as frowns. It normally requires some woe on the level of a toothache to make George's features display displeasure.

"J.," he began, then broke off. Eppley's typewriter continued to chatter away. The frown on George's face was replaced by a look of uncertainty, tempered with worry; once again, not an expression one generally looks for in George.

The conclusion to which I came was that George wished to remark upon something, but either felt too uncertain to do so, or thought it might be indelicate. Consequently, I did not respond to him in words of my own, but simply tilted my head to the side, and raised a silent eyebrow.

I was pleased to find that my deduction was evidently correct, for George made a gesture with his forefinger, in a subtle way most unlike him, beckoning me over to him.

I arose from my seat and drifted over to George, in a casual fashion. It was evident that George wanted to be discreet, for once in his life. Really, he need not have feared; for Eppley was still focused entirely upon composing his copy, and Harris was standing alongside Eppley, reading over his shoulder. I have often had cause to chide Harris about this insufferable habit of his, which in my case renders me quite unable to continue writing. For a moment, I envied Eppley, who seemed wholly unperturbed by his audience of one.

"I say, J.," said George, sotto voce, once I was up close to him. "Do you still have that facsimile of the bank robber's note – the one Neville and Oakes gave you on Oakapple?"

I started to dig through my jacket pockets, before I remembered.

"Did I not give it to Miss Lexlake?" I said, digging instead through my memory. "I almost think – "

"You jolly well ought to," said George, sharply. And upon seeing me momentarily at a loss, he added "Think, that is. Come along."

Returning to his normal voice, he said to Eppley and Harris

"We'll be back in a jiffy, you fellows." With that, he turned and operated the crank which opened the door of our quarters. Still puzzled, I followed him through; whereupon he cranked the door closed once again, with an energy more befitted to a chauffeur trying to start a car on a cold morning than George's customary lethargy.

"Do you know what the trouble is," he puffed once the door was once again sealed closed, "with these confounded Selene City doors?"

"You can't slam them," I said, which I thought a shrewd observation.

"I meant," said George, "that you can't sneak through them quietly."

"Why did you want – "

"Never mind that," interrupted George. "We need to speak to Miss Lexlake."

Feeling ourselves quite daring and modern to approach a single lady's hotel chambers in this manner, even on the Moon rather than stick-in-the-mud old Earth, we made our way through the hotel passageways in search of Miss Lexlake and her companions. I followed in George's footsteps, still trying to puzzle out what he might possibly have in mind as he arrived at his destination and rapped upon the door.

It cranked steadily open, to reveal Miss Dickson, to whom George raised his cap.

"I hope you'll forgive me for impinging upon you in this way," he said, self-consciously.

"Consider yourself freely forgiven," said Miss Dickson. "It's always a pleasure to encounter you gentlemen."

At this, George blushed. He is very often a self-conscious noodle where women are concerned.

"I really wished to consult Miss Lexlake upon something," he said, apologetically, as though he expected Miss Dickson to be disappointed that he hadn't come visiting in order to see her.

Miss Dickson called out "Celia!" and within a moment, Miss Lexlake appeared behind her.

"May I be of assistance?" As previously, Miss Lexlake did not seem so delighted as her friend to find herself in our presence.

George raised his cap again as a substitute for speech, then found his tongue. "I... I say, Miss Lexlake," he ground out awkwardly, "J. here tells me that he left you with that ransom-note thingummy – the facsimile copy of the one used in the bank robbery on Oakapple Orbital."

"I believe he did." Miss Lexlake seemed as perplexed as I had been by George's reference to that note. "I think I left it in my reticule."

George took a step toward the door, then retraced it hastily when Miss Lexlake's steely eyes lowered at him from under her brow. I noted, once again, that Miss Lexlake seemed content to discard traditional ideas of female propriety when they did not suit her purposes, but to cling to them when they did. George was plainly not going to be granted access to the ladies' quarters.

"I say, Miss Lexlake," he groaned, "this may be fearfully important. May we speak privately?"

Miss Lexlake looked at me, whereupon George did too. "Oh, J. doesn't signify," he added, which I thought a little unfeeling of him.

With a keen look growing in her eye, Miss Lexlake retrieved her small clutch-bag, and looked inside it. "I have it here. Now, may I enquire just why you need it? You're all of a fluster," she said, with accuracy if not with complete civility.

George's cheeks grew more and more pink. "I'd really rather not speak of it here," he said. "Most likely it's all just a foolish fancy of mine and a waste of all our time."

Whether he intended it or not, this admission seemed to find favour with Miss Lexlake. "Well, well," she said, "perhaps you'll allow me to be the judge of that, and advise you as a friend? Arabel, will you crank the door shut behind me, while I go to hold council with these gentlemen, and assist them as best I may?"

The door cranked closed, leaving us in the passage outside the hotel room. Miss Lexlake extracted from her little bag the photographic facsimile of the bank robber's note.

"Pray, what is this excitement all about?" she said, as she passed it to George.

George took it in one hand, and held the discarded draft of Eppley's news copy in the other. He blinked at one, then at the other; then he changed hands, as though he thought that might make some difference; then he squinted under the harsh, cold electric light of Selene City.

"I'm dashed if I can believe it," he said after a few seconds, "but I'd swear these two were both typed upon the same machine."

"That's hardly a surprise," I said. "It's a Van Gortel Foldaway. I know half a dozen chaps who use one, over and above Eppley – "

"Hold," said Miss Lexlake, interrupting me. I held.

She took the two sheets from George, and peered at them intently.

"You see," said George. "The capital K has a chip on one side, and the bottom of the Y is missing the end of its tail – and the typebar of the S must be a little askew, because every S is a shade too far to the right –"

"I see," said Miss Lexlake. "No doubt a fuller examination would find further points of correspondence; but given what we have noted with the unaided eye already, there appears only one conclusion to draw." She passed the papers back to George, in order to put her hand up to her head and straighten her coiffure, as though the thoughts in it were so powerful that they had made her hair go astray.

"You mean," I said, "they were typed on the very same machine?"

"Well, yes," said George. "And it scarcely seems possible, but – "

"But?"

"But," said Miss Lexlake, "the obvious inference is that Mr. Eppley typed the note presented during the bank robbery; and the inference from that, is that it was he who carried out that robbery."

To this day, I could not tell you whether my slowness on the uptake was because my mind was working slower than normal on that day, for some reason; or whether I was shying away from the conclusion that Eppley – a fellow to whom I had taken, who had proved a charming and convivial travelling companion – a chap I had broken bread with, nay, drunk whisky with – could possibly be guilty of such a crime.

Yet the evidence was there. I grabbed the papers from George, and compared the jelly-graph note to the crumpled sheet which Eppley had typed. The very first letter of the former, the K of "Kindly", did indeed display a chip of damage as George had pointed out; so, too, did the letters Y and S appear identical in both documents.

"But – but, I say," I stammered, "isn't it possible that two different machines could sustain damage – "

"Don't be an ass, J.," said George. "The odds against so many correspondences between more than one machine must be incredible."

"And the odds of two such typewriters both being found away from the earth's surface, still more so," said Miss Lexlake, in tones which would brook no denial. "It is plain. Marsh's party stand exonerated in full; Eppley must be the bank-robber."

"That gladstone-bag of his!" exclaimed George. "Why, it must be full of banknotes."

"But what shall we do?" I said, still trying to come to terms with the news.

"You will keep quiet, and you will follow my instructions."

I jerked around at the sound of a new voice. We had been so intent on examining the evidence, and then discussing it, that none of us had seen Eppley approach from behind us – from the direction of our rooms.

He did not speak loudly, or even sharply; but then, he scarcely needed to. More than sufficient emphasis was lent to his words by the fact that in his right hand, he was holding a small gun, its barrel pointed directly at us.

21

"For pity's sake, Eppley – " I started.

"Oh, do button your foolish lip, J.," he retorted. "Move – all of you – yes, you too, madam. Back to our quarters. Out of the public gaze."

"You realise," said Miss Lexlake, calmly, "that if you discharge that weapon, and it were to blow a hole in the protective shield of Selene City, we would all be asphyxiated?"

"Then," said Eppley, "you had better not give me any reason to fire it, hadn't you? Move, I say. Quick and sharp."

He gestured with the gun, and sheepishly, the three of us began to make our way back along the metal passage which led to the rooms which George and I had so recently quitted. Eppley marched close behind us. I could no longer see his gun, but I had no cause to doubt that he still held it at our backs. I wondered dizzily what Eppley would do if we encountered someone else along the way, but we reached our rooms without encounter and without further incident.

"Open it," said Eppley. I cranked the door open, and we all hastened inside.

"Hulloa," said Harris, "all of you back together, what? You were quicker than I expected, Eppley – "

He broke off as Eppley swung the gun around in his direction.

"W-what the deuce – "

"Shut your idiotic mouth," said Eppley. "And you, J. – you shut the door."

Harris did not shut his mouth; it continued to hang open. He did, however, cease speaking. I bent over to deal with the door-crank, still struggling to comprehend the events of the past five minutes.

"Wait," said Miss Lexlake. She stepped between me and Eppley's gun-hand. For a moment I was filled with relief, before shame overtook me at the prospect of her being shot down like a pheasant while I stood by.

I paused, my hand still on the crank, trying desperately to think what to do.

"You – you insane woman," growled Eppley. "Do you truly want me to put a bullet through your foolish head?" He raised his gun, pointing it directly into her face from a distance at which a mere child could hardly have failed to miss his mark.

"Mr. Eppley," said Miss Lexlake, "your manners are atrocious, and your memory equally deficient." She stood her ground, without the slightest sign of fear or of nervousness. "You may recall that only hours ago, I was willing to die by my own hand for the cause of my movement. Do you think that I would not welcome the opportunity to sacrifice my life for the publicity it would gain us, were you to fire that gun?"

"Miss Lexlake – " blurted George.

"Hush," said Miss Lexlake gently to George; and George subsided.

"I'll shoot," said Eppley again.

"Will you?" said Miss Lexlake. "Shoot an unarmed woman? I rather think you lack the nerve. Put up that weapon." She took a step closer to Eppley. Eppley's hand wavered.

"I thought not."

Eppley bared his teeth, and instead of aiming at Miss Lexlake, swung his gun around to aim it at me.

By instinct, I threw myself to the ground – which hurt less than I expected; Lunar gravity, once again. Miss Lexlake sprang toward Eppley, and reached for the gun.

Eppley growled a monosyllabic oath, which was certainly unfit for Miss Lexlake's ears, and his finger tightened upon the trigger. As it did so, she jerked up a hand to deflect his aim; this combined with the force from the shot to jerk the gun out of Eppley's grip. The bullet struck the armchair next to me, burying itself in the padding of its seat. The gun hit the ground, with a clash of one metal against another.

As it did so, Eppley snatched up the gladstone-bag which we had brought to the Moon alongside him, and hurled himself out of the still-open doors to our quarters.

I hauled myself, dazed, to my feet. George stooped to pick up the gun.

"Don't touch that," called out Miss Lexlake. "No doubt the police will need to prove that it carries his finger-prints. Quick – after him."

"After him?" I repeated.

"You surely don't want to let him get away scot-free?" she said, stepping through the door with great purposefulness.

"What, in the name of all that's holy," said Harris faintly, "was that all about?"

"No time for that," cried George, hurrying after Miss Lexlake. I followed him, and Harris, still protesting inarticulately, followed me.

Half a dozen yards outside the door, Miss Lexlake paused, and hastily tore off first one shoe, and then the other.

"I'll run – faster – without these damn' things," she panted, and as though to prove the point, set off, at a speed which Norman Pritchard might have envied, in the direction of Selene City's port. Harris stooped, and picked one of the shoes up, blinking at it.

"No time for that either, Harris, you ass," shouted George, chasing along in Miss Lexlake's wake.

And so the four of us set out in pursuit of Eppley and his gladstone-bag, which I could no longer doubt was crammed with the proceeds of the Oakapple Orbital bank robbery.

It has never before (or since) been my lot to chase after a bank-robber through an artificial, metal city in lunar gravity. As I sit to write this, at a good firm desk in the comfort of a leather-padded chair, I find it strange to cast my mind back to that moment. I have lived an entertaining enough existence, and have quite the arsenal of stories upon which I can draw at dinner-parties and in public houses – yet this must be one of the strangest and wildest.

To begin with, running on the moon is an art-form in its own right. Your mind and body have been trained to run in full earthly gravity, ever since your youthful experiences at school sports-days. Upon the moon, you find yourself bounding lightly along, and yet your body retains its full earthly mass; which is liable to lead to trouble, especially if your mass is in the nature of George's.

And so, if you need to turn a corner or to dodge around some obstacle, you need to see it coming well in advance, and make a quick mental calculation as to the path you need to follow; and if some wretched person then intersects your trajectory, the worse for both that person, and for you.

The intelligent reader will, I hope, understand that in the circumstances, we had neither the time nor the capacity of mind to think about anything else save the chase. With hindsight, it is facile for me to remark that the sensible course of action would have been for us to separate; for one of us to return to Miss Craddock and Miss Dickson to notify them of the situation, for one of us to find a member of the local constabulary, and for a third to run to Oakes and his men to warn them of what we had discovered; leaving one of us still to pursue Eppley.

But, as it was, we none of us reasoned this out, and all four of us raced after our quarry, in a confused and chaotic manner which I can only imagine must have provided a sight to behold. All of our party, even the efficient Celia Lexlake, left a trail of chaos in our wake as we ran, colliding with people, and luggage-trolleys, and newspaper-stands; and Harris, who must always go one step beyond everyone else, ran into a little barrow selling moon-made chocolate-creams, which were supposedly lighter than air upon the tongue. I don't know how those sweetmeats tasted, but they certainly scattered themselves to the four points of the compass as though they weighed scarcely more than a feather each.

Our blundering pursuit would surely have proven fruitless, were it not for the fact that Eppley, too, was no dab hand at sprinting in low gravity. As we drew close to the embarking area, we saw signs of a fracas ahead, which proved to be a tangle of Eppley, two stout matrons, a luggage-porter, several cases, and an umbrella.

As we came charging toward them, Eppley regained his feet. One of the ladies, not unreasonably seeming annoyed, thrust the umbrella at him; Eppley unsportingly snatched it from her, and broke it over his knee – a caddish thing to do, I think, even though there can be no conceivable reason for anyone to bring an umbrella to the moon. He turned, and ran hell-for-leather once again toward the train platform as we came tumbling by the struggling group upon the floor. George touched his cap in passing, which (he afterwards said) he meant to convey the meaning of "I should like to have stopped and helped you to your feet, but I'm in a confounded hurry". I venture to doubt whether he adequately conveyed that meaning.

We had gained upon Eppley, but not enough; as he ran onto the platform, the station-master was grasping his flag, and had his whistle to his lips.

"Stand away, there!" he shouted; but a fellow who has lately robbed a bank sees it as a mere bagatelle to disobey the command of a humble station-master. Eppley hurled himself at the train, found a footing on the running-board, and as it began to inch into motion, jerked the door open with one hand. He crammed his gladstone-bag of loot into the carriage. For a moment he teetered, on the verge of falling back; then he regained his balance, and tumbled inside. The train, with its door still swinging open, picked up speed on its journey to the sphere-docks; and the four of us were left, panting for breath, to watch it as it departed.

22

I could think of a great many remarks and observations I might justly have made, but I had no breath remaining to voice any of them.

"Another train in five minutes, sirs, madam."

The station-master was standing next to us, flag furled.

"That man – " George panted, straightening his cap – "that man was a thief – a criminal."

"You don't say, sir?" said the station-master stolidly, as though a daily part of his duties might involve bank-robbers diving onto departing trains under his nose.

"We do say," rejoindered Miss Lexlake. "It was he who robbed the bank, up there on Oakapple, the other day."

"And that bag he had is stuffed with the boodle," I added.

The station-master looked perplexed.

"Is there nothing you can do?" Miss Lexlake said, in what I would have described as a bark, had she been of a different gender.

"I could telegraph," said the servant of the railway. "Yes – I could telegraph – do please excuse me – " And he walked away towards a door marked PRIVATE: NO ADMITTANCE.

"That should put paid to him," said George, looking up at the telegraph wires with a hopeful expression.

"Except," said Miss Lexlake," that by the time he telegraphs, the train will have arrived and Eppley will have escaped. Also, that man plainly thought we were a party of – you'll excuse the phrase, given our location – lunatics, and he has probably gone to lock himself in his office away from us, rather than to telegraph down the line."

"Then what – " I began.

Miss Lexlake raised her arm straight and extended her forefinger.

"The next train – there, waiting at the alternate platform. We may catch him yet, if he isn't quick on his heels at the far end."

We ran around the buffer-stops from the platform upon which we stood to the adjacent one, George still gasping for breath. There was no point, now, in racing pell-mell, and we threaded our way between passengers leaving the second train.

"Now," Harris exclaimed as we climbed aboard, "will someone please tell me what has happened?"

George and I began to explain. Miss Lexlake sat, silent and impatient, drumming her fingers on her lap. After a little while, she stood up and first peered out of the window, then opened the carriage door.

"Miss Lexlake – " I began.

"We have been more than five minutes, and the train has not moved," she said. "Neither is there any sign of it preparing to."

We all piled back out, and joined her once again on the platform.

"I dare say," she continued, "that the railwayman told us five minutes, simply to be rid of us."

"What sauce!" George scowled in the direction of PRIVATE: NO ADMITTANCE.

As we stood there, movement caught my eye from an unexpected direction; from directly above. I paused, with my hand on the carriage door-handle, and looked up.

"Stargazing again, J.?" asked Harris.

"Isn't that sphere coming awfully close?" said George, who was quicker on the uptake than Harris, and was also looking upward.

"The railwayman will be rid of us, all right," I said, "if it doesn't turn aside pretty sharpish."

Through the reinforced atmospherium hemisphere which enclosed the railway, we could all see clearly – too clearly – a space vessel. Rather than rising straight up from the lunar surface, as such things ought, this one was veering and wobbling upon a trajectory which was sure to bring it back down to the moon in short order; and not just down to the moon, but to the very spot where we stood, faces upturned.

We were not the only ones to observe this imminent convergence of the twain; other eyes were also staring into the heavens, now. There were gasps around us. Then came a scream; then more.

"There is no point in running," said Miss Lexlake, as someone fled past us. "If that thing hits the glass and breaks it, it will release the air into vacuum. It will kill us, and everyone in this station."

As the truth of her statement began to sink into me, the errant sphere dipped, then sluggishly rose, its pilot desperately trying to recover control.

"He's going back up – " George breathed.

"Too late," said Harris.

"I told you back on Earth," I said, "that going into space was a crack-pot idea, and – "

Before I could conclude what I fully expected to be my last ever sentence with "and I was quite right", the sphere struck the roof of the station.

There was a cacophony of ominous sounds; creaks, scrapes, grinding. The impact had come almost at the zenith of the roof's curve, and nearly at a right-angle. The sphere's momentum carried it onward, over our heads, dragging over the roof. The transparent atmospherium-glass made it easy to follow its progress. I wished that the architects had chosen smoked glass instead.

"It must be Eppley," said Miss Lexlake, still sounding calmer than anyone in imminent danger of their life had any right to sound.

She was right, of course – again. From where we stood, it was impossible to catch a glimpse of the sphere's pilot, or to see inside it at all; but plainly no experienced operator could make such a ham-fisted launch. It could only be an utter novice, or else someone in a desperate hurry to leave the satellite's surface; such as a bank-robber in fear of being laid by his heels.

The horrid scrapes continued to reverberate throughout the station. Then the sphere bounced sluggishly off the roof, and inched its way upward once more, before it seemed to find its second wind, take a sharp vertical twist, and shoot properly away from the moon at last.

The sounds and echoes of the collision died slowly away, leaving the station's protective enclosure unbroken.

"That," said Harris, "was a close shave." He turned to look at me. "J., I don't like to bother you at a moment like this, but you were just explaining to me what's been going on?"

I started out to resume explaining to him, since after all, it was

I to whom he had put this request; but George and Miss Lexlake both began to speak as well, and I doubt whether Harris took in so many as one word in a dozen.

I raised my hand for silence. "Can we not have this conversation aboard the train?"

"I suppose we could," said Miss Lexlake, "but I doubt there will be any more departures from the station after what just occurred; and in any case, by now Eppley will be somewhere up there in space."

"We could go after him," said George tentatively.

"How would we find him," responded Miss Lexlake, "in the vast void between here and Earth?"

"I'm still confused," muttered Harris.

"I think, then," I said, "that we should find the authorities and make a clean breast of the whole dashed thing to them."

"That should be simple enough," said Miss Lexlake, "for here comes Neville, and – is that Oakes with him?"

Miss Lexlake's powers of observation once again came up to the mark. We were joined by Neville, and Oakes, and quite a cluster of lunar police officers, some of whom seemed quite keen to take us into custody first and ask questions afterwards. I do not know what arrangements they have for locking up wicked people on the moon – evidently they must, for I suppose criminals and rogues exist there as everywhere – but Oakes sternly commanded them to rein in their natural urge to arrest anyone they saw in the vicinity; and they subsided, and let us explain what had taken place, and how we had discovered Eppley to be the bank robber, and how he had escaped us and nearly crashed his sphere through the station's roof as he made his getaway.

"That," said Oakes, "would have pierced the vacuum and – "

"– and killed us all," I said, finding myself suddenly in a touchy mood and inclined to speak sharply. "Is there nothing that can be done to pursue him, or must we reconcile ourselves to him escaping scot-free back to Earth with all that stolen money?"

"I can't believe that he took us all in," sighed Harris. "He was such a pleasant young man – affable, I'd call him." He looked down in sorrow, which reminded him that he was still holding one of Miss Lexlake's shoes.

He held it out toward her, with the air of a man with a guilty conscience making a peace-offering. Miss Lexlake arched an eyebrow.

"Thank you, I'm sure," she said, "but really, I should leave the role of Prince Charming alone, if I were you, for I've no desire to play Cinderella against you, or against anyone else."

"You might have picked them both up," said George. "What earthly use – "

"Lunar use," I couldn't resist interjecting.

" – earthly use," George went on, ignoring my correction, "did you think one shoe was going to be? What if we'd had to chase after him in a space-vessel – would you have expected Miss Lexlake to travel half-way across the cosmos with one stockinged foot?"

But Miss Lexlake took the shoe from Harris nonetheless, with a grave expression and a very slight curtsey. She did not put it on. Instead, she turned to Oakes once more.

"As J. here was saying, is there any way at all in which we can stop Eppley now? I expect he'll be making haste to return to Earth; surely, at the very least, Selene City can radio a warning so that the police down there may be on their watch for his arrival?"

At this, Oakes swung into decisive action and started to bark commands at those surrounding him. I don't believe that, technically, he had any right to order the local constabulary about; but whether because they recognised him as the owner of Oakapple, or whether because of the manner in which he arrogated to himself the role of monarch of all he surveyed, they obeyed. He sent them off in various different directions; one to the Morse room, to spread the news of Eppley's flight to Earth and to all the orbital stations; one to Selene City's municipal maintenance department, to arrange for a team to check that Eppley's careless piloting had caused no significant damage to the roof above our heads; one, at Miss Lexlake's prompting, to find and notify Miss Craddock and Miss Dickson of what had transpired; one to the station-master's office, to advise of developments and arrange for the station to re-open and for trains to recommence running; still another to warn the newspaper offices that they should not expect Eppley to be filing any more copy in the foreseeable future. Finally, he sent Neville back with the last lunar constable, to tell Gorman that the mystery of the bank robbery was solved, and that Bustany's party was, as they had maintained, innocent at least of that.

I began to comprehend how it had come to pass that Oakes had risen from coal-mining to make good his fortunes as the proprietor of a successful orbital station.

When, finally, he had run out both of commands to give, and of minions to whom he might give them, he paused for breath, enabling me to speak.

"Mr Oakes," I began.

"Gareth, Gareth, please," he corrected me.

I am old-fashioned enough that I still prefer to address a man by his surname with whom I am not on terms of close friendship, but Oakes commanded such an air of authority that I could not but accede to his request.

"Gareth, then – what action do you have in mind, now?"

He looked around as though to satisfy himself that he had taken every step which it was possible to take in the current time and place. Evidently he thought he had, for he nodded in satisfaction.

"I shall return to Oakapple without delay," he said. "Now that the bank robber's been identified, I shall need to speak again to the bank's representatives there. A senior partner of theirs was to depart from Earth to take charge of the enquiries on the station, following the robbery, and I'm sure he must be there by now." He rubbed his hands contemplatively, as the man he had sent to speak to the station-master returned. "Ah, back already? May we expect a train to leave for the docking port soon?"

The answer was in the affirmative, and Oakes rubbed his hands again, then placed one of them on the handle of the train carriage's door. But he paused before opening it.

"Would you care to accompany me in the Rhondda Cynon Taff? Your evidence will be vital for the bank people, as well as for the bobbies; not to mention that your company on my way back to

Oakapple will be very welcome, if I'm leaving Neville in charge of my immediate interests here for the moment."

"I should deem it a pleasure," said Miss Lexlake, before any of the rest of us could respond, "but where are Emily and Arabel – ah!"

As though on a theatrical cue, Miss Lexlake's friends were hurrying toward us.

"Celia, I believe this is yours?" said Miss Dickson, holding out the companion shoe to the one which Harris had carried to the station.

"Thank you so much, Arabel," said Miss Lexlake, using the carriage step to once again return herself to a fully shod state. "Gareth, here, wishes us to return to Oakapple with him and assist the police and the bank with their investigations into this sordid affair."

"Then we should do so," said Miss Craddock, "as good, law-abiding citizens."

That remark made Miss Dickson chuckle aloud, and hastily hide her mirth behind her hand.

"What about our luggage?" asked George.

"I'll arrange for it to be sent on," said Oakes, and detailed the man who had returned from the station-master to take care of that chore.

"And the vessel we came here in?" I said, as I climbed aboard the carriage, and then helped the ladies in after me. "It's not ours, you know; it's hired from Peckover of Maplin."

"Peckover? I know him well," said Oakes blithely. "I'll straighten anything out that needs straightening with Jimmy Peckover."

I was wondering, by this point, whether there was anything on the Earth's surface or above it which Gareth Oakes wasn't able to arrange to his will.

23

I consider myself a thoughtful and contemplative person; one who observes things around him. I think it, indeed, a great handicap to any writer not to be of such a nature.

And, I dare say, the reason why it is I and not Harris who chronicles for the public consumption the jollities and misadventures which befall us when we enjoy (well, I say "enjoy") a holiday together, is that Harris never notices a dashed thing unless you shove it so close under his nose that it threatens to get tangled up with his moustache. I count William Samuel Harris as a dear friend, and have for most of my adult life; but my regard for truth forces me to set this fact down in stark simplicity.

As for George – well, he does at least notice what's around him; but where George falls down is when he needs to distinguish what is important from what is trivial.

So it was that as we found ourselves aboard the large and luxuriously fitted-out spacecraft that was the property of Gareth Oakes, we each of us acted true to our respective forms. George made straight for a porthole, where he could enjoy the views of the stars and of the lunar mountains as we launched; Harris pottered about, getting in everyone's way and asking pointless and irritating questions.

I, myself, more than either of my companions, felt myself truly superfluous to requirements. Oakes, we soon learned, could pilot a ship just as well as he seemed able to do anything else he might find useful to his purposes; the unmasking of Eppley's thievery was down not to me, but to George and to Miss Lexlake; in short, as the Moon's surface receded from us, I began to feel more and more as though a case of "the blues" were stealing over me. We had intended to spend a brief and refreshing spell of time in space for the good of our health, both of body and mind, and to leave all our cares behind us on Earth; instead, we had begun by blundering around the aether like the veriest novices, and had then proceeded to entangle ourselves in both the affair of the fake Lord Freckleton, and the mystery of the bank theft on Oakapple.

Mulling things over, I concluded that – far from enjoying a relaxing holiday away from it all – we had been swept away in a series of events which had really prevented us from achieving much at all by way of relaxation.

As I formed this conclusion, I realised that Miss Dickson, who was sitting alongside me, was regarding me with a quizzical air.

"A penny for your thoughts, J.?" she said. "Or, since everything is so awfully expensive once you leave Earth, perhaps I'd better offer you a bob."

Miss Dickson was the youngest, the prettiest, and (to my eyes) the least forbidding of the three suffragettes; and a little to my own surprise, I found myself explaining to her what had been running through my head, and why I felt so unrefreshed by what we had intended as a jolly holiday.

She listened with every appearance of solemn interest as I unburdened myself. When at length I ran out of grumbling words, and not before then, she spoke up in reply.

"Don't you see," she said, "that this is one of the reasons I and my fellow fighters for women's suffrage have in mind?"

I did not see, and I told her as much. My failure to comprehend did not appear to vex her, and she explained.

"Well, at present, men claim the positions of power in every field of human society, do they not? This is all very well, on the face of it; but it's my belief – I'm most sincere in this, J. – that for them to have to hold the reins all the time not only keeps women enslaved and oppressed, but also enslaves and oppresses them. You poor men must always have your hands on the reins, whether in government or in industry or in any other walk of life; and it isn't good for you. Do you know," she said, looking into my eyes with an intensity which in other circumstances I might have found enchanting, "that the average man lives fully four years fewer than his female counterpart?"

I was seized by the feeling that it would be impolite to enter into a dispute with Miss Dickson; but I reminded myself that if women were to be the equal of men in all regards, they would have to be prepared to enter into conversational debates with men, with no quarter given to them out of old-fashioned chivalry.

So I said, "But surely much of that is down to men having to work in strenuous positions – factories and coal-mines – " (At this, Oakes glanced over his shoulder, and put me off my line of thought.) " – and... and what about the Army?"

"In due course," said Miss Dickson, as though she had been expecting my reply, "we shall reach the point where conflict between nations is seen as the childish pastime it is; as a habit unworthy of the human race, if it is to have any prospect of long enduring. And as for factory accidents – have you ever visited a factory where women work?"

I had to concede that I had not.

"Women," she said, her eyes shining more moistly than ever, "die in factories just as do men – perhaps less violently, but no less horribly. I should have thought, as a literary man," (I didn't like the emphasis which she put on 'literary'; it sounded as though she doubted my claim), "you would have read Charles Dickens' article about the evils of match-factories, written some seventy years since? And yet little or nothing has changed – unless it be," she concluded, "that women are now employed in them more often than men, and suffer the woes that were once denied them. No! When women have the vote – nay, more, when women may enter Parliament alongside men – we shall soon see to it that we no longer lose our sisters or our brothers to the terrors of war, or to the unnecessary tragedies of industrial accidents which may, with but a little care, be safeguarded against. What do you say to that?"

She delivered this oration with such force and such a heartfelt manner that I was at a loss to come up with any argument against it; I felt it my duty to at least try to find a weak spot in her words, but while I was still cudgelling my wits for one, Harris spoke up.

"I say," he said, glancing from the porthole to address us over his shoulder, "stars aren't meant to flash on and off, are they?"

"They don't," said George scornfully. "You must be seeing things."

Miss Craddock, at the next porthole to Harris, shook her head. "I declare, I can see it too."

George swung himself weightlessly across the cabin, and bumped into the wall between Harris and Miss Craddock. "Let me look," he said, elbowing Harris, and the two of them jostled for position for a few seconds.

Before either of them could displace the other from their vantage-point, Oakes brought the Rhondda Cynon Taff round with a gentle touch upon the controls, until we could all see the blinking light through the large front window which his vessel boasted.

"That is no star," said Miss Lexlake.

"Of course it bl – of course it isn't," said Oakes. "That's a distress beacon." His hands adjusted the controls once more.

"Are we going to investigate?" asked Harris, which earned him a scornful glance from Oakes.

"Why else," he replied, "do you think I have just set a course for it?"

Harris subsided, crushed, and we all clustered up against the front window, until Oakes testily ordered us to stop blocking his view.

"I wonder what the emergency may be," said Miss Dickson to Oakes.

As a conversational gambit, this worked very well.

"Probably loss of control," said Oakes. "There are two major causes of accidents in space – control failures, and vacuum failures. And with vacuum failures, you don't generally find anyone living for long enough to turn their emergency beacon on – begging your pardon," he added, as a look of dismay stole over Miss Dickson's face. "But control failures are common enough, though more often it's some ass who has managed to snarl them up, rather than the controls themselves breaking down."

"I heard tell," said Harris, eager to regain face, "about a fellow who jammed his controls up by shaving off his beard with a souvenir razor – "

"That's all my eye," snorted Oakes. "You hear all kind of stories up in the space stations, and they all happened to a friend of a friend – never to anyone who can tell the story at first-hand and say it happened to them. Now, pipe down, everyone, and let me concentrate on bringing this ship over to the distress beacon. Odds are that we either won't need to do anything, or else won't be able to, but you men might as well get yourselves ready in case there's something we can do."

"We shall all be at readiness," said Miss Lexlake firmly.

"Begging your pardon," said Oakes. "Let us all be ready to do whatever we may."

The emergency lights on space-vessels are, as you'd expect, designed to penetrate as far as possible through the blackness of space; but space is, as I have remarked already, vast. There was no sign of any other ship, save ourselves, approaching the beacon. We were all determined to spring into action if required; but there was little we could really do to prepare ourselves. George made a show of puffing out his cheeks and flexing his muscles, which made Miss Dickson smile. Miss Lexlake had opened the compartment which held the space-suits; luckily, they take up a great deal less space when folded and stowed than they do when they are being worn, and puff themselves out like a tropical fish warning away a predator.

The light grew ever brighter as we drew closer, and continued to pulse. Eventually we reached a proximity where we could distinguish the outline of the vessel to which it was attached.

"That's a peculiar shape for a ship," said George. "A double sphere, rather than a single one?"

Oakes pulled open a drawer set in the plinth upon which were fixed the controls. It contained a sextant, but thankfully he left that alone, and took out instead a pair of opera-glasses. He peered through them a moment, then laid them aside.

"That is not one ship, but two," he said, "and I think they're tethered together."

Miss Craddock and I both reached for the opera-glasses at the same moment; I let her have first go at them.

"How strange!" she said, passing them not to me but to Miss Dickson. By the time all three ladies had taken a good look of the scene which we were approaching at speed, I could see pretty well for myself that Oakes had been right. There were two spheres, of a similar size; one was attached to the other by what seemed to be some kind of grapple, which had taken hold of it by one of the external hand-holds. Both ships were jerking and rocking about as though they were down on Earth and bobbing in a lively sea, rather than in the supposedly tranquil vacuum of space, where neither waves nor wind can affect a vessel's stability.

"Strange," muttered Oakes, as he steered our ship closer.

As we tacked around the two vessels, though, the position became clear. The cable between them was taut; taut almost to breaking-point. The two were pulling in different directions, as though they hoped to re-enact the famous competition between the Rattler and the Alecto; but they were more evenly matched than that historical contest between paddle and screw, and neither seemed able to gain an advantage over the other.

George gave a cry as Oakes brought us to a stand at a little distance from this peculiar tug-of-war.

"That's Eppley," he said. "It's as we thought – he must have forced his way aboard a ship and tried to flee in it."

"But who's that in the other ship?" I asked.

Oakes snatched up his opera-glasses again, peered through them, and threw them down, so that they drifted in mid-air on the end of their tethering cord.

"This ship," he said, "has more Cavorite slats than either of the others. We could tow Eppley where the hell we please, if we can just fasten ourselves to his ship. But – we don't carry a grapple like that one." He pointed to the attachment at the end of the cable that bound the two rival ships together.

"I assume that we have cables," said Miss Lexlake. "Surely we need only to clothe ourselves in these suits, pass through the double hatch into space, and attach them with our own hands?"

"We?" said Oakes. "Madam, this is my job. I would never ask anyone else – be they man or woman – to run a risk I wasn't prepared to undertake myself."

"I thought," said Miss Lexlake, "that there was a general rule in space travel that one should not go out into space alone, unless no other option is possible."

"That's so," said Oakes. "But someone needs to remain at the controls; and – begging you gentlemen's pardons – from what I understand, you're none of you veterans at that billet."

The feeling of superfluousness which had hung around me since our failed pursuit of Eppley on the Moon rose to overwhelm me.

"Look here," I said. "If Miss Lexlake will take the helm, I'll clamber into one of these beastly suits, and go outside with you, Oakes – Gareth, I mean."

"I say, J.," murmured Harris. But Oakes gave me a nod of approval.

"Very well. There shouldn't be any real danger," he reassured me, "so long as you don't allow yourself to become trapped in between two ships; and if you do, then between being crushed flat, and having your suit pop its seals and lose all its air, you wouldn't suffer for more than an instant."

I have seldom regretted so deeply and so quickly any statement that I have made on the spur of the moment, as I did at those words of Oakes. But I thrust away from me any temptation to resile from my offer to go with the intrepid little Welshman. To show the white feather in front of the three suffragettes, not to mention Harris and George, was not to be thought of.

"Let's both take good care," I said, in as casual a voice as I could muster, "not to do so, then."

Miss Lexlake pushed herself over to me.

"If I may say so," she said to me, "you are a braver and more decent man than you appear externally; and probably than you believe yourself. Do be careful."

She took my hand and gave it a firm squeeze. I was silent; I wished I could reply to her, but no words that I could find on my tongue seemed anything but superfluous and vapid.

"Now," she said, "let's get you two men safely into your suits. Emily, Arabel? Will you assist, while I relieve Mr. Oakes at the helm?"

Oakes pushed himself over to join me, and we were bundled into our space-suits. This was only the second time I had worn one, and the first time had been on the surface of Oakapple Orbital, where there had been no need for me to leave the station's exterior and go floating in the vacuum between the planets.

"You know how to use the air-gun?" said Oakes.

"In theory," I said.

Oakes grunted. "I suppose that's the best I could hope for. Remember, you point it in the opposite direction to the way you want to move; action and reaction. We'll be linked together; I suggest you allow me to take the lead. We shall need to touch helmets, if you truly need to speak to me; otherwise we must use signs. And don't let yourself get enraptured."

I paused in the act of placing my helm over my head. "Enraptured?"

"Letting the stars hypnotise you. I shouldn't worry; it only tends to happen to the feeble-minded, and to poetic types." Oakes fastened his own helm, and picked up the coil of cable which stood ready for him.

I wondered whether books of essays and sketches and so forth qualified me to be a "poetic type"; and wished that Harris had been quicker to volunteer for this duty than I.

Then again, given how tight a squeeze it was for Oakes and myself to fit in the hatch together even before the outer door was thrown open to vacuum and our suits inflated like a child's balloons, perhaps it was as well that Harris and his non-poetic mind were remaining inside.

Oakes fastened the belt of his suit to mine by means of a device resembling an oversized karabiner, gave it a tug to test it, and – evidently satisfied that we were linked closely together, as though we were about to compete in a three-legged race – cranked open the door. I could neither see nor hear the atmosphere of the hatchway vent itself to space, but knew all too well that it was escaping. A certain tight feeling began to manifest itself behind my ribs.

Oakes beckoned, then reached for the first hand-hold outside the door.

I was pleased to find that Oakes' ship had even more hand-holds and belaying-points than the one we had hired from Peckover's yard. I took hold of one, and gripped it as firmly as I could manage, given that my hands were enclosed in the gloves of my space-suit, and that the fingers of those gloves were blown up like a row of saveloys. I knew full well that Oakes and I were possessed of the same velocity of the ship that had brought us here, and that it was not about to streak away at hundreds of relative miles per hour and leave us stranded; and yet I found it hard to dispel the fear that it was about to do just that – a fear which had not worried me in the least when I was moving over the surface of Oakapple Orbital. The response of the human mind to the depths of space is fascinating, but I find it best contemplated in full gravity, and preferably from an armchair.

Oakes threaded the cable through the karabiner that connected us, and began to climb from handhold to handhold. I followed him, from necessity, marvelling at the calm and precise way in which he made progress. I knew he had begun his adult life working miles underground, and the irony forced itself upon me that here he was now, further above the earth's surface than he had ever been below it, and in a situation where a false move would lead to a death more certain than ever a man might encounter in a coal-mine. But he displayed no sign of "nerves" or of hesitation.

I told myself that if he did not, then neither should I; and together we made our way over the ship's surface until the other two vessels, still straining against one another, were in full view.

Oakes touched his head to mine.

"I'm going to unfasten us," he said. "You belay yourself here. I'll take the cable over and lash it to Eppley. All you need to do is pay the cable out as I go – and then we'll pay that b_____ Eppley out." He chuckled, which was more than I would have been able to do in his shoes.

The karabiner attached me to Oakes' ship, leaving me with both hands free to hold the cable. Oakes was unattached, now, and floating free. With one hand he took the end of the cable; with the other, he drew from its housing his air-gun.

He pointed at the hand-hold to which I was fastened. Now that our heads were no longer touching, he could not speak, but his meaning was clear: "hold on tight!"

Taking careful aim, he pointed the air-gun. He must have squeezed its trigger, for he began to move backward, leaving his own ship and steadily drifting over to Eppley's. He was only in transit for a few seconds, though that was enough for me to imagine him fetching up against some sharp protruberance, tearing his suit open, and expiring in full sight of me while I was helpless to do anything to save him.

But he had judged well; he landed gently, gave me an insouciant wave to show that he was in no bother, and quickly hitched the cable to the nearest belaying-point on Eppley's sphere. Next, he extended his arm in my direction, and beckoned me to join him.

I took a deep breath, then wished I hadn't; there is nothing like being outside a space-sphere in a vacuum-suit to impress upon a chap that every breath should be treated as precious.

Then – summoning up all my courage – I unfastened myself from Oakes' ship and began to crawl along the cable toward Eppley's. I took especial care always to have one hand in contact with the line; and presently, I was very glad for that precaution.

Eppley had evidently realised the predicament he was in, and began to jerk his ship around; I could see the Cavorite slats rolling up and down. The cable I was clutching began to undulate, and soon, I was moving up and down with it, with sufficient force to make me feel queasy.

It did seem rather harsh that I should find myself suffering from mal-de-mer, here, with the nearest ocean hundreds if not thousands of miles away – and that ocean the dry, dusty ones which are all the Moon can boast.

I clung to that cable with all my might, and wondered dizzily for how long I could maintain a grip, and whether the cable would break, and how the deuce they would bury me if I were jerked loose and tumbled off into space. It's astonishing, the morbid depths to which one's thoughts descend in such circumstances.

But I was saved by the alertness of Miss Lexlake. She quickly comprehended what Eppley was resorting to in his desperation, and set Oakes's larger ship under way. The cable tautened once more and Eppley, unable to overcome the force of the more powerful vessel, found himself strung along behind. I inched along the cable, fist over fist, yard by yard, and finally caught hold of the same hand-hold where Oakes perched.

Oakes thumped me on the shoulder encouragingly; which is a sheer waste of time in a vacuum-suit, for the air inside it cushions your body from such minor external forces. All the same, I felt ridiculously grateful, for I had feared for a minute that I would never feel the touch of another human being.

Oakes pointed to the hatch. I held up my hand like a traffic policeman, and then raised two fingers, hoping to convey to Oakes that I required a couple of minutes to compose myself. After all, I reasoned, Eppley was now secure, a fish on the end of a line, and could evidently not escape.

And so I clung to the outside of the metal sphere, as it skimmed along at the end of its cable under the power of Miss Lexlake's capable hand at the helm, and looked at the stars – so many of them, more than any eye can see from the surface of our dear dirty old Earth with its atmosphere full of fog and smoke and dust – and at that self-same Earth with its white clouds and blue oceans and brown deserts. Somewhere between me and Earth, I knew, lay Oakapple and the other orbital stations; but either we were too far from them to pick them up by sight, or else I was looking in the wrong place for them.

Oakes waited patiently beside me, looking out into infinity together with me, like two tiny birds perched on the end of a branch above some vast canyon. I had the sudden feeling that – even though the little Welshman was so much more experienced a space-sailor than I – he too was enjoying the sights spread before us, and as grateful as I to be able still to do so.

I was about to give Oakes a gesture to show that I was recovered and ready to penetrate into Eppley's ship, when I felt a hand on my shoulder once again; not the light, friendly blow which Oakes had just given me, but a firm grasp.

Before I could even start to wonder what fresh trouble was besetting me, a small board or placard appeared in my field of vision, a gloved hand holding it by its edge. There were four words written on that placard, in large and clearly legible letters.

YOU ARE UNDER ARREST.

I twisted around with such force that I nearly lost my grip on the hand-hold. A third space-suited figure had joined Oakes and myself. Through the visor of its helm, I dimly saw a face with pink cheeks, black hair, a bristling moustache and a look of righteousness in its eye.

It was the face of Constable Nuttall of the Atmospheric and Orbital Link.

24

Well, what do you do when you are clinging, surrounded by vacuum, to the exterior of a space-ship, which contains a bank-robber who evidently makes up in desperation what he lacks in being a criminal mastermind, and a constabulary gentleman comes and pushes a sign at you advising that it is you who are under arrest?

I have given this question considerable thought, since, and still have not come up with a good answer; so it's hardly a surprise that I could think of none at the time. The sudden worry came to me that Nuttall was going to try to drag me away by force; I clung onto the hand-hold more firmly, filled with determination that if Nuttall wanted to take me away and throw me in gaol, he would have to saw off the rail I was clutching, and take that along with me.

Nuttall climbed over me and up to Oakes, and pushed the same notice in his face, then pointed imperiously to the hatch of Eppley's ship.

My first thought was to protest against his order; my second was that there was no way to do so in any manner which would have effect, or be comprehensible to Nuttall. Following hard on this came a third thought, which was that once inside Eppley's ship I could remove my wretched space-helm and plead my innocence.

By the time this third thought had formed, Oakes – ahead of me once again – was already cranking the external door open. As soon as it lay wide enough to admit him, he clambered inside, and as Nuttall and I joined him, he cranked it shut again with a swift ferocity. As soon as air filled the hatchway, he unlocked and removed his helm, revealing his face – very irascible.

Nuttall, too, doffed his helm. "Why," he said, "it's Mr. Oakes. Whatever are you doing here?"

I was convinced, by now, that Gareth Oakes enjoyed the personal acquaintance of every single human being who had travelled beyond the confines of Earth. I began to try and unfasten my helm, but with three of us crammed together in the hatch, I couldn't find space enough to lift my left arm enough to reach.

"I might ask the same of you," growled Oakes. "Esgob annwyl! Whatever are you doing hitched up to that thieving shinach Eppley's ship?"

Nuttall drew himself up to his full height, giving me even less room to manoeuvre.

"I signalled to that ship," he said, "because it was being piloted at a hexcessive speed and in a manner dangerous to other vessels. Instead of 'eaving to and permitting me to board and take happropriate haction, its pilot hattempted to hescape, forcing me to grapple it – "

"It's small bloody wonder he tried to slip past you," said Oakes. "The man in that ship is the rascal who robbed the bank on my own bloody space station, the other day. And you were going to arrest us, and give him a speeding-fine!"

"I thought you was confederates of his," retorted Nuttall, "come to hinterfere with me in the course of my hofficial duties."

I finally managed to twist around and crack open my helm, allowing me to enter the conversation. "I say, hadn't we better do something about him?" I said.

Both Oakes and Nuttall seemed quite ready to shout at one another till the air in the hatch was exhausted; but thankfully, my words restored their perspective.

"I don't know habout bank-robberies," said Nuttall, blowing out his cheeks as a precursor to action, "but resisting harrest, and furious driving in charge of a space vessel... " He glanced at me. "Is he likely to be harmed?"

"Well, I don't suggest we should hurt him – Oh," I said, "armed. I don't think so. He had a gun, but he dropped it back in Selene City."

"Armed or not," said Oakes, "nobody brings my station's good name into the dirt by robbing bloody banks aboard it." He reached for the inner door control, and cranked it open.

Despite my words, I believe all three of us were ready for a tussle; but when we burst into the sphere, Eppley sat at the helm as meek as any lamb. His head was downcast, but he glanced up at us as we pushed our weightless way into his presence.

"So," he said with a rueful smile at me, "it's come to this, after all."

Nuttall pushed himself forward, then addressed Oakes and myself in a stage whisper. "What's this fellow's name?"

"Eppley," said Oakes.

"Harold Eppley," I added.

"'Arold Heppley," said Nuttall, rolling the words around his mouth as though they were a savoury delight upon his tongue, "I harrest you for piloting a space-vessel to the public danger; for resisting harrest; for... for larceny, to wit, the robbery of a bank hupon the space station named Hoakapple Horbital; for... for..."

"Don't forget that I stole this ship," said Eppley.

"Piracy!" breathed Nuttall.

"No, is it really? Even nowadays?" Eppley rubbed his chin. "At least tell me it doesn't carry the death penalty. I haven't damaged it, I think; but I had to get off the Moon in a tremendous hurry, with J. here and his buffoonish chums on my heels, and stealing a ship was the only way. I say, J., what have you done with the suffragettes?"

"Miss Lexlake," I said stiffly – for while I could sympathise with his judgment of Harris and George, I felt very much as though it included me also – "is piloting Oakes' ship – the one that reined you in."

"I might have known it," said Eppley. "There is nothing in the world, or off it, that beastly old catamaran can't turn her hand to. I should have shot her while I had the chance. What rancid, rotten luck I've had!" he groaned. "First my sphere breaks down at the moment I need it to escape from Oakapple with the money; then you see through my scheme to make Bustany shoulder the blame, which nine people out of ten would have fallen for; then that confounded ass, George – who, to look at, you would not think has two thoughts in his silly head – turns out to have been understudying Sherlock Holmes on typewriters."

I clicked my tongue in a vaguely sympathetic fashion, finding no easy response to his plaint. Meantime, Nuttall wrote his words down in a notebook with an air of great satisfaction; and Oakes, having retrieved Eppley's gladstone bag, and was glancing inside it.

"Here's the boodle," he said. "Nuttall, shall I take charge of this, while you deal with Eppley?"

Now, most people, if they offered to take charge of a suitcase full of stolen banknotes in front of a policeman, would probably receive an answer that was decidedly negative. But Gareth Oakes, as I had observed many times since our first meeting, was not by any means most people – not he! Nuttall readily acceded to his suggestion, and it was agreed that Oakes and I would return to Oakes's vessel, while Nuttall remained in charge of Eppley; and that we would all proceed to Oakapple, with Oakes towing the two smaller ships. There seemed to be no fight left, now, in Eppley; but Nuttall made assurance doubly sure by first handcuffing him, and then lashing him to a hammock-pole.

25

The pleasant popping sound of a champagne cork leaving its bottle echoed around the room, and Oakes looked on with approval as the waiter filled his glass. When my turn came, I also gave an approving look.

George, whom the waiter had reached before me, wore a more thoughtful expression as he sipped.

"Is it not to your liking?" queried Miss Dickson.

"Oh, it's splendid," said George. "But I can't help thinking that it tastes slightly different to how it would back on Earth."

"I suppose it's the gravity again," said Harris, who can never resist a chance to show off what he thinks is his knowledge. "Do you know, Miss Dickson, J. here brought no end of bottled beer with us, and didn't realise you can't drink it properly when there's no gravity to make the bubbles work."

"I noticed it, back at Maplin," replied Miss Dickson evenly, "but you all seemed to eager to try to keep it from my eyes that I thought it more polite not to remark upon it."

Which – for once – silenced Harris, and brought George out in a broad grin. George has no head for champagne – even more of no head, I mean, than he displays in the course of routine.

Oakes seized the opportunity to tap on his glass with a teaspoon, and while the waiter went around with our plates, he rose to his feet.

"Ladies and gentlemen," he began, "it is my very great honour to sit at table with you all. In the last few days, since I made all your acquaintances, we have enjoyed – ahem! – we have undergone some singular experiences, and some very trying ones. But thanks to you – thanks to you all – what might have been an event which caused great damage to Oakapple's reputation as a watering-hole, up here in orbit, has instead been turned into an opportunity to increase its fame and draw still more people here to its charms – and," he went on, turning to Miss Lexlake and bowing slightly, "all of 'em will see the message which, as a consequence of your intrepid daring and self-sacrifice, may soon bear fruit back down below."

"Increase its fame?" murmured Miss Lexlake, arching a delicate eyebrow.

Oakes chuckled. "Publicity is invaluable – you as a political campaigner must know this, ma'am. I have made sure that every journalist here on Oakapple – I except, of course, that wretch Eppley, in his gaol cell – has been briefed with the story of how the bank robber was chased down and apprehended. It will bring me prominence over all the other orbital stations, and do me the world of good. Really and truly, I cannot thank you all enough, for I could never have achieved this without your aid. This dinner-party, I'm afraid, is quite insufficient to display my gratitude, but – oh well – I mean to say – " He waved a hand, finding himself suddenly at a loss for words. "That is, look you – ah – peg away!"

We pegged away. The food was splendid; so was the wine; so was the waiter, who must have been the most superior chap of his calling to be hired on Oakapple, and who took care that we lacked for nothing and that our glasses were never allowed to even think for a moment of approaching emptiness.

I had wondered, before leaving Earth, how it would affect a fellow's stomach to eat when away from the planet's surface. I was now able to satisfy myself that, at least in the gravity of Oakapple, one might feel a pleasant sensation of repleteness after an excellent meal, in just the same way as one would back at home. The realisation cheered me; for there are so many things which are very different in orbit to how they are on Earth, that it was a relief to encounter one which wasn't.

"Normally," said Oakes, rising to his feet once again after the plates had been cleared, "I would say this was the point where the port should be brought out, and the ladies should retire. I shall not say that, upon this occasion."

Miss Lexlake nodded, very firmly, as the port came out.

"Really, when you think about it," said Oakes, his Welsh accent becoming stronger and more fire-filled with every word, "there isn't a scintilla of a reason for such a thing. Soon enough, I dare say, it will be seen as a quaint, old-fashioned custom for men and women to separate at this point in a dinner. To dine up here, with our home planet far below us, gives a man – I do beg your pardon; I mean, it gives anyone a perspective on such things. We see how insignificant they are in the broad scheme; we see how the difference between the sexes, if I may so refer to it, seems trivial compared to the vastness of space, and the prospect of the future stretching before us. And so," he concluded, beaming, "I give a toast; votes for women!"

"Votes for women!" we all echoed, raising our glasses.

A less honest writer than I might have chosen to break off at this point. Instead, in the interest of truth and full disclosure, I shall go on to chronicle the rest of that dinner.

We were all, I think, in that slightly cracked state of mind which besets you when you have been through excitement and peril and danger, and emerged upon the other side in one piece and a little wiser for the experience.

When in that position, you know that you will soon need to mull it over, and think upon how you reacted in a crisis, and what you might have done better, or at least differently. You will mentally relive your every thought and action, in odd moments of leisure, or in bed at night before sleep claims you. And in the end you will reach, to your own satisfaction, a clear picture of exactly what you must do should you ever find yourself in that dilemma again.

But before you come to the point of revolving the affair in your mind, you discover you wish to congratulate yourself on having survived it at all, and to celebrate in appropriate manner; or sometimes even inappropriate.

And so it was that all of us around that table, having already eaten heartily, now proceeded to enjoy the port on top of the champagne to which Oakes had already treated us. Oakes – his Welsh tones still to the fore – told us some tales of his mining days, both in his homeland and upon the Moon; some of them were perhaps of questionable delicacy, but none of the ladies present seemed to mind, and if they didn't mind, I saw no reason why I should.

Miss Lexlake, indeed, regaled us with some stories from her own experience – of the treatment some cruel young men meted out to her as a female undergraduate, culminating in them picking her lock and placing a sheep inside her room; and how she stood up to it and paid them out for it by returning the favour with a litter of piglets. Miss Dickson, on my other side from Miss Lexlake, laughed like a peal of bells, although I knew she must have heard the tale before; and George, on Miss Dickson's other side, positively guffawed.

In other words, we all became thoroughly merry, and I confess I felt very modern indeed to be doing so in mixed company.

The party finally came to a conclusion when Harris, by now very pink in the face, said that 'pon his word, he was more than half tempted to sing a comic song. At this, George and I exchanged a glance; and that glance contained a silent compact that, no matter what other indiscretions we might have committed over that dinner, we were on no account going to allow Harris to sing a comic song.

I have written previously of how strong men come staggering away, with a look in their eye that shows they have seen too much, when Harris sings Gilbert and Sullivan. Since then, he has diversified his repertoire, so to speak, and if not firmly headed off, he is liable to deliver you a number from "Our Miss Gibbs" or "The Spring Chicken"; and while Harris's Gilbert and Sullivan may have the power of a speeding bullet, his attempts at the more modern comic songs are capable of wreaking as much havoc an exploding bomb.

And so George and I rose in unison, and made loud remarks about how time was drawing on, and how we really could not presume upon Oakes' generosity any further, and how we needed to rest and refresh ourselves ready to return to Earth on the morrow (for Oakes, with his customary efficiency, had had Peckover's hired sphere brought back from the moon and made ready for us).

I don't know what would have happened had George and I not been so prompt to act, for as we made our way back to our quarters, Harris burst into a dreadful rendition of "A fashionable band of brothers are we"; and, quite apart from being wholly inapplicable to the three of us, the chump delivered it in so reedy a falsetto that anyone might have mistaken it for the station having sprung a leak and its air hissing out of the hole.

We bundled him out of public sight, and having done so, George and I shook hands.

"I suppose we should turn in," I said.

"I don't know," said George. "You can, old chap, but there's something I rather want to do before I go to bed."

"Oh; what?"

"Never mind, J. Please don't take offence, but this is the sort of thing a fellow needs to do alone, like old Coriolanus in Shakespeare."

And he wouldn't say any more than that; he straightened his cap on his head, and marched out.

There is no arguing with George when he gets into a mood like that, and besides, I felt disinclined to go chasing him all over Oakapple; a distinct and unusual lethargy had hold of me, for some reason. Instead, I decided to find a position of comfortable repose, and make some notes upon my recent adventures. But I couldn't even do that, for Harris somehow got his second wind – perhaps the champagne had triumphed over the port, somewhere internally – and the man would come and chatter at me about how much he had enjoyed our travels above the atmosphere, and how he had played the major part in all our exploits (this he sincerely appeared to believe), and how he could scarcely wait to return to the bosom of his family and regale his wife with every detail of his exploits.

Not for the first time in my life, I felt a pang of sympathy for Clara Harris.

Fortunately, I was able to satisfy Harris with a string of "mm-hmm" and "really?" and "you don't say, old man" and so forth, while I surreptitiously held my notebook on my knee and jotted down remarks and reminiscences. If I have been harsher upon Harris than he deserves, during this narrative – it is not impossible – you may put it down to it largely being based upon the notes I made that night on Oakapple.

After a while, George returned. His cap had gone crooked once again – I never knew such a man for not being able to keep a hat or a tie on straight for five minutes – and he bore what struck me as a thoughtful look.

"Did you achieve what you went off to do, George?" I asked pleasantly.

"No, I did not," he said, taking the cap off and throwing it across the room.

This seemed a reply not wholly in keeping with the kindness and politeness of my question; and I believe George realised it too, for he gave a long sigh and threw himself into a chair, and began to fiddle with his middle waistcoat button.

"I'm sorry, J.," he said after a few seconds. "I've made a confounded fool of myself."

My initial thought was to say "Again?"; but I am a man of some tact and judgment, and restrained myself. Instead, I said "Oh? What's wrong, old bean?"

"Yes, do tell," Harris said. Harris's face is not one which naturally falls into a sympathetic expression, but he tried very hard, and achieved something approximating to it.

"You'll laugh at me," he said, still twiddling his waistcoat button.

We assured him that we would not – that we wouldn't dream of so cruel a thing.

"You will. You married men are always beastly to us bachelors."

That seemed rather unfair; in my experience, we tend to envy them their freedom, rather than pour scorn upon them; but once again we promised to listen with tender delicacy. It was plain to me that George wanted to disburden himself, and finally he plucked up the courage to.

"You see, it's Arabel Dickson. I know she's a suffragette, and I used to believe the stories about how they were all angular old harridans who were too ugly to find a man; but it ain't so. She's a very charming and beautiful young woman, and – and – and," he stammered, going even pinker than Harris, "for a while, since we met, I've wondered – "

"You're spoons on Miss Dickson?" blurted Harris.

"I knew you'd laugh."

"Harris wasn't laughing, George," I said. "I quite see what you mean. There are very many women less pleasing to the eye than Miss Dickson."

"There, you see!" exclaimed George. "Even you noticed how beautiful she is."

I didn't like that "even", but for my friend's sake, I let it pass.

"Well," he went on, "tonight, I think I may have taken a little Dutch courage – I wasn't drunk, naturally – " (We both assured him that of course, that was impossible.) " – and I said to myself, tomorrow we plan to return home, and if I wanted to – to – to say anything to Miss Dickson, it would have to be tonight – so – Harris, would you be a good chap and pass me my flask?"

Silently, Harris passed it; George unscrewed it and refreshed himself from it.

"Suffice it to say," George resumed, "that there's nothing doing. Oh, she was perfectly lovely about it, as you'd expect; she let me down as gently as she could."

"Is there another man?" said Harris. "Or – goodness! – perhaps one of those other lady companions – "

"Don't be so vulgar, Harris," growled George. "No; she told me that she had no interest in romantic entanglements – never had, and never expected to – certainly had no desire to start a family – and a lot more of that kind of talk. I'd have believed it unfeminine, if it weren't for the fact that I never met a woman so feminine as her. Well, I may have looked a spot down in the mouth, for she said she thought me a charming man and a jolly good sort; and somehow that felt worse than if she'd simply turned me down flat and sent me away. And she must have noticed that, as well, for she invited me to kiss her hand. Which I did. A very well-manicured, sweet little hand, too," he sighed. "And she said that if I truly wished to please her – which Lord knows, I do – I should align myself with the women's suffrage movement when I get back to London."

"Are you going to?" said I.

"Absolutely, I am," said George, giving me a look which dared me to disbelieve him.

"You're going to smash windows," said Harris, "and set pillar-boxes alight?"

"I don't say I shall go quite that far," George said, and reached for his hip-flask again.

Next morning, we were none of us what you might call lively, and we were rather slow to get going; but happily, we were in no hurry. Gareth Oakes – from an excess of generosity, or a desire to make sure that we arrived home in one piece, or both – had assigned to us a professional helmsman. We met him over a late breakfast. He was barely more than half my age; said he had known he wanted to go into space as soon as he heard about it. When we confided in him regarding the problems we had had with that wretched sextant, he just nodded sympathetically.

"Everyone has trouble with sextants," he said.

I suspect that he was just hoping to soothe us, because he didn't seem to find them difficult. Or perhaps it is easier going down in a sphere than it is going up. Going up, one is trying to locate an orbital station. Going down, your target is a planet some eight thousand miles in diameter; and the closer you get to it, the more it looks that size, until it fills the whole of your front window, and you feel the tug of its gravity once more begin to act upon you. Soon, you know, you will once more weigh what you are accustomed to weighing; soon you will no longer be able to bound about effortlessly, and your feet will once again protest at having to carry you about.

So it was for us. And without having the need to pilot the ship to distract us, we fell to discussing this topic.

"I already feel as though I weigh a ton," grumbled George, "and we're still miles away from landing."

"I swear I weigh two tons," groaned Harris. "Dear me! Still, at least our pipes are waiting for us, down below. I declare, I shall smoke like a chimney for a full hour, once I'm reunited with tobacco."

"You said," I pointed out to George, "that this trip would be as good as a rest-cure."

"Well, so it has been," said George. "Or at least, it would have been if we hadn't got ourselves tangled up in all that excitement."

"That's the trouble with holidays," said Harris. "If you spend them doing nothing, you feel that you've wasted them; and if you spend them running around playing tourist, by the time you're finished, you need a holiday to recover from the holiday."

"Well," said George,"there's an idea."

I gave George a sharp look. I had a dreadful premonition that I knew what he was about to suggest.

"What do you mean, George?" said Harris.

"We've barely seen a fraction of all the things there are to see off Earth. There's so much more a chap can do up there, after all! There's all the other orbital stations, and Farsideville and Maceburg and the rest of the Moon – why," said George, "we could try Mars next time."

I shall close my narrative at this point; for otherwise, I should have to set down in print my exact reply to that remark.

ACKNOWLEDGMENTS

This book's existence is owed to the emotional, physical, moral or literary support of many people, including (but not limited to) Russ Copeland, Joey Hamilton, John D. Berry, Dan Steffan, Claire Brialey, Farah Mendlesohn, Emmy Gregory, Alison Scott, Kari Sperring, Geri Sullivan, Ted White, Dave Langford (Zero-G Inertia Consultant), Stephen Lawton (Zero-G Beer Consultant), the members of Greenwich Writers, the members of Wordwars, and most of all the crazed loon who supported me in this bugsy project – my editor and publisher, Michael Dobson.

Printed in Great Britain
by Amazon